THE LAST BIRTHDAY

"I really am having the most wonderful birthday," said Miss Bunner.

The party broke up with renewed thanks to the hostess.

"Enjoy yourself, Bunny?" asked Miss Blacklock.

"Oh, I did. But I've got a terrible headache."

"It's the cake," said Patrick. "I feel a bit livery myself."

"I'll go lie down, I think," said Miss Bunner. "I'll take a couple of aspirin and try and have a nice sleep."

Miss Bunner had a very nice sleep indeed. She never woke up again!

AGATHA CHRISTIE

A JANE MARPLE MURDER MYSTERY

A MURDER IS ANNOUNCED

PUBLISHED BY POCKET BOOKS NEW YORK

POCKET BOOKS, a division of Simon & Schuster, Inc.
1230 Avenue of the Americas, New York, N.Y. 10020

ISBN: 0-671-55267-8

First Pocket Books printing October, 1951

25   24   23   22   21   20   19

POCKET and colophon are registered trademarks
of Simon & Schuster, Inc.

Printed in the U.S.A.

To Ralph and Anne Newman
at whose house I first tasted—
"delicious death!"

Contents

CONTENTS

Cast of Characters

A MURDER WAS ANNOUNCED—
AND THESE HOUSEHOLDS WERE AFFECTED:

A
MURDER IS
ANNOUNCED

CHAPTER 1

"A Murder Is Announced"

BETWEEN 7:30 and 8:30 every morning except Sundays, Johnnie Butt made the round of the village of Chipping Cleghorn on his bicycle, whistling vociferously through his teeth and alighting at each house or cottage to shove through the letter box such morning papers as had been ordered by the occupants of the house in question from Mr. Totman, stationer, of the High Street. Thus at Colonel and Mrs. Easterbrook's he delivered *The Times* and the *Daily Graphic;* at Mrs. Swettenham's he left *The Times* and the *Daily Worker;* at Miss Hinchliffe and Miss Murgatroyd's he left the *Daily Telegraph* and the *News Chronicle;* at Miss Blacklock's he left the *Telegraph, The Times* and the *Daily Mail*.

At all these houses, and indeed at practically every house in Chipping Cleghorn, he delivered every Friday a copy of the *North Benham News and Chipping Cleghorn Gazette,* known locally simply as the *Gazette.*

Thus, on Friday mornings, after a hurried glance at the headlines in the daily paper (INTERNATIONAL SITUATION CRITICAL! U.N. MEETS TODAY! BLOODHOUNDS SEEK BLOND TYPIST'S KILLER! THREE COLLIERIES IDLE. TWENTY-THREE DIE OF FOOD POISONING IN SEASIDE HOTEL, *etc.*), most of the inhabitants of Chipping Cleghorn eagerly opened the *Gazette* and plunged into the local news. After a cursory glance at CORRESPONDENCE (in which the passionate hates and feuds of rural life found full play), nine out of ten subscribers then turned to the PERSONAL column. Here were grouped together higgledy-piggledy articles for sale or wanted, frenzied appeals for domestic help, innumerable insertions regarding dogs, announcements concerning poultry and garden equipment; and various other items of an interesting nature to those living in the small community of Chipping Cleghorn.

This particular Friday, October 29th—was no exception to the rule. . . .

2

Mrs. Swettenham, pushing back the pretty little gray curls from her forehead, opened *The Times*, looked with a lackluster eye at the left-hand center page, decided that, as usual, if there *was* any exciting news, *The Times* had succeeded in camouflaging it in an impeccable manner; took a look at the BIRTHS, MARRIAGES and DEATHS, particularly the latter; then, her duty done, she put aside *The Times* and eagerly seized the Chipping Cleghorn *Gazette*.

When her son Edmund entered the room a moment later, she was already deep in the PERSONAL column.

"Good morning, dear," said Mrs. Swettenham. "The Smedleys are selling their Daimler. A 1935—that's rather a long time ago, isn't it?"

Her son grunted, poured himself a cup of coffee, helped himself to a couple of kippers, sat down at the table and opened the *Daily Worker* which he propped up against the toast rack.

"Bull mastiff puppies," read out Mrs. Swettenham. "I really don't know how people manage to feed big dogs nowadays—I really don't. . . . H'm, Selina Lawrence is advertising for a cook again. I could tell her it's just a waste of time advertising in these days. She hasn't put her address, only a box number—that's quite fatal —I could have told her so—servants simply insist on knowing where they are going. They like a good address. . . . False teeth—I can't think why false teeth are so popular. Best prices paid. . . . Beautiful bulbs. Our special selection. They sound rather cheap. . . . Here's a girl wants an Interesting post—would travel. I daresay! Who wouldn't? Dachshunds . . . I've never really cared for dachshunds myself—I don't mean because they're German, because we've got over all that—I just don't care for them, that's all. Yes, Mrs. Finch?"

The door had opened to admit the head and torso of a grim-looking female in an aged velvet beret.

"Good morning, mum," said Mrs. Finch. "Can I clear?"

"Not yet. We haven't finished," said Mrs. Swettenham. "Not quite finished," she added ingratiatingly.

Casting a look at Edmund and his paper, Mrs. Finch sniffed and withdrew.

"I've only just begun," said Edmund, just as his mother remarked:

"I do wish you wouldn't read that horrid paper, Edmund. Mrs. Finch doesn't like it at all."

"I don't see what my political views have to do with Mrs. Finch."

"And it isn't," pursued Mrs. Swettenham, "as though you were a worker. You don't do any work at all."

"That's not in the least true," said Edmund indignantly. "I'm writing a book."

"I meant real work," said Mrs. Swettenham. "And Mrs. Finch does matter. If she takes a dislike to us and won't come, who else could we get?"

"Advertise in the *Gazette*," said Edmund grinning.

"I've just told you that's no use. Oh, dear me, nowadays unless one has an old Nannie in the family, who will go into the kitchen and do everything, one is simply sunk."

"Well, why haven't we an old Nannie? How remiss of you not to have provided me with one! What were you thinking about?"

"You had an ayah, dear."

"No foresight," murmured Edmund.

Mrs. Swettenham was once more deep in the PERSONAL column.

"Second-hand motor-mower for sale. Now I wonder —Goodness, what a price! . . . More dachshunds. . . . Do write or communicate, desperate, Woggles. What silly nicknames people have. . . . Cocker Spaniels . . . do you remember darling Susie, Edmund? She really was human. Understood every word you said to her. . . . Sheraton sideboard for sale. Genuine family antique. Mrs. Lucas, Dayas Hall. What a liar that woman is! Sheraton indeed!"

Mrs. Swettenham sniffed and then continued her reading:

"All a mistake, darling. Undying love. Friday as usual. J. I suppose they've had a lovers' quarrel—or do you think it's a code for burglars? More dachshunds! Really, I do think people have gone a little crazy about breeding dachshunds. I mean, there are other dogs. Your uncle Simon used to breed Manchester terriers. Such graceful little things. I do like dogs with legs. . . . Lady going abroad will sell her navy two-piece suiting . . . no measurements or price given. A marriage is announced—no, a *murder* . . . *what?* Well, I never! Edmund, *Edmund*, listen to this: *A murder is announced and will take place on Friday, October 29th, at Little Paddocks, at 6:30 p.m. Friends please accept this, the only intimation.* What an extraordinary thing! *Edmund!*"

"What's that?" Edmund looked up from his newspaper.

"Friday, October 29th—why, that's today."

"Let me see." Her son took the paper from her.

"But what does it mean?" Mrs. Swettenham asked with lively curiosity.

Edmund Swettenham rubbed his nose doubtfully.

"Some sort of party, I suppose. The Murder Game—that kind of thing."

"Oh," said Mrs. Swettenham doubtfully. "It seems a very odd way of doing it. Just sticking it in the advertisements like that. Not at all like Letitia Blacklock, who always seems to me such a sensible woman."

"Probably got up by the bright young things she has in the house."

"It's very short notice. Today. Do you think we're just supposed to go?"

"It says, 'Friends please accept this, the only intimation,'" her son pointed out.

"Well. I think these new-fangled ways of giving invitations are very tiresome," said Mrs. Swettenham decidedly.

"All right, Mother, you needn't go."

"No," agreed Mrs. Swettenham.

There was a pause.

"Do you really want that last piece of toast, Edmund?"

"I should have thought my being properly nourished mattered more than letting that old hag clear the table."

"Sh, dear, she'll hear you . . . Edmund, what happens at a Murder Game?"

"I don't know exactly. They pin pieces of paper upon you, or something—no, I think you draw them out of a hat. And somebody's the victim and somebody else is a detective—and then they turn the lights out and some-

body taps you on the shoulder and then you scream and
lie down and sham dead."

"It sounds quite exciting."

"Probably a beastly bore. I'm not going."

"Nonsense, Edmund," said Mrs. Swettenham resolutely. "I'm going and you're coming with me. That's
settled!"

3

"Archie," said Mrs. Easterbrook to her husband,
"listen to this."

Colonel Easterbrook paid no attention, because he
was already snorting with impatience over an article in
The Times.

"Trouble with these fellows is," he said, "that none
of them know the first thing about India! Not the first
thing!"

"I know, dear, I know."

"If they did, they wouldn't write such piffle."

"Yes, I know. Archie, do listen. *A murder is announced and will take place on Friday, October 29th*
(that's today), *at Little Paddocks, at 6:30 p.m. Friends
please accept this, the only intimation.*"

She paused triumphantly. Colonel Easterbrook looked
at her indulgently but without much interest.

"Murder Game," he said.

"Oh."

"That's all it is. Mind you," he unbent a little, "it
can be very good fun if it's well done. But it needs good
organizing by someone who knows the ropes. You draw
lots. One person's the murderer, nobody knows who.
Lights out. Murderer chooses his victim. The victim has
to count twenty before he screams. Then the person

who's chosen to be the detective takes charge. Questions everybody. Where they were, what they were doing, tries to trip the real fellow up. Yes, it's a good game—if the detective—er—knows something about police work."

"Like you, Archie. You had all those interesting cases to try in your district."

Colonel Easterbrook smiled indulgently and gave his mustache a complacent twirl.

"Yes, Laura," he said. "I daresay I could give them a hint or two." And he straightened his shoulders.

"Miss Blacklock ought to have asked you to help her in getting the thing up."

The colonel snorted.

"Oh, well, she's got that young cub staying with her. Expect this is his idea. Nephew or something. Funny idea, though, sticking it in the paper."

"It was in the PERSONAL column. We might never have seen it. I suppose it is an invitation, Archie?"

"Funny kind of invitation. I can tell you one thing. They can count me out."

"Oh, Archie," Mrs. Easterbrook's voice rose in a shrill wail.

"Short notice. For all they know I might be busy."

"But you are not, are you, darling?" Mrs. Easterbrook lowered her voice persuasively. "And I do think, Archie, that you really ought to go—just to help poor Miss Blacklock out. I'm sure she's counting on you to make the thing a success. I mean, you know so much about police work and procedure. The whole thing will fall flat if you don't go and help to make it a success. After all, one must be neighborly."

Mrs. Easterbrook put her synthetic blond head on one side and opened her blue eyes very wide.

"Of course, if you put it like that, Laura . . ." Colonel

Easterbrook twirled his gray mustache again important-
ly, and looked with indulgence on his fluffy little wife.
Mrs. Easterbrook was at least thirty years younger than
her husband.

"If you put it like that, Laura," he said.

"I really do think it's your duty, Archie," said Mrs.
Easterbrook solemnly.

4

The Chipping Cleghorn *Gazette* had also been delivered at Boulders, the picturesque three cottages knocked
into one, inhabited by Miss Hinchliffe and Miss Murgatroyd.

"Hinch?"

"What is it, Murgatroyd?"

"Where are you?"

"Henhouse."

"Oh."

Paddling gingerly through the long wet grass, Miss
Amy Murgatroyd approached her friend. The latter,
attired in corduroy slacks and battle-dress tunic, was
conscientiously stirring in handfuls of balancer meal to
a repellently steaming basin full of cooked potato peel-
ings and cabbage stumps.

She turned her head with its short manlike crop and
weatherbeaten countenance towards her friend.

Miss Murgatroyd, who was fat and amiable, wore a
checked tweed skirt and a shapeless pullover of brilliant royal blue. Her curly bird's-nest of gray hair was
in a good deal of disorder and she was slightly out of
breath.

"In the *Gazette*," she panted. "Just listen—what can
it mean? *A murder is announced and will take place on*

Friday, October 29th, at Little Paddocks, at 6:30 p.m. Friends please accept this, the only intimation."

She paused, breathless, as she finished reading, and awaited some authoritative pronouncement.

"Daft," said Miss Hinchliffe.

"Yes, but what do you think it means?"

"Means a drink, anyway," said Miss Hinchliffe.

"You think it's a sort of invitation?"

"We'll find out what it means when we get there," said Miss Hinchliffe. "Bad sherry, I expect. You'd better get off the grass, Murgatroyd. You've got your bedroom slippers on still. They're soaked."

"Oh, dear." Miss Murgatroyd looked down ruefully at her feet. "How many eggs today?"

"Seven. That damned hen's still broody. I must get her into the coop."

"It's a funny way of putting it, don't you think?" Amy Murgatroyd asked, reverting to the notice in the *Gazette*. Her voice was slightly wistful.

But her friend was made of sterner and more single-minded stuff. She was intent on dealing with recalcitrant poultry and no announcement in a paper, however enigmatic, could deflect her.

She squelched heavily through the mud and pounced upon a speckled hen. There was a loud and indignant squawking.

"Give me ducks every time," said Miss Hinchliffe. "Far less trouble."

5

"Oo, scrumptious!" said Mrs. Harmon across the breakfast table to her husband, the Rev. Julian Harmon. "There's going to be a murder at Miss Blacklock's."

"A murder?" said her husband, slightly surprised. "When?"

"This afternoon . . . at least this evening. Six-thirty. Oh, bad luck, darling; you've got your preparations for confirmation then. It is a shame. And you do so love murders!"

"I don't really know what you're talking about, Bunch."

Mrs. Harmon, the roundness of whose form and face had early led to the sobriquet of "Bunch" being substituted for her baptismal name of Diana, handed the *Gazette* across the table.

"There. All among the second-hand pianos and the old teeth."

"What a very extraordinary announcement."

"Isn't it?" said Bunch happily. "You wouldn't think that Miss Blacklock cared about murders and games and things, would you? I suppose it's the young Simmonses put her up to it—though I should have thought Julia Simmons would find murders rather crude. Still, there it is, and I do think, darling, it's a shame you can't be there. Anyway, I'll go and tell you all about it, though it's rather wasted on me, because I don't really like games that happen in the dark. They frighten me, and I do hope I shan't have to be the one who's murdered. If someone suddenly puts a hand on my shoulder and whispers. 'You're dead,' I know my heart will give such a big thump that perhaps it really might kill me! Do you think that's likely?"

"No, Bunch. I think you're going to live to be an old, old woman—with me."

"And die on the same day and be buried in the same grave. That would be lovely."

Bunch beamed from ear to ear at this agreeable prospect.

"You seem very happy, Bunch," said her husband, smiling.

"Who'd not be happy if they were me?" demanded Bunch rather confusedly. "With you and Susan and Edward, and all of you fond of me and not caring if I'm stupid— And the sun shining! And this lovely big house to live in!"

The Rev. Julian Harmon looked round the big bare dining room and assented doubtfully.

"Some people would think it was the last straw to have to live in this great rambling draughty place."

"Well, I like big rooms. All the nice smells from outside can get in and stay there. And you can be untidy and leave things about and they don't clutter you."

"No labor-saving devices or central heating. It means a lot of work for you, Bunch."

"Oh, Julian, it doesn't. I get up at half past six and light the boiler and rush round like a steam-engine, and by eight it's all done. And I keep it nice, don't I, with beeswax and polish and big jars of autumn leaves? It's not really harder to keep a big house clean than a small one. You go round with mops and things much quicker, because your behind isn't always bumping into things like it is in a small room. And I like sleeping in a big cold room—it's so cosy to snuggle down with just the tip of your nose telling you what it's like up above. And whatever size house you live in, you peel the same amount of potatoes and wash up the same amount of plates and all that. Think how nice it is for Edward and Susan to have a big empty room to play in where they can have railways and dolls' tea parties all over the floor and never have to put them away. And then it's nice to have extra bits of the house that you can let people have to live in. Jimmy Symes and Johnnie Finch —they'd have had to live with their in-laws otherwise. And you know, Julian, it isn't nice living with your in-laws. You're devoted to mother, but you wouldn't really have liked to start our married life living with her and father. And I shouldn't have liked it either. I'd have gone on feeling like a little girl."

Julian smiled at her.

"You're rather like a little girl still, Bunch."

Julian Harmon himself had clearly been a model designed by nature for the age of sixty. He was still about twenty-five years short of achieving Nature's purpose.

"I know I'm stupid—"

"You're not stupid, Bunch. You're very clever."

"No, I'm not. I'm not a bit intellectual. Though I do try . . . and I really love it when you talk to me about books and history and things. I think perhaps it wasn't an awfully good idea to read Gibbon aloud to me in the evenings, because if it's been a cold wind out, and it's nice and hot by the fire, there's something about Gibbon that does rather make me go to sleep."

Julian laughed.

"But I do love listening to you, Julian. Tell me the story again about the old vicar who preached about Ahasuerus."

"You know that by heart, Bunch."

"Just tell it to me again. Please."

Her husband complied.

"It was old Scrymgour. Somebody looked into his church one day. He was leaning out of the pulpit and preaching fervently to a couple of old charwomen. He was shaking his finger at them and saying, 'Aha! I know what you are thinking. You think that the Great Ahasuerus of the First Lesson was Artaxerxes the Second. But he wasn't!' And then with enormous triumph, 'He was Artaxerxes the Third!'"

It had never struck Julian Harmon as a particularly funny story, but it never failed to amuse Bunch.

Her clear laugh floated out.

"The old pet!" she exclaimed. "I think you'll be exactly like that some day, Julian."

Julian looked rather uneasy.

"I know," he said with humility. "I do feel very strongly that I can't always get the proper simple approach."

"I shouldn't worry," said Bunch, rising and beginning to pile the breakfast plates on a tray. "Mrs. Butt told me yesterday that Butt, who never went to church and used to be practically the local atheist, comes every Sunday now on purpose to hear you preach."

She went on, with a very fair imitation of Mrs. Butt's super refined voice:

" 'And Butt was saying only the other day, Madam, to Mr. Timkins from Little Worsdale, that we'd got real culture here in Chipping Cleghorn. Not like Mr. Goss, at Little Worsdale, who talks to the congregation as though they were children who hadn't had any education. Real culture, Butt said, that's what we've got. Our vicar's a highly educated gentleman—Oxford, not Milchester—and he gives us the full benefit of his education. All about the Romans and the Greeks he knows, and the Babylonians and the Assyrians, too. And even the vicarage cat, Butt says, is called after an Assyrian king!' So there's glory for you," finished Bunch triumphantly. "Goodness, I must get on with things or I shall never get done. Come along, Tiglath-Pileser, you shall have the herring bones."

Opening the door and holding it dexterously ajar with her foot, she shot through with the loaded tray, singing in a loud and not particularly tuneful voice, her own version of a sporting song:

> "It's a fine murdering day" (sang Bunch),
> "And as balmy as May,
> And the sleuths from the village are gone,"

A rattle of crockery being dumped in the sink drowned the next lines, but as the Rev. Julian Harmon left the house, he heard the final triumphant assertion:

"And we'll all go a'murdering today!"

CHAPTER 2

Breakfast at Little Paddocks

AT LITTLE PADDOCKS also breakfast was in progress.

Miss Blacklock, a woman of sixty-odd, the owner of the house, sat at the head of the table. She wore country tweeds—and with them, rather incongruously, a choker necklace of large false pearls. She was reading Lane Norcott in the *Daily Mail*. Julia Simmons was languidly glancing through the *Telegraph*. Patrick Simmons was checking up on the crossword in *The Times*. Miss Dora Bunner was giving her attention wholeheartedly to the local weekly paper.

Miss Blacklock gave a subdued chuckle, Patrick muttered, "Adherent—not adhesive—that's where I went wrong."

Suddenly a loud cluck, like a startled hen, came from Miss Bunner.

"Letty—Letty—have you seen this? Whatever can it mean?"

"What's the matter, Dora?"

"The most extraordinary advertisement. It says Little Paddocks quite distinctly. But whatever can it mean?"

"If you'd let me see, Dora dear—"

Miss Bunner obediently surrendered the paper into Miss Blacklock's outstretched hand, pointing to the item with a tremulous forefinger.

"Just look, Letty."

Miss Blacklock looked. Her eyebrows went up. She threw a quick scrutinizing glance round the table. Then she read the advertisement out loud:

"A murder is announced and will take place on Friday, October 29th, at Little Paddocks, at 6:30 p.m. Friends please accept this, the only intimation."

Then she said sharply:

"Patrick, is this your idea?"

Her eyes rested searchingly on the handsome devil-may-care face of the young man at the other end of the table.

Patrick Simmons' disclaimer came quickly.

"No, indeed, Aunt Letty. Whatever put that idea into your head? Why should I know anything about it?"

"I wouldn't put it past you," said Miss Blacklock grimly. "I thought it might be your idea of a joke."

"A joke? Nothing of the kind."

"And you, Julia?"

Julia, looking bored, said: "Of course not."

Miss Bunner murmured: "Do you think Mrs. Haymes—" and looked at an empty place where someone had breakfasted earlier.

"Oh, I don't think our Phillipa would try and be funny," said Patrick. "She's a serious girl, she is."

"But what's the idea, anyway?" said Julia, yawning. "What does it mean?"

Miss Blacklock said slowly, "I suppose—it's some silly sort of hoax."

"But why?" Dora Bunner exclaimed. "What's the point of it? It seems a very stupid sort of joke. And in very bad taste."

Her flabby cheeks quivered indignantly, and her short-sighted eyes sparkled with indignation.

Miss Blacklock smiled at her.

"Don't work yourself up over it, Bunny," she said. "It's just somebody's idea of humor, but I wish I knew whose."

"It says today," pointed out Miss Bunner. "Today at 6:30 p.m. What do you thing is going to happen?"

"Death!" said Patrick in sepulchral tones. "Delicious Death."

"Be quiet, Patrick," said Miss Blacklock as Miss Bunner gave a little yelp.

"I only meant the special cake that Mitzi makes," said Patrick apologetically. "You know we always call it Delicious Death."

Miss Blacklock smiled a little absent-mindedly.

Miss Bunner persisted, "But, Letty, what do you really think——"

Her friend cut across the words with reassuring cheerfulness.

"I know one thing that will happen at 6:30," she said dryly. "We'll have half the village up here, agog with curiosity. I'd better make sure we've got some sherry in the house."

2

"You are worried, aren't you, Lotty?"

Miss Blacklock started. She had been sitting at her writing table, absent-mindedly drawing little fishes on the blotting paper. She looked up into the anxious face of her old friend.

She was not quite sure what to say to Dora Bunner. Bunny, she knew, mustn't be worried or upset. She was silent for a moment or two, thinking.

She and Dora Bunner had been at school together. Dora then had been a pretty, fair-haired, blue-eyed, rather stupid girl. Her being stupid hadn't mattered, because her gaiety and high spirits and her prettiness had made her an agreeable companion. She ought, her friend thought, to have married some nice Army officer, or a country solicitor. She had so many good qualities —affection, devotion, loyalty. But life had been unkind to Dora Bunner. She had had to earn her living. She had been painstaking but never competent at anything she undertook.

The two friends had lost sight of each other. But six months ago a letter had come to Miss Blacklock, a rambling, pathetic letter. Dora's health had given way. She was living in one room, trying to subsist on her old-age pension. She endeavored to do needlework, but her fingers were stiff with rheumatism. She mentioned their schooldays—since then life had driven them apart —but could—possibly—her old friend help?

Miss Blacklock had responded impulsively. Poor Dora, poor, pretty, silly, fluffy Dora. She had swooped down upon Dora, had carried her off, had installed her at Little Paddocks with the comforting fiction that "the housework is getting too much for me. I need someone to help me run the house." It was not for long—the doctor had told her that—but sometimes she found poor old Dora a sad trial. She muddled everything, upset the temperamental foreign "help," miscounted the laundry, lost bills and letters—and sometimes reduced the competent Miss Blacklock to an agony of exasperation. Poor old muddleheaded Dora, so loyal, so anxious to help, so pleased and proud to think she was of assistance—and, alas, so completely unreliable.

Miss Blacklock said sharply:

"Don't, Dora. You know I asked you—"

"Oh." Miss Bunner looked guilty. "I know. I forgot. But—but you are, aren't you?"

"Worried? No. At least," she added truthfully, "not

exactly. You mean about that silly notice in the *Gazette?*"

"Yes—even if it's a joke, it seems to me it's a—a spiteful sort of joke."

"Spiteful?"

"Yes. It seems to me there's spite there somewhere. I mean—it's not a nice kind of joke."

Miss Blacklock looked at her friend. The mild eyes, the long obstinate mouth, the slightly upturned nose. Poor Dora, so maddening, so muddle-headed, so devoted and such a problem. A dear fussy old idiot and yet, in a queer way, with an instinctive sense of values.

"I think you're right, Dora," said Miss Blacklock. "It's not a nice joke."

"I don't like it at all," said Dora Bunner with unsuspected vigor. "It frightens me." She added suddenly: "And it frightens you, Letitia."

"Nonsense," said Miss Blacklock with spirit.

"It's dangerous. I'm sure it is. Like those people who send you bombs done up in parcels."

"My dear, it's just some silly idiot trying to be funny."

"But it isn't funny."

It wasn't really very funny . . . Miss Blacklock's face betrayed her thoughts, and Dora cried triumphantly, "You see. You think so, too!"

"But, Dora, my dear—"

She broke off. Through the door there surged a tempestuous young woman with a well-developed bosom heaving under a tight jersey. She had on a dirndl skirt of a bright color and had greasy dark braids wound round and round her head. Her eyes were dark and flashing.

She said gustily: "I can speak to you, yes, please, no?"

Miss Blacklock sighed.

"Of course, Mitzi, what is it?"

Sometimes she thought it would be preferable to do the entire work of the house as well as the cooking rather than be bothered with the eternal nerve storms of her refugee "lady help."

"I tell you at once—it is in order, I hope? I give you my notices and I go—I go at once!"

"For what reason? Has somebody upset you?"

"Yes, I am upset," said Mitzi dramatically. "I do not wish to die! Already in Europe I escape. My family they all die—they are all killed—my mother, my little brother, my so sweet little niece—all, all they are killed. But me I run away—I hide. I get to England. I work. I do work that never—never would I do in my own country —I—"

"I know all that," said Miss Blacklock crisply. It was, indeed, a constant refrain of Mitzi's lips. "But why do you want to leave now?"

"Because again they come to kill me!"

"Who do?"

"My enemies. The Nazis! Or perhaps this time it is the Bolsheviks. They find out I am here. They come to kill me. I have read it—yes—it is in the newspaper!"

"Oh, you mean in the *Gazette?*"

"Here, it is written here." Mitzi produced the *Gazette* from where she had been holding it behind her back. "See—here it says murder. At Little Paddocks. That is here, is it not? This evening at six-thirty. Ah! I do not wait to be murdered—no."

"But why should this apply to you? It's—we think it is a joke."

"A joke? It is not a joke to murder someone."

"No, of course not. But, my dear child, if anyone wanted to murder you, they wouldn't advertise the fact in the paper, would they?"

"You do not think they would?" Mitzi seemed a little shaken. "You think, perhaps, they do not mean to murder anyone at all? Perhaps it is you they mean to murder, Miss Blacklock."

"I certainly can't believe anyone wants to murder me," said Miss Blacklock lightly. "And, really, Mitzi, I don't see why anyone should want to murder you. After all, why should they?"

"Because they are bad peoples . . . very bad peoples. I tell you, my mother, my little brother, my so sweet niece . . ."

"Yes, yes," Miss Blacklock stemmed the flow adroitly. "But I cannot really believe anyone wants to murder you, Mitzi. Of course, if you want to go off like this at a moment's notice, I cannot possibly stop you. But I think you will be very silly if you do."

She added firmly, as Mitzi looked doubtful:

"We'll have that beef the butcher sent stewed for lunch. It looks very tough."

"I make you a goulash, a special goulash."

"If you prefer to call it that, certainly. And perhaps you could use up that rather hard bit of cheese in making some cheese straws. I think some people may come in this evening for drinks."

"This evening? What do you mean, this evening?"

"At half past six."

"But that is the time in the paper? Who should come then? Why should they come?"

"They're coming to the funeral," said Miss Blacklock with a twinkle. "That'll do now, Mitzi. I'm busy. Shut the door after you," she added firmly.

"And that's settled her for the moment," she said as the door closed behind a puzzled-looking Mitzi.

"You are so efficient, Letty," said Miss Bunner admiringly.

CHAPTER 3

At 6:30 P.M.

"WELL, here we are, all set," said Miss Blacklock. She looked round the double drawing-room with an appraising eye. The rose-patterned chintzes—the two bowls of bronze chrysanthemums, the small vase of violets and the silver cigarette box on a table by the wall, the tray of drinks on the center table.

Little Paddocks was a medium-sized house built in the early Victorian style. It had a long shallow veranda and green-shuttered windows. The long narrow drawing-room, which lost a good deal of light owing to the veranda roof, had originally had double doors at one end, leading into a small room with a bay window. A former generation had removed the double doors and replaced them with portières of velvet. Miss Blacklock had dispensed with the portières so that the two rooms had become definitely one. There was a fireplace at each end, but neither fire was lit, although a gentle warmth pervaded the room.

"You've had the central heating lit," said Patrick.

Miss Blacklock nodded.

"It's been so misty and damp lately. The whole house felt clammy. I got Evans to light it before he went."

"The precious, precious coke?" said Patrick, mockingly.

"As you say, the precious coke. But otherwise there would have been the even more precious coal. You know the Fuel Office won't even let us have the little bit that's due us each week—not unless we can say definitely that we haven't any other means of cooking."

"I suppose once there were heaps of coke and coal for everybody?" said Julia, with the interest of one hearing about an unknown country.

"Yes, and cheap, too."

"And anyone could go and buy as much as they wanted, without filling in anything, and there wasn't any shortage? There was lots of it then?"

"All kinds and qualities—and not all stones and slates like what we get nowadays."

"It must have been a wonderful world," said Julia with awe in her voice.

Miss Blacklock smiled. "Looking back on it, I certainly think so. But then I'm an old woman. It's natural for me to prefer my own times. But you young things oughtn't to think so."

"I needn't have had a job then," said Julia. "I could just have stayed at home and done the flowers, and written notes . . . why did one write notes and who were they to?"

"All the people that you now ring up on the telephone," said Miss Blacklock with a twinkle. "I don't believe you even know how to write, Julia."

"Not in the style of that delicious *Complete Letter Writer* I found the other day. Heavenly! It told you the correct way of refusing a proposal of marriage from a widower."

"I doubt if you would have enjoyed staying at home as much as you think," said Miss Blacklock. "There were duties, you know." Her voice was dry. "However, I don't really know much about it. Bunny and I," she smiled affectionately at Dora Bunner, "went into the labor market early."

"Oh, we did, we did indeed," agreed Miss Bunner. "Those naughty, naughty children. I'll never forget them. Of course Letty was clever. She was a business woman, secretary to a big financier."

The door opened and Phillipa Haymes came in. She was tall and fair and placid-looking. She looked round the room in surprise.

"Hullo," she said. "Is it a party? Nobody told me."

"Of course," cried Patrick. "Our Phillipa doesn't know. The only woman in Chipping Cleghorn who doesn't, I bet."

Phillipa looked at him inquiringly.

"Here you behold," said Patrick dramatically, waving a hand, "the scene of a murder!"

Phillipa Haymes looked faintly puzzled.

"Here," Patrick indicated the two big bowls of chrysanthemums, "are the funeral wreaths and these dishes of cheese straws and olives represent the funeral baked meats."

Phillipa looked inquiringly at Miss Blacklock.

"Is it a joke?" she asked. "I'm always terribly stupid at seeing jokes."

"It's a very nasty joke," said Dora Bunner with energy. "I don't like it at all."

"Show her the advertisement," said Miss Blacklock. "I must go and shut up the ducks. It's dark. They'll be in by now."

"Let me do it," said Phillipa.

"Certainly not, my dear. You've finished your day's work."

"I'll do it, Aunt Letty," offered Patrick.

"No, you won't," said Miss Blacklock with energy. "Last time you didn't latch the door properly."

"I'll do it, Letty dear," cried Miss Bunner. "Indeed,

I should love to. I'll just slip on my galoshes—and now where did I put my cardigan?"

But Miss Blacklock, with a smile, had already left the room.

"It's no good, Bunny," said Patrick. "Aunt Letty's so efficient that she can never bear anybody else to do things for her. She really much prefers to do everything herself."

"She loves it," said Julia.

"I didn't notice you making any offers of assistance," said her brother.

Julia smiled lazily.

"You've just said Aunt Letty likes to do things herself," she pointed out. "Besides," she held out a well-shaped leg in a sheer stocking, "I've got my best stockings on."

"Death in silk stockings!" declaimed Patrick.

"Not silk; nylons, you idiot."

"That's not nearly such a good title."

"Won't somebody please tell me," cried Phillipa plaintively, "why there is all this insistence on death?"

Everybody tried to tell her at once—nobody could find the *Gazette* to show her because Mitzi had taken it into the kitchen.

Miss Blacklock returned a few minutes later.

"There," she said briskly, "that's done." She glanced at the clock. "Twenty past six. Somebody ought to be here soon—unless I'm entirely wrong in my estimate of my neighbors."

"I don't see why anybody should come," said Phillipa, looking bewildered.

"Don't you, dear? I daresay you wouldn't. But most people are rather more inquisitive than you are."

"Phillipa's attitude to life is that she just isn't interested," said Julia, rather nastily.

Phillipa did not reply.

Miss Blacklock was glancing round the room. Mitzi had put the sherry and three dishes containing olives, cheese straws and some little fancy pastries on the table in the middle of the room.

"You might move that tray—or the whole table if you like—round the corner into the bay window in the other room, Patrick, if you don't mind. After all, I am not giving a party! I haven't asked anyone. And I don't intend to make it obvious that I expect people to turn up."

"You wish, Aunt Letty, to disguise your intelligent anticipation?"

"Very nicely put, Patrick. Thank you, my dear boy."

"Now we can all give a lovely performance of a quiet evening at home," said Julia, "and be quite surprised when somebody drops in."

Miss Blacklock had picked up the sherry bottle. She stood holding it uncertainly in her hand.

Patrick reassured her.

"There's quite half a bottle there. It ought to be enough."

"Oh, yes—yes . . ." She hesitated. Then, with a slight flush, she said, "Patrick, would you mind . . . there's a new bottle in the cupboard in the pantry . . . bring it and a corkscrew. I—we—might as well have a new bottle. This—this has been opened some time."

Patrick went on his errand without a word. He returned with the new bottle and drew the cork. He looked up curiously at Miss Blacklock as he placed it on the tray.

"Taking things seriously, aren't you, darling?" He asked gently.

"Oh," cried Dora Bunner, shocked. "Surely, Letty, you can't imagine—"

"Hush," said Miss Blacklock quickly. "That's the

bell. You see, my intelligent anticipation is being justified."

2

Mitzi opened the door of the drawing-room and admitted Colonel and Mrs. Easterbrook. She had her own methods of announcing people.

"Here is Colonel and Mrs. Easterbrook to see you," she said conversationally.

Colonel Easterbrook was very bluff and breezy to cover some slight embarrassment.

"Hope you don't mind us dropping in," he said. (A subdued gurgle came from Julia.) "Happened to be passing this way—eh, what? Quite a mild evening. Notice you've got your central heating on. We haven't started ours yet."

"Aren't your chrysanthemums lovely?" gushed Mrs. Easterbrook. "Such beauties!"

"They're rather scraggy really," said Julia.

Mrs. Easterbrook greeted Phillipa Haymes with a little extra cordiality to show that she quite understood that Phillipa was not really an agricultural laborer.

"How is Mrs. Lucas's garden getting on?" she asked. "Do you think it will ever be straight again? Completely neglected all through the war—and then only that dreadful old man Ashe who simply did nothing but sweep up a few leaves and put in a few cabbage plants."

"It's yielding to treatment," said Phillipa. "But it will take a little time."

Mitzi opened the door again and said, "Here are the ladies from Boulders."

"Evening," said Miss Hinchliffe, striding over and taking Miss Blacklock's hand in her formidable grip. "I said to Murgatroyd: 'Let's just drop in at Little Paddocks!' I wanted to ask you how your ducks are laying."

"The evenings do draw in so quickly now, don't they?" said Miss Murgatroyd to Patrick in a rather fluttery way. "What lovely chrysanthemums!"

"Scraggy!" said Julia.

"Why can't you be co-operative?" murmured Patrick to her in a reproachful aside.

"You've got your central heating on," said Miss Hinchliffe. She said it accusingly. "Very early."

"The house gets so damp this time of year," said Miss Blacklock.

Patrick signaled with his eyebrows: "Sherry yet?" and Miss Blacklock signaled back: "Not yet."

She said to Colonel Easterbrook:

"Are you getting any bulbs from Holland this year?"

The door again opened and Mrs. Swettenham came in rather guiltily, followed by a scowling and uncomfortable Edmund.

"Here we are!" said Mrs. Swettenham, gaily, gazing round her with frank curiosity. Then, feeling suddenly uncomfortable, she went on: "I just thought I'd pop in and ask you if by any chance you wanted a kitten, Miss Blacklock? Our cat is just—"

"About to be brought to bed of the progeny of a ginger tom," said Edmund. "The result will, I think, be frightful. Don't say you haven't been warned!"

"She's a very good mouser," said Mrs. Swettenham hastily. And added: "What lovely chrysanthemums!"

"You've got your central heating on, haven't you?" asked Edmund with an air of originality.

"Aren't people just like gramophone records?" murmured Julia.

"I don't like the news," said Colonel Easterbrook to Patrick, buttonholing him fiercely. "I don't like it at all. If you ask me, war's inevitable—absolutely inevitable."

"I never pay any attention to news," said Patrick.

Once more the door opened and Mrs. Harmon came in.

Her battered felt hat was stuck on the back of her head in a vague attempt to be fashionable and she had put on a rather limp frilly blouse instead of her usual pullover.

"Hullo, Miss Blacklock," she exclaimed, beaming all over her round face. "I'm not too late, am I? When does the murder begin?"

3

There was an audible series of gasps. Julia gave an approving little giggle, Patrick crinkled up his face and Miss Blacklock smiled at her latest guest.

"Julian is just frantic with rage that he can't be here," said Mrs. Harmon. "He adores murders. That's really why he preached such a good sermon last Sunday—I suppose I oughtn't to say it was a good sermon as he's my husband—but it really was good, didn't you think? So much better than his usual sermons. But as I was saying it was all because of *Death Does the Hat Trick*. Have you read it? The girl at Boots kept it for me specially. It's simply baffling. You keep thinking you know—and then the whole thing switches round—and there are a lovely lot of murders, four or five of them. Well, I left it in the study when Julian was shutting himself up there to do his sermon, and he just picked it up and simply could not put it down! And consequently he had to write his sermon in a frightful hurry and had to just put down what he wanted to say very simply—without any scholarly twists and bits and learned references—and naturally it was heaps better.

Oh, dear, I'm talking too much. But do tell me, when is the murder going to begin?"

Miss Blacklock looked at the clock on the mantelpiece.

"If it's going to begin," she said cheerfully, "it ought to begin soon. It's just a minute to the half hour. In the meantime, have a glass of sherry."

Patrick moved with alacrity through the archway. Miss Blacklock went to the table by the archway where the cigarette box was.

"I'd love some sherry," said Mrs. Harmon. "But what do you mean by if?"

"Well," said Miss Blacklock. "I'm as much in the dark as you are. I don't know what—"

She stopped and turned her head as the little clock on the mantelpiece began to chime. It had a sweet, silvery, bell-like tone. Everybody was silent and nobody moved. They all stared at the clock.

It chimed a quarter—and then the half. As the last note died away all the lights went out.

4

Delighted gasps and feminine squeaks of appreciation were heard in the darkness. "It's beginning," cried Mrs. Harmon in an ecstasy. Dora Bunner's voice cried out plaintively, "Oh, I don't like it!" Other voices said, "How terribly, terribly frightening!" "It gives me the creeps." "Archie, where are you?" "What do I have to do?" "Oh dear—did I step on your foot? I'm so sorry."

Then, with a crash, the door swung open. A powerful flashlight played rapidly round the room. A man's hoarse nasal voice, reminiscent to all of pleasant afternoons at the movies, directed the company crisply to:

"Stick 'em up! Stick 'em up, I tell you!" the voice barked.

Delightedly, hands were raised willingly above heads. "Isn't it wonderful?" breathed a female voice. "I'm so thrilled."

And then, unexpectedly, a revolver spoke. It spoke twice. The ping of two bullets shattered the complacency of the room. Suddenly the game was no longer a game. Somebody screamed . . .

The figure in the doorway whirled suddenly around, it seemed to hesitate, a third shot rang out, it crumpled and then it crashed to the ground. The flashlight dropped and went out. There was darkness once again. And gently, with a little Victorian protesting moan, the drawing-room door, as was its habit when not propped open, swung gently to and latched with a click.

5

Inside the drawing-room there was pandemonium. Various voices spoke at once. "Lights!" "Can't you find the switch?" "Who's got a lighter?" "Oh, I don't like it, I don't like it." "But those shots were real!" "It was a real revolver he had." "Was it a burglar?" "Oh, Archie, I want to get out of here." "Please, has somebody got a lighter?"

And then, almost at the same moment, two lighters clicked and burned with small steady flames.

Everybody blinked and peered at each other. Startled face looked into startled face. Against the wall by the archway Miss Blacklock stood with her hand up to her face. The light was too dim to show more than that something dark was trickling over her fingers.

Colonel Easterbrook cleared his throat and rose to the occasion.

"Try the switches, Swettenham," he ordered.

Edmund, near the door, obediently jerked the switch up and down.

"Off at the main, or a fuse," said the colonel. "Who's making that awful row?"

A female voice had been screaming steadily from somewhere beyond the closed door. It rose now in pitch and with it came the sound of fists hammering on a door.

Dora Bunner, who had been sobbing quietly, called out, "It's Mitzi. Somebody's murdering Mitzi . . ."

Patrick muttered: "No such luck."

Miss Blacklock said: "We must get candles. Patrick, will you—"

The colonel was already opening the door. He and Edmund, their lighters flickering, stepped into the hall. They almost stumbled over a recumbent figure there.

"Seems to have knocked him out," said the colonel. "Where's that woman making that hellish noise?"

"In the dining-room," said Edmund.

The dining-room was just across the hall. Someone was beating on the panels and howling and screaming.

"She's locked in," said Edmund, stooping down. He turned the key and Mitzi came out like a bounding tiger.

The dining-room light was still on. Silhouetted against it, Mitzi presented a picture of insane terror and continued to scream. A touch of comedy was introduced by the fact that she had been engaged in cleaning silver and was still holding a chamois leather and a large fish slice.

"Be quiet, Mitzi," said Miss Blacklock.

"Stop it," said Edmund, and as Mitzi showed no disposition to stop screaming, he leaned forward and gave her a sharp slap on the cheek. Mitzi gasped and hiccuped into silence.

"Get some candles," said Miss Blacklock. "In the kitchen cupboard. Patrick, you know where the fuse-box is?"

"The passage behind the scullery? Right, I'll see what I can do."

Miss Blacklock had moved forward into the light thrown from the dining-room and Dora Bunner gave a sobbing gasp. Mitzi let out another full-blooded scream.

"The blood, the blood!" she gasped. "You are shot— Miss Blacklock, you bleed to death."

"Don't be so stupid," snapped Miss Blacklock. "I'm hardly hurt at all. It just grazed my ear."

"But, Aunt Letty," said Julia, "the blood."

And indeed Miss Blacklock's white blouse and pearls and her hand were a horrifyingly gory sight.

"Ears always bleed," said Miss Blacklock. "I remember fainting in the hairdresser's when I was a child. The man had only just snipped my ear. There seemed to be a basin of blood at once. But we must have some light."

"I get the candles," said Mitzi.

Julia went with her and they returned with several candles stuck into saucers.

"Now let's have a look at our malefactor," said the colonel. "Hold the candles down low, will you, Swettenham? As many as you can."

"I'll come the other side," said Phillipa.

With a steady hand she took a couple of saucers. Colonel Easterbrook knelt down.

The recumbent figure was draped in a roughly made black cloak with a hood to it. There was a black mask over the face and he wore black cotton gloves. The hood had slipped back disclosing a ruffled fair head.

Colonel Easterbrook turned him over, felt the pulse, the heart . . . then drew away his fingers with an exclamation of distaste, looking down on them. They were sticky and red.

"Shot himself," he said.

"Is he badly hurt?" asked Miss Blacklock.

"H'm. I'm afraid he's dead. May have been suicide —or he may have tripped himself up with that cloak thing and the revolver went off as he fell. If I could see better—"

At that moment, as though by magic, the lights came on again.

With a queer feeling of unreality those inhabitants of Chipping Cleghorn who stood in the hall of Little Paddocks realized that they stood in the presence of violent and sudden death. Colonel Easterbrook's hand was stained red. Blood was still trickling down Miss Blacklock's neck over her blouse and skirt, and the grotesquely sprawled figure of the intruder lay at their feet.

Patrick, coming from the dining-room, said, "It seemed to be just one fuse gone . . ." He stopped.

Colonel Easterbrook tugged at the small black mask. "Better see who the fellow is," he said. "Though I don't suppose it's anyone we know."

He detached the mask. Necks were craned forward. Mitzi hiccuped and gasped, but the others were very quiet.

"He's quite young," said Mrs. Harmon with a note of pity in her voice.

And suddenly Dora Bunner cried out excitedly:

"Letty, Letty, it's the young man from the Spa Hotel in Medenham Wells. The one who came out here and wanted you to give him money to get back to Switzerland and you refused. I suppose the whole thing was just a pretext—to spy out the house. . . . Oh, dear—he might easily have killed you."

Miss Blacklock, in command of the situation, said incisively, "Phillipa, take Bunny into the dining-room

and give her a half glass of brandy. Julia dear, just
run up to the bathroom and bring me the sticking
plaster out of the bathroom cupboard—it's so messy
bleeding like a pig. Patrick, will you ring up the police
at once?"

CHAPTER 4

The Royal Spa Hotel

GEORGE RYDESDALE, Chief Constable of Middleshire, was a quiet man. Of medium height, with shrewd eyes under rather bushy brows, he was in the habit of listening rather than talking. Then, in his unemotional voice, he would give a brief order—and the order was obeyed.

He was listening now to Detective Inspector Dermot Craddock. Craddock was now officially in charge of the case. Rydesdale had recalled him last night from Liverpool where he had been sent to make certain inquiries in connection with another case. Rydesdale had a good opinion of Craddock. He not only had brains and imagination, he had also, which Rydesdale appreciated even more, the self-discipline to go slow, to check and examine each fact and to keep an open mind until the very end of a case.

"Constable Legg took the call, sir," Craddock was saying. "He seems to have acted very well, with promptitude and presence of mind. And it can't have been easy. About a dozen people all trying to talk at once, including one of those Mittel Europas who go off the deep end at the mere sight of a policeman. Made sure she was going to be locked up, and fairly screamed the place down."

"Deceased has been identified?"

"Yes, sir. Rudi Scherz. Swiss nationality. Employed

36

at the Royal Spa Hotel, Medenham Wells, as a receptionist. If you agree, sir. I thought I'd take the Royal Spa
Hotel first, and go out to Chipping Cleghorn afterwards. Sergeant Fletcher is out there now. He'll see
the bus people and then go on to the house."

Rydesdale nodded approval.

The door opened and the Chief Constable looked
up.

"Come in, Henry," he said. "We've got something
here that's a little out of the ordinary."

Sir Henry Clithering, ex-Commissioner of Scotland
Yard, came in with slightly raised eyebrows. He was a
tall, distinguished-looking, elderly man.

"It may appeal to even your blasé palate," went on
Rydesdale.

"I was never blasé," said Sir Henry indignantly.

"The latest idea," said Rydesdale, "is to advertise
one's murders beforehand. Show Sir Henry that advertisement, Craddock."

"The *North Benham News and Chipping Cleghorn
Gazette*," said Sir Henry. "Quite a mouthful." He read
the half inch of print indicated by Craddock's finger.
"Hm, yes, somewhat unusual."

"Any line on who inserted this advertisement?" asked
Rydesdale.

"By the description, sir, it was handed in by Rudi
Scherz himself—on Wednesday."

"Nobody questioned it? The person who accepted
it didn't think it odd?"

"The adenoidal blonde who receives the advertisements is quite incapable of thinking, I should say, sir.
She just counted the words and took the money."

"What was the idea?" asked Sir Henry.

"Get a lot of the locals curious," suggested Rydesdale. "Get them all together at a particular place at a
particular time, then hold them up and relieve them of

their spare cash and valuables. As an idea, it's not without originality."

"What sort of a place is Chipping Cleghorn?" asked Sir Henry.

"A large, sprawling, picturesque village. Butcher, baker, grocer, quite a good antique shop—two tea shops. Self-consciously a beauty spot. Caters to the motoring tourist. Also highly residential. Cottages formerly lived in by agricultural laborers now converted and lived in by elderly spinsters and retired couples. A certain amount of building done around about in Victorian times."

"I know," said Sir Henry. "Nice old pussies and retired colonels. Yes, if they noticed that advertisement they'd all come sniffing round at 6:30 to see what was up. Lord, I wish I had my own particular old pussy here. Wouldn't she like to get her nice ladylike teeth into this? Right up her street it would be."

"Who's your own particular pussy, Henry? An aunt?"

"No." Sir Henry sighed. "She's no relation." He said reverently: "She's just the finest detective God ever made. Natural genius cultivated in a suitable soil."

He turned upon Craddock.

"Don't you despite the old pussies in this village of yours, my boy," he said. "In case this turns out to be a high-powered mystery, which I don't suppose for a moment it will, remember that an elderly unmarried woman who knits and gardens is streets ahead of any detective sergeant. She can tell you what might have happened and what ought to have happened and even what actually did happen! And she can tell you why it happened!"

"I'll bear that in mind, sir," said Detective Inspector Craddock in his most formal manner, and nobody would have guessed that Dermot Eric Craddock was actually

Sir Henry's godson and was on easy and intimate terms with his godfather.

Rydesdale gave a quick outline of the case to his friend.

"They'd all turn up at 6:30, I grant you that," he said. "But would that Swiss fellow know they would? And another thing, would they be likely to have much loot on them to be worth the taking?"

"A couple of old-fashioned brooches, a string of seed pearls—a little loose change, perhaps a note or two—not more," said Sir Henry thoughtfully. "Did this Miss Blacklock keep much money in the house?"

"She says not, sir. Five pounds odd, I understand."

"Mere chicken feed," said Rydesdale.

"What you're getting at," said Sir Henry, "is that this fellow liked to play-act—it wasn't the loot, it was the fun of playing and acting the holdup. Movie stuff, eh? It's quite possible. How did he manage to shoot himself?"

Rydesdale drew a paper towards him.

"Preliminary medical report. The revolver was discharged at close range—singeing . . . h'm . . . nothing to show whether accident or suicide. Could have been done deliberately, or he could have tripped and fallen and the revolver which he was holding close to him could have gone off. Probably the latter." He looked at Craddock. "You'll have to question the witnesses very carefully and make them say exactly what they saw."

Detective Inspector Craddock said sadly, "They'll all have seen something different."

"It's always interested me," said Sir Henry, "what people do see at a moment of intense excitement and nervous strain. What they do see and, even more interesting, what they don't see."

"Where's the report on the revolver?"

"Foreign make—fairly common the the Continent— Scherz did not hold a permit for it—and did not declare it on coming into England."

"Bad lad," said Sir Henry.

"Unsatisfactory character all round. Well, Craddock, go and see what you can find out about him at the Royal Spa Hotel."

2

At the Royal Spa Hotel Inspector Craddock was taken straight to the manager's office.

The manager, Mr. Rowlandson, a tall florid man with a hearty manner, greeted Inspector Craddock with expansive geniality.

"Glad to help you in any way we can, Inspector," he said. "Really, a most surprising business. I'd never have credited it—never. Scherz seemed a very ordinary, pleasant young chap—not at all my idea of a holdup man."

"How long has he been with you, Mr. Rowlandson?"

"I was looking that up before you came. A little over three months. Quite good credentials, the usual permits, etc."

"And you found him satisfactory?"

Without seeming to do so, Craddock marked the infinitesimal pause before Rowlandson replied,

"Quite satisfactory."

Craddock made use of a technique he had found efficacious before now.

"No, no, Mr. Rowlandson," he said, gently shaking his head. "That's not really quite the case, is it?"

"We-ll—" The manager seemed slightly taken aback.

"Come now, there was something wrong. What was it?"

"That's just it. I don't know."

"But you thought there was something wrong?"

"Well—yes—I did . . . but I've nothing really to go upon. I shouldn't like my conjectures to be written down and quoted against me."

Craddock smiled pleasantly.

"I know just what you mean. You needn't worry. But I've got to get some idea of what this fellow Scherz was like. You suspected him of—what?"

Rowlandson said, rather reluctantly, "Well, there was trouble, once or twice, about the bills. Items charged that oughtn't to have been there."

"You mean you suspected that he charged up certain items which didn't appear in the hotel records, and that he pocketed the difference when the bill was paid?"

"Something like that. Put it at the best, there was gross carelessness on his part. Once or twice quite a big sum was involved. Frankly, I got our accountant to go over his books, suspecting that he was—well, a wrong 'un; but though there were various mistakes and a good deal of slipshod method, the actual cash was quite correct. So I came to the conclusion that I must be mistaken."

"Supposing you hadn't been wrong? Supposing Scherz had been helping himself to various small sums here and there, he could have covered himself, I suppose, by making good the money?"

"Yes, if he had the money. But people who help themselves to 'small sums' as you put it—are usually hard up for those sums and spend them offhand."

"So if he wanted money to replace missing sums, he would have had to get money—by a holdup or other means?"

"Yes. I wonder if this is his first attempt."

"Might be. It was certainly a very amateurish one. Is there anyone else he could have got money from? Any woman in his life?"

"One of the waitresses in the Grill. Her name's Myrna Harris."

"I'd better have a talk with her."

3

Myrna Harris was a pretty girl with a glorious head of red hair and a pert nose.

She was alarmed and wary, and deeply conscious of the indignity of being interviewed by the police.

"I don't know a thing about it, sir. Not a thing," she protested. "If I'd known what he was like I'd never have gone out with Rudi at all. Naturally, seeing as he worked as receptionist here, I thought he was all right. Naturally I did. What I say is, the hotel ought to be more careful when they employ people—especially foreigners. Because you never know where you are with foreigners. I suppose he might have been in with one of these gangs you read about."

"We think," said Craddock, "that he was working quite on his own."

"Fancy—and him so quiet and respectable. You'd never think. Though there have been things missed—now I come to think of it. A diamond brooch—and a little gold locket, I believe. But I never dreamed that it could have been Rudi."

"I'm sure you didn't," said Craddock. "Anyone might have been taken in. You knew him fairly well?"

"I don't know that I'd say well."

"But you were friendly?"

"Oh, we were friendly—that's all, just friendly. Nothing serious at all. I'm always on my guard with foreigners, anyway. They've often got a way with them, but you never know, do you? Some of those Poles during the war! And even some of the Americans! Never let on they're married men until it's too late. Rudi talked big and all that—but I always took it with a grain of salt."

Craddock seized on the phrase.

"Talked big, did he? That's very interesting, Miss Harris. I can see you're going to be a lot of help to us. In what way did he talk big?"

"Well, about how rich his people were in Switzerland—and how important. But that didn't go with his being as short of money as he was. He always said that because of the money regulation he couldn't get money from Switzerland over here. That might be, I suppose, but his things weren't expensive. His clothes, I mean. They weren't really class. I think, too, that a lot of the stories he used to tell me were so much hot air. About climbing in the Alps, and saving people's lives on the edge of a glacier. Why, he turned quite giddy just going along the edge of Boulter's Gorge. Alps, indeed!"

"You went out with him a good deal?"

"Yes—well—yes, I did. He had awfully good manners and he knew how to—to look after a girl. The best seats at the pictures, always. And even flowers he'd buy me sometimes. And he was just a lovely dancer—lovely."

"Did he mention this Miss Blacklock to you at all?"

"She comes in and lunches here sometimes, doesn't she? And she's stayed here once. No, I don't think Rudi ever mentioned her. I didn't know he knew her."

"Did he mention Chipping Cleghorn?"

He thought a faintly wary look came into Myrna Harris's eyes but he couldn't be sure.

"I don't think so . . . I think he did once ask about buses—what time they went—but I can't remember if that was Chipping Cleghorn or somewhere else. It wasn't just lately."

He couldn't get more out of her. Rudi Scherz had seemed just as usual. She hadn't seen him the evening before. She'd had no idea—no idea at all—she stressed the point, that Rudi Scherz was a crook.

And probably, Craddock thought, that was quite true.

CHAPTER 5

Miss Blacklock and Miss Bunner

LITTLE PADDOCKS was very much as Detective Inspector Craddock had imagined it to be. He noted ducks and chickens, and what had been until lately an attractive herbaceous border and in which a few late Michaelmas daisies showed a last dying splash of purple beauty. The lawn and the paths showed signs of neglect.

Summing up, Detective Inspector Craddock thought: Probably not much money to spend on gardeners— fond of flowers and a good eye for planning and massing a border. House needs painting. Most houses do nowadays. Pleasant little property.

As Craddock's car stopped before the front door, Sergeant Fletcher came round the side of the house. With an erect military bearing, Sergeant Fletcher looked like a guardsman, and was able to impart several different meanings to the one monosyllable: "Sir."

"So there you are, Fletcher."

"Sir," said Sergeant Fletcher.

"Anything to report?"

"We've finished going over the house, sir. Scherz doesn't seem to have left any fingerprints anywhere. He wore gloves, of course. No signs of any of the doors or windows being forced to effect an entrance. He seems to have come out from Medenham on the bus, arriving here at six o'clock. Side door of the house was locked at 5:30, I understand. Looks as though he must have walked in through the front door. Miss Blacklock states that that door isn't usually locked until the house is shut up for the night. The maid, on the other hand, states that the front door was locked all the afternoon—but she'd say anything. Very temperamental you'll find her. Mittel Europa refugee of some kind."

"Difficult, is she?"

"Sir!" said Sergeant Fletcher, with intense feeling.

Craddock smiled.

Fletcher resumed his report.

"Lighting system is quite in order everywhere. We haven't spotted yet how he operated the lights. It was just the one circuit went. Drawing-room and hall. Of course, nowadays, the wall brackets and lamps wouldn't all be on one fuse—but this is old-fashioned installation and wiring. Don't see how he could have tampered with the fuse box because it's out by the scullery and he'd have had to go through the kitchen, so the maid would have seen him."

"Unless she was in it with him?"

"That's very possible. Both foreigners—and I wouldn't trust her a yard—not a yard."

Craddock noticed two enormous frightened black eyes peering out of a window by the front door. The face, flattened against the pane, was hardly visible.

"That her there?"

"That's right, sir."

The face disappeared.

Craddock rang the front doorbell.

After a long wait the door was opened by a good-looking young woman with chestnut hair and a bored expression.

"Detective Inspector Craddock," said Craddock.

The young woman gave him a cool stare out of very

attractive hazel eyes and said, "Come in. Miss Blacklock is expecting you."

The hall, Craddock noted, was long and narrow and
seemed almost incredibly full of doors.

The young woman threw open one on the left, and
said: "Inspector Craddock, Aunt Letty. Mitzi wouldn't
go to the door. She's shut herself up in the kitchen and
she's making the most marvelous moaning noises. I
shouldn't think we'd get any lunch."

She added in an explanatory manner to Craddock,
"She doesn't like the police," and withdrew, shutting
the door behind her.

Craddock advanced to meet the owner of Little
Paddocks.

He saw a tall active-looking woman of about sixty.
Her gray hair had a slight natural wave and made a
distinguished setting for an intelligent resolute face.
She had keen gray eyes and a square determined chin.
There was a surgical dressing on her left ear. She
wore no make-up and was plainly dressed in a well-cut
tweed coat and skirt and pullover. Round the neck of
the latter she wore, rather unexpectedly, a set of old-
fashioned cameos—a Victorian touch which seemed to
hint at a sentimental streak not otherwise apparent.

Close beside her, with an eager round face and untidy hair escaping from a hairnet, was a woman of
about the same age whom Craddock had no difficulty
in recognizing as the "Dora Bunner—companion" of
Constable Legg's notes—to which the latter had added
an off-the-record commentary of "Scatty!"

Miss Blacklock spoke in a pleasant well-bred voice.

"Good morning, Inspector Craddock. This is my
friend, Miss Bunner, who helps me run the house.
Won't you sit down? You won't smoke, I suppose?"

"Not on duty, I'm afraid, Miss Blacklock."

"What a shame!"

Craddock's eyes took in the room with a quick, practiced glance. Typical Victorian double drawing-room. Two long windows in this room, built-out bay window in the other . . . chairs . . . sofa . . . center table with a big bowl of chrysanthemums—another bowl in the window—all fresh and pleasant without much originality. The only incongruous note was a small silver vase with dead violets in it on a table near the archway into the further room. Since he could not imagine Miss Blacklock tolerating dead flowers in a room, he imagined it to be the only indication that something out of the way had occurred to distract the routine of a well-run household.

He said, "I take it, Miss Blacklock, that this is the room in which the—incident occurred?"

"Yes."

"And you should have seen it last night," Miss Bunner exclaimed. "Such a mess. Two little tables knocked over, and the leg off one—people barging about in the dark—and someone put down a lighted cigarette and burnt one of the best bits of furniture. People—young people especially—are so careless about these things . . . Luckily none of the china got broken—"

Miss Blacklock interrupted gently but firmly, "Dora, all these things, vexatious as they may be, are only trifles. It will be best, I think, if we just answer Inspector Craddock's questions."

"Thank you, Miss Blacklock. I shall come to what happened last night presently. First of all, I want you to tell me when you first saw the dead man—Rudi Scherz."

"Rudi Scherz?" Miss Blacklock looked slightly surprised. "Is that his name? Somehow, I thought—Oh, well, it doesn't matter. My first encounter with him was when I was in Medenham Spa for a day's shopping about—let me see—about three weeks ago. We—Miss

Bunner and I—were having lunch at the Royal Spa
Hotel. As we were just leaving after lunch, I heard
my name spoken. It was this young man. He said: 'It
is Miss Blacklock, is it not?' And went on to say that
perhaps I did not remember him, but that he was the
son of the proprietor of the Hôtel des Alpes at Montreux, where my sister and I had stayed for nearly a year
during the war."

"The Hôtel des Alpes, Montreux," noted Craddock.
"And did you remember him, Miss Blacklock?"

"No, I didn't. Actually, I had no recollection of ever
having seen him before. These boys at hotel reception
desks all look exactly alike. We had had a very pleasant
time at Montreux and the proprietor there had been
extremely obliging, so I tried to be as civil as possible
and said I hoped he was enjoying being in England, and
he said, yes, that his father had sent him over for six
months to learn the hotel business. It all seemed quite
natural."

"And your next encounter?"

"About—yes, it must have been ten days ago, he
suddenly turned up here. I was very surprised to see
him. He apologized for troubling me, but said I was
the only person he knew in England. He told me that
he urgently needed money to return to Switzerland as
his mother was dangerously ill."

"But Letty didn't give it to him," Miss Bunner put
in breathlessly.

"It was a thoroughly fishy story," said Miss Blacklock with vigor. "I made up my mind that he was
definitely a wrong 'un. That story about wanting the
money to return to Switzerland was nonsense. His father
could easily have wired for arrangements to have been
made in this country. These hotel people are all in with
each other. I suspected that he'd been embezzling money
or something of that kind." She paused and said dryly,

"In case you think I'm hardhearted, I was secretary for many years to a big financier and one becomes wary about appeals for money. I know simply all the hard luck stories there are.

"The only thing that did surprise me," she added thoughtfully, "was that he gave in so easily. He went away at once without any more argument. It's as though he had never expected to get the money."

"Do you think now, looking back on it, that his coming was really by way of a pretext to spy out the land?"

Miss Blacklock nodded her head vigorously.

"That's exactly what I do think—now. He made certain remarks as I let him out—about the rooms. He said, 'You have a very nice dining-room' (which, of course, it isn't—it's a horrid dark little room), just as an excuse to look inside. And then he sprang forward and unfastened the front door; he said, 'Let me.' I think now he wanted to have a look at the fastening. Actually, like most people round here, we never lock the front door until it gets dark. Anyone could walk in."

"And the side door? There is a side door to the garden, I understand?"

"Yes. I went out through it to shut up the ducks not long before the people arrived."

"Was it locked when you went out?"

Miss Blacklock frowned.

"I can't remember . . . I think so. I certainly locked it when I came in."

"That would be about quarter past six?"

"Somewhere about then."

"And the front door?"

"That's not usually locked until later."

"Then Scherz could have walked in quite easily that way. Or he could have slipped in whilst you were out shutting up the ducks. He'd already spied out the lay of the land and had probably noted various places of concealment—cupboards, etc. Yes, that all seems quite clear."

"I beg your pardon, it isn't at all clear," said Miss Blacklock. "Why on earth should anyone take all that elaborate trouble to come and burgle this house and stage that silly sort of holdup?"

"Do you keep money in the house, Miss Blacklock?"

"About five pounds in that desk there, and perhaps a pound or two in my purse."

"Jewelry?"

"A couple of rings and brooches and the cameos I'm wearing. You must agree with me, Inspector, that the whole thing's absurd."

"It wasn't burglary at all," cried Miss Bunner. "I've told you so, Letty, all along. It was revenge! Because you wouldn't give him that money! He deliberately shot at you—twice."

"Ah," said Craddock. "We'll come now to last night. What happened exactly, Miss Blacklock? Tell me in your own words as nearly as you can remember."

Miss Blacklock reflected a moment.

"The clock struck," she said. "The one on the mantelpiece. I remember saying that if anything were going to happen it would have to happen soon. And then the clock struck. We all listened to it without saying anything. It chimes, you know. It chimed the two quarters and then, quite suddenly, the lights went out."

"What lights were on?"

"The wall brackets in here and in the further room. The standard lamp and the two small reading lamps weren't on."

"Was there a flash first, or a noise when the lights went out?"

"I don't think so."

"I'm sure there was a flash," said Dora Bunner. "And a crackling noise. Dangerous!"

"And then, Miss Blacklock?"

"The door opened—"

"Which door? There are two in the room."

"Oh, this door in here. The one in the other room doesn't open. It's a dummy. The door opened and there he was, a masked man with a revolver. It just seemed too fantastic for words, but, of course, at the time I just thought it was a silly joke. He said something —I forget what—"

"Hands up or I shoot!" supplied Miss Bunner dramatically.

"Something like that," said Miss Blacklock, rather doubtfully.

"And you all put your hands up?"

"Oh yes," said Miss Bunner. "We all did. I mean it was part of it."

"I didn't," said Miss Blacklock crisply. "It seemed so utterly silly. And I was annoyed by the whole thing."

"And then?"

"The flashlight was right in my eyes. It dazzled me. And then, quite incredibly, I heard a bullet whiz past me and hit the wall by my head. Somebody shrieked and then I felt a burning pain in my ear and heard the second report."

"It was terrifying," put in Miss Bunner.

"And what happened next, Miss Blacklock?"

"It's difficult to say—I was so staggered by the pain and the surprise. The—the figure turned away and seemed to stumble and then there was another shot and his flashlight went out and everybody began pushing and calling out. All banging into each other."

"Where were you standing, Miss Blacklock?"

"She was over by the table. She'd got the vase of violets in her hand," said Miss Bunner breathlessly.

"I was over here." Miss Blacklock went over to the small table by the archway. "Actually, it was the cigarette box I'd got in my hand."

Inspector Craddock examined the wall behind her. The two bullet holes showed plainly. The bullets themselves had been extracted and had been sent for comparison with the revolver.

He said quietly, "You had a very near escape, Miss Blacklock."

"He did shoot at her," said Miss Bunner. "Deliberately at her! I saw him. He turned the flash round on everybody until he found her and then he held it right at her and just fired at her. He meant to kill you, Letty."

"Dora dear, you've just got that into your head from mulling the whole thing over and over."

"He shot at you," repeated Dora stubbornly. "He meant to shoot you and when he'd missed, he shot himself. I'm certain that's the way it was!"

"I don't think he meant to shoot himself for a minute," said Miss Blacklock. "He wasn't the kind of man who shoots himself."

"You tell me, Miss Blacklock, that until the revolver was fired you thought the whole business was a joke?"

"Naturally. What else could I think it was?"

"Who did you think was the author of this joke?"

"You thought Patrick had done it at first," Dora Bunner reminded her.

"Patrick?" asked the Inspector, sharply.

"My young cousin, Patrick Simmons," Miss Blacklock continued sharply, annoyed with her friend. "It did occur to me when I saw this advertisement that it might be some attempt at humor on his part, but he denied it absolutely."

"And then you were worried, Letty," said Miss Bunner. "You were worried, although you pretended not to be. And you were quite right to be worried. It said a murder is announced—and it was announced—your murder! And if the man hadn't missed, you would have been murdered. And then where should we all be?"

Dora Bunner was trembling as she spoke. Her face was puckered up and she looked as though she were going to cry.

Miss Blacklock patted her on the shoulder.

"It's all right, Dora dear—don't get excited. It's so bad for you. Everything's quite all right. We've had a nasty experience, but it's over now." She added, "You must pull yourself together for my sake, Dora. I rely on you, you know, to keep the house going. Isn't it the day for the laundry to come?"

"Oh, dear me, Letty, how fortunate you reminded me! I wonder if they'll return that missing pillowcase. I must make a note in the book about it. I'll go and see to it at once."

"And take these violets away," said Miss Blacklock. "There's nothing I hate more than dead flowers."

"What a pity. I picked them fresh yesterday. They haven't lasted at all—Oh, dear, I must have forgotten to put any water in the vase. Fancy that! I'm always forgetting things. Now I must go and see about the laundry. They might be here any moment."

She bustled away, looking quite happy again.

"She's not very strong," said Miss Blacklock, "and excitements are bad for her. Is there anything more you want to know, Inspector?"

"I just want to know exactly how many people make up your household here and something about them."

"Yes, well in addition to myself and Dora Bunner, I have two young cousins living here at present, Patrick and Julia Simmons."

"Cousins? Not a nephew and niece?"

"No, they call me Aunt Letty, but actually they are distant cousins. Their mother was my second cousin."

"Have they always made their home with you?"

"Oh, dear, no; only for the last two months. They lived in the South of France before the war. Patrick went into the Navy and Julia, I believe, was in one of the Ministries. She was at Llandudno. When the war was over their mother wrote and asked me if they could possibly come to me as paying guests—Julia is training as a dispenser in Milchester General Hospital, Patrick is studying for an engineering degree at Milchester University. Milchester, as you know, is only fifty minutes by bus, and I was very glad to have them here. This house is really too large for me. They pay a small sum for board and lodging and it all works out very well." She added with a smile, "I like having somebody young about the place."

"Then there is a Mrs. Haymes, I believe?"

"Yes. She works as an assistant gardener at Dayas Hall, Mrs. Lucas's place. The cottage there is occupied by the old gardener and his wife and Mrs. Lucas asked if I could billet her here. She's a very nice girl. Her husband was killed in Italy, and she has a boy of eight who is at a prep school and whom I have arranged to have here in the holidays."

"And by way of domestic help?"

"A Mrs. Huggins from the village comes up five mornings a week and I have a foreign refugee with a most unpronounceable name as a kind of lady cook help. You will find Mitzi rather difficult, I'm afraid. She has a kind of persecution mania."

Craddock nodded. He was conscious in his own mind of yet another of Constable Legg's invaluable commentaries. Having appended the word "Scatty" to Dora Bunner, and "All right" to Letitia Blacklock, he had embellished Mitzi's record with the one word, "Liar."

As though she had read his mind Miss Blacklock said, "Please don't be too prejudiced against the poor thing because she's a liar. I do really believe that, like so many liars, there is a real substratum of truth behind her lies. I mean that though, to take an instance, her atrocity stories have grown and grown until every kind of unpleasant story that has ever appeared in print has happened to her or her relatives personally; she did have a bad shock initially and did see one, at least, of her relatives killed. I think a lot of these displaced persons feel, perhaps justly, that their claim to our notice and sympathy lies in their atrocity value and so they exaggerate and invent."

She added, "Quite frankly, Mitzi is a maddening person. She exasperates and infuriates us all, she is suspicious and sulky, is perpetually having 'feelings' and thinking herself insulted. But in spite of it all, I really am sorry for her." She smiled. "And, also, when she wants to, she can cook very nicely."

"I'll try not to ruffle her more than I can help," said Craddock soothingly. "Was that Miss Julia Simmons who opened the door to me?"

"Yes. Would you like to see her now? Patrick has gone out. Phillipa Haymes you will find working at Dayas Hall."

"Thank you, Miss Blacklock. I'd like to see Miss Simmons now if I may."

CHAPTER 6

Julia, Mitzi and Patrick

JULIA, when she came into the room and sat down in the chair vacated by Letitia Blacklock, had an air of composure that Craddock, for some reason, found annoying. She fixed a limpid gaze on him and waited for his questions.

Miss Blacklock had tactfully left the room.

"Please tell me about last night, Miss Simmons."

"Last night?" murmured Julia with a blank stare. "Oh, we all slept like logs. Reaction, I suppose."

"I mean last night from six o'clock onwards."

"Oh, I see. Well, a lot of tiresome people came—"

"They were?"

She gave him another limpid stare.

"Don't you know all this already?"

"I'm asking the questions, Miss Simmons," said Craddock pleasantly.

"My mistake. I always find repetitions so dready. Apparently you don't . . . Well, there were Colonel and Mrs. Easterbrook, Miss Hinchliffe and Miss Murgatroyd, Mrs. Swettenham and Edmund Swettenham, and Mrs. Harmon, the vicar's wife. They arrived in that order. And if you want to know what they said—they all said the same things in turn. 'I see you've got your central heating on' and 'What lovely chrysanthemums!' "

Craddock bit his lip. The mimicry was good.

"The exception was Mrs. Harmon. She's rather a pet. She came in with her hat falling off and her shoelaces untied and she asked straight out when the murder was going to happen. It embarrassed everybody because they'd all been pretending they'd dropped in by chance. Aunt Letty said in her dry way that it was due to happen quite soon. And then that clock chimed and just as it finished the lights went out, the door was flung open and a masked figure said, 'Stick 'em up, guys,' or something like that. It was exactly like a bad film. Really, quite ridiculous. And then he fired two shots at Aunt Letty and suddenly it wasn't ridiculous any more."

"Where was everybody when this happened?"

"When the light went out? Well, just standing about, you know. Mrs. Harmon was sitting on the sofa— Hinch (that's Miss Hinchliffe) had taken up a manly stance in front of the fireplace."

"You were all in this room, or the far room?"

"Mostly, I think, in this room. Patrick had gone into the other to get the sherry. I think Colonel Easterbrook went after him, but I don't really know. We were —well—as I said, just standing about."

"Where were you, yourself?"

"I think I was over by the window. Aunt Letty went to get the cigarettes."

"On that table by the archway?"

"Yes—and then the lights went out and the bad film started."

"The man had a powerful flashlight. What did he do with it?"

"Well, he shone it on us. Horribly dazzling. It just made you blink."

"I want you to answer this very carefully, Miss Simmons. Did he hold it steady or did he move it about?"

Julia considered. Her manner was now definitely less weary.

"He moved it," she said slowly. "Like a spotlight in a dance hall. It was full in my eyes and then it went on round the room and then the shots came. Two shots."

"And then?"

"He whirled round—and Mitzi began to scream like a siren from somewhere and his flashlight went out and there was another shot. And then the door closed (it does, you know, slowly, with a whining noise—quite uncanny) and there we were all in the dark, not knowing what to do, and poor Bunny squealing like a pig and Mitzi going all out across the hall."

"Would it be your opinion that the man shot himself deliberately, or do you think he stumbled and the revolver went off accidentally?"

"I haven't the faintest idea. The whole thing was so stagy. Actually, I thought it was still some silly joke—until I saw the blood from Aunt Letty's ear. But even if you were actually going to fire a revolver to make the thing more real, you'd be careful to fire it well above someone's head, wouldn't you?"

"You would indeed. Do you think he could see clearly who he was firing at? I mean, was Miss Blacklock clearly outlined in the light of the torch?"

"I've no idea. I wasn't looking at her. I was looking at the man."

"What I'm getting at is—do you think the man was deliberately aiming at her—at her in particular, I mean?"

Julia seemed a little startled by the idea.

"You mean deliberately picking on Aunt Letty? Oh, I shouldn't think so . . . After all, if he wanted to take a pot shot at Aunt Letty, there would be heaps of more suitable opportunities. There would be no point in collecting all the friends and neighbors just to make it more difficult. He could have shot her from behind a hedge in the good old Irish fashion any day of the week, and probably got away with it."

And that, thought Craddock, was a very complete reply to Dora Bunner's suggestion of a deliberate attack on Letitia Blacklock.

He said, with a sigh. "Thank you, Miss Simmons. I'd better go and see Mitzi now."

"Mind her fingernails," warned Julia. "She's a tartar!"

2

Craddock, with Fletcher in attendance, found Mitzi in the kitchen. She was rolling pastry and looked up suspiciously as they entered.

Her black hair hung over her eyes; she looked sullen and the purple jumper and brilliant green skirt she wore were not becoming to her pasty complexion.

"What do you come in my kitchen for, Mr. Policeman? You are police, yes? Always, always there is persecution—ah! I shoud be used to it by now. They say it is different here in England, but no, it is just the same. You come to torture me, yes, to make me say things, but I shall say nothing. You will tear off my fingernails, and put lighted matches on my skin—oh, yes, and worse than that. But I will not speak, do you hear? I shall say nothing—nothing at all. And you will send me away to a concentration camp, and I shall not care."

Craddock looked at her thoughtfully, selecting what was likely to be the best method of attack. Finally he sighed and said, "O.K. then; get your hat and coat."

"What is that you say?" Mitzi looked startled.

"Get your hat and coat and come along, I haven't got my nail-pulling apparatus and the rest of the bag of tricks with me. We keep all that down at the station. Got the handcuffs handy, Fletcher?"

"Sir!" said Sergeant Fletcher, with appreciation.

"But I do not want to come!" screeched Mitzi, backing away from him.

"Then you'll answer civil questions civilly. If you like, you can have a solicitor present."

"A lawyer? I do not like a lawyer. I do not want a lawyer."

She put the rolling-pin down, dusted her hands on a cloth and sat down.

"What do you want to know?" she asked sulkily.

"I want your account of what happened here last night."

"You know very well what happened."

"I want your account of it."

"I tried to go away. Did she tell you that? When I saw that in the paper saying about murder, I wanted to go away. She would not let me. She is very hard—not at all sympathetic. She made me stay. But I knew—I knew what would happen. I knew I should be murdered."

"Well, you weren't murdered, were you?"

"No," admitted Mitzi grudgingly.

"Come now, tell me what happened."

"I was nervous. Oh, I was nervous. All that evening. I hear things. People moving about. Once I think someone is in the hall moving stealthily—but it is only that Mrs. Haymes coming through the side door so as not to dirty the front steps, she says. Much she cares! She is a Nazi herself, that one, with her fair hair and her blue eyes, so superior and looking at me and thinking that I—I am only dirt—"

"Never mind Mrs. Haymes."

"Who does she think she is? Has she had expensive university education like I have? Has she a degree in

Economics? No, she is just a paid laborer. She digs and mows grass and is paid so much every Saturday. Who is she to call herself a lady?"

"Never mind Mrs. Haymes, I said. Go on."

"I take the sherry and the glasses, and the little pastries that I have made so nice into the drawing-room. Then the bell rings and I answer the door. Again and again and again I answer the door. It is degrading —but I do it. And then I go back into the pantry and I start to polish the silver, and I think it will be very handy, that, because if someone comes to kill me, I have there close at hand the big carving knife, all sharp."

"Very foresighted of you."

"And then, suddenly—I hear shots. I think: It has come—it is happening. I run through the dining-room (the other door—it will not open). I stand a moment to listen and then there comes another shot and a big thud, out there in the hall, and I turn the door handle, but it is locked outside. I am shut in there like a rat in a trap. And I go mad with fear. I scream and I scream and I beat upon the door. And at last—at last—they turn the key and let me out. And then I bring candles, many, many candles—and the lights go on, and I see blood— blood! Ah, *Gott in Himmel,* the blood! It is not the first time I have seen blood. My little brother—I see him killed before my eyes—I see the blood in the street —people shot, dying—I—"

"Yes," said Inspector Craddock. "Thank you very much."

"And now," said Mitzi dramatically, "you can arrest me and take me to prison!"

"Not today," said Inspector Craddock.

3

As Craddock and Fletcher went through the hall to the front door, it was flung open and a tall, handsome young man almost collided with them.

"Sleuths, as I live!" cried the young man.

"Mr. Patrick Simmons?"

"Quite right, Inspector. You're the Inspector, aren't you, and the other's the Sergeant?"

"You are quite right, Mr. Simmons. Can I have a word with you, please?"

"I am innocent, Inspector. I swear I am innocent."

"Now then, Mr. Simmons, don't play the fool. I've a good many other people to see and I don't want to waste time. What's this room? Can we go in here?"

"It's the so-called study—but nobody studies."

"I was told that you were studying," said Craddock.

"I found I couldn't concentrate on mathematics, so I came home."

In a businesslike manner Inspector Craddock demanded full name, age, details of war service.

"And now, Mr. Simmons, will you describe what happened last night?"

"We killed the fatted calf, Inspector. That is, Mitzi set her hand to making savory pastries, Aunt Letty opened a new bottle of sherry—"

Craddock interrupted.

"A new bottle? Was there an old one?"

"Yes, half full. But Aunt Letty didn't seem to fancy it."

"Was she nervous then?"

"Oh, not really. She's extremely sensible. It was old Bunny, I think, who had put the wind up—prophesying disaster all day."

"Miss Bunner was definitely apprehensive then?"

"Oh, yes, she enjoyed herself thoroughly."

"She took the advertisement seriously?"

"It scared her into fits."

"Miss Blacklock seems to have thought, when she first read that advertisement, that you had had something to do with it. Why was that?"

"Ah, sure, I get blamed for everything round here!"

"You didn't have anything to do with it, did you, Mr. Simmons?"

"Me? Never in the world."

"Had you ever seen or spoken to this Rudi Scherz?"

"Never saw him in my life."

"It was the kind of joke you might have played, though?"

"Who's been telling you that? Just because I once made Bunny an apple pie bed—and sent Mitzi a postcard saying the Gestapo was on her track—"

"Just give me your account of what happened."

"I'd just gone into the small drawing-room to fetch the drinks when, hey, presto, the lights went out. I turned round and there's a fellow standing in the doorway saying, 'Stick your hands up,' and everybody gasping and squealing, and just when I'm wondering if I can rush him, he starts firing a revolver and then crash down he goes and his flashlight goes out and we're in the dark again, and Colonel Easterbrook starts shouting orders in his barrack-room voice. 'Lights!' he says, and will my lighter go on? No, it won't, as is the way of those cussed inventions."

"Did it seem to you that the intruder was definitely aiming at Miss Blacklock?"

"Ah, how could I tell? I should say he just loosed off his revolver for the fun of the thing—and then found, maybe, he'd gone too far."

"And shot himself?"

"It could be. When I saw the face of him, he looked

like the kind of little pasty thief who might easily lose his nerve."

"And you're sure you had never seen him before?"

"Never."

"Thank you, Mr. Simmons. I shall want to interview the other people who were here last night. What would be the best order in which to take them?"

"Well, our Phillipa—Mrs. Haymes—works at Dayas Hall. The gates of it are nearly opposite this gate. After that, the Swettenhams are the nearest. Anyone will tell you."

CHAPTER 7

Among Those Present

DAYAS HALL had certainly suffered during the war years. Couch grass grew enthusiastically over what had once been an asparagus bed, as evidenced by a few waving tufts of asparagus foliage. Groundsel, bindweed and other garden pests showed every sign of vigorous growth.

A portion of the kitchen garden bore evidence of having been reduced to discipline and here Craddock found a sour-looking old man leaning pensively on a spade.

"It's Mrs. 'Aymes you want? I couldn't say where you'd find 'er. 'As 'er own ideas, she 'as, about what she'll do. Not one to take advice. I could show 'er—show 'er willing—but what's the good? Won't listen, these young ladies won't! Think they know everything because they've put on breeches and gone for a ride on a tractor. But it's gardening that's needed here. And that isn't learned in a day. Gardening, that what this place needs."

"It looks as though it does," said Craddock.

The old man chose to take this remark as an aspersion.

"Now, look here, mister, what do you suppose I can do with a place this size? Three men and a boy, that's what it used to 'ave. And that's what it wants. There's not many men could put in the work on it that I do.

'Ere sometimes, I am, till eight o'clock at night. Eight o'clock."

"What do you work by? An oil lamp?"

"Naterally I don't mean this time o' year. Naterally. Summer evenings I'm talking about."

"Oh," said Craddock. "I'd better go and look for Mrs. Haymes."

The rustic displayed some interest.

"What are you wanting 'er for? Police, aren't you? She been in trouble, or is it the do there was up to Little Paddocks? Masked man bursting in and holding up a roomful of people with a revolver. Ah! That sort of thing wouldn't 'ave 'appened afore the war. Deserters, that's what it is. Desperate men roaming the countryside. Why don't the military round 'em up?"

"I've no idea," said Craddock. "I suppose this holdup caused a lot of talk?"

"That it did. What's us coming to? That's what Ned Barker said. Comes of going to the pictures so much, he said. But Tom Riley, he says it comes of letting these furriners run about loose. And depend on it, he says, that girl as cooks up there for Miss Blacklock and 'as such a nasty temper—she's in it, he said. She's a Communist or worse, he says, and we don't like that sort 'ere. And Marlene, who's behind the bar, you understand, she will 'ave it that there must be something very valuable up at Miss Blacklock's. Not that you'd think it, she says, for I'm sure Miss Blacklock goes about as plain as plain, except for them great rows of false pearls she wears. And, then she says—supposin' as them pearls is real; and Florrie (that's old Bellamy's daughter), she says, 'Nonsense,' she says—'noovo art—that's what they are—costume jewelry,' she says. Costume jewelry—that's a fine way of labeling a string of false pearls. Roman pearls, the gentry used to call 'em once—and Parisian diamonds—my wife was a lady's maid and I know. But what does it all mean—just glass! I suppose it's costume jewelry that young Miss Simmons wears—gold ivy leaves and dogs and such like. 'Tisn't often you see a real bit of gold nowadays—even wedding rings they make of this gray plattinghum stuff. Shabby, I call it—for all that it costs the earth."

Old Ashe paused for breath and then continued, " 'Miss Blacklock don't keep much money in the 'ouse, that I do know,' says Jim Huggins, speaking up. He should know, for it's his wife as goes up and does for 'em at Little Paddocks, and she's a woman as knows most of what's going on. Nosy, if you get me."

"Did he say what Mrs. Huggins's view was?"

"That Mitzi's mixed up in it, that's what she thinks. Awful temper she 'as, and the airs she gives herself! Called Mrs. Huggins a working woman to her face the other morning."

Craddock stood a moment, checking over in his orderly mind the substance of the old gardener's remarks. It gave him a good cross section of rural opinion in Chipping Cleghorn, but he didn't think there was anything to help him in his task. He turned away and the old man called after him grudgingly:

"Maybe you'd find her in the apple orchard. She's younger than I am for getting the apples down."

And sure enough, in the apple orchard Craddock found Phillipa Haymes. His first view was a pair of nice legs encased in breeches, sliding easily down the trunk of a tree. Then Phillipa, her face flushed, her hair ruffled by the branches, stood looking at him in a startled fashion.

Make a good Rosalind, Craddock thought automatically, for Detective Inspector Craddock was a Shakespeare enthusiast and had played the part of the melancholy Jaques with great success in a performance of *As You Like It* for the Police Orphanage.

A moment later he amended his view. Phillipa Haymes was too wooden for Rosalind, her fairness and her impassivity were intensely English, but English of the twentieth rather than of the sixteenth century. Well-bred, unemotional English, without a sparkle of mischief.

"Good morning, Mrs. Haymes. I'm sorry if I startled you. I'm Detective Inspector Craddock of the Middleshire Police. I wanted to have a word with you."

"About last night?"

"Yes."

"Will it take long? Shall we——"

She looked about her rather doubtfully.

Craddock indicated a fallen tree trunk.

"Rather informal," he said pleasantly, "but I don't want to interrupt your work longer than necessary."

"Thank you."

"It's just for the record. You came in from work at what time last night?"

"At about half past five. I'd stayed about twenty minutes later in order to finish some watering in the greenhouse."

"You came in by which door?"

"The side door. One cuts across by the ducks and the hen-house from the drive. It saves going round and, besides, it avoids dirtying up the front porch. I'm in rather a mucky state sometimes."

"You always come in that way?"

"Yes."

"The door was unlocked?"

"Yes. During the summer it's usually wide open. This time of the year it's shut but not locked. We all go out and in that way a good deal. I locked it when I came in."

"Do you always do that?"

"I've been doing it for the last week. You see, it gets

dark at six. Miss Blacklock goes out to shut up the ducks and the hens sometimes in the evening, but she very often goes out through the kitchen door."

"And you are quite sure you did lock the side door this time?"

"I really am quite sure about that."

"Quite so, Mrs. Haymes. And what did you do when you came in?"

"Kicked off my muddy footwear and went upstairs, had a bath and changed. Then I came down and found that a kind of party was in progress. I hadn't known anything about this funny advertisement until then."

"Now please describe just what occurred when the holdup happened."

"Well, the lights went out suddenly—"

"Where were you?"

"By the mantelpiece. I was searching for my lighter which I thought I had put down there. The lights went out—and everybody giggled. Then the door was flung open and this man shone a flashlight on us and flourished a revolver and told us to put our hands up."

"Which you proceeded to do?"

"Well, I didn't actually. I thought it was just fun, and I was tired and didn't think I really needed to put them up."

"In fact, you were bored by the whole thing?"

"I was, rather. And then the revolver went off. The shots sounded deafening and I was really frightened. The flashlight went whirling round and dropped and went out, and then Mitzi started screaming. It was just like a pig being killed."

"Did you find the flashlight very dazzling?"

"No, not particularly. It was quite a strong one, though. It lit up Miss Bunner for a moment and she looked quite like a turnip ghost—you know, all white and staring with her mouth open and her eyes starting out of her head."

"The man moved the flashlight?"

"Oh, yes, he played it all round the room."

"As though he were looking for someone?"

"Not particularly, I should say."

"And after that, Mrs. Haymes?"

Phillipa Haymes frowned.

"Oh, it was all a terrible muddle and confusion. Edmund Swettenham and Patrick Simmons switched on their lighters and they went out into the hall and we followed, and someone opened the dining-room door— the lights hadn't gone out there—and Edmund Swettenham gave Mitzi a terrific slap on the cheek and brought her out of her screaming fit, and after that it wasn't so bad."

"You saw the body of the dead man?"

"Yes."

"Was he known to you? Had you ever seen him before?"

"Never."

"Have you any opinion as to whether his death was accidental, or do you think he shot himself deliberately?"

"I haven't the faintest idea."

"You didn't see him when he came to the house previously?"

"No. I believe it was in the middle of the morning and I wouldn't have been there."

"Thank you, Mrs. Haymes. One thing more. You haven't any valuable jewelry? Rings, bracelets, anything of that kind?"

Phillipa shook her head.

"My engagement ring—a couple of brooches."

"And, as far as you know, there was nothing of particular value in the house?"

"No. I mean there is some quite nice silver—but nothing out of the ordinary."

"Thank you, Mrs. Haymes."

2

As Craddock retraced his steps through the kitchen garden he came face to face with a large, red-faced lady, carefully corseted.

"Good morning," she said belligerently. "What do you want here?"

"Mrs. Lucas? I am Detective Inspector Craddock."

"Oh, that's who you are. I beg your pardon. I don't like strangers forcing their way into my garden, wasting the gardener's time. But I quite understand you have to do your duty."

"Quite so."

"May I ask if we are to expect a repetition of that outrage last night at Miss Blacklock's? Is it a gang?"

"We are satisfied, Mrs. Lucas, that it was not the work of a gang."

"There are far too many robberies nowadays. The police are getting slack." Craddock did not reply. "I suppose you've been talking to Phillipa Haymes?"

"I wanted her account as an eyewitness."

"You couldn't have waited until one o'clock, I suppose? After all, it would be fairer to question her in her time, rather than in mine."

"I'm anxious to get back to headquarters."

"Not that one expects consideration nowadays. Or a decent day's work. On duty late, half an hour's pottering. A break for relief at ten o'clock. No work done at all the moment the rain starts. When you want the lawn mowed there's always something wrong with the mower.

And off duty five or ten minutes before the proper time."

"I understand from Mrs. Haymes that she left here at twenty minutes past five yesterday instead of five o'clock."

"Oh, I daresay she did. Give her her due, Mrs. Haymes is quite keen on her work, though there have been days when I have come out here and not been able to find her anywhere. She is a lady by birth, of course, and one feels it one's duty to do something for these poor young war widows. Not that it isn't very inconvenient. Those long school holidays, and the arrangement is that she has extra time off then. I told her that there are really excellent camps nowadays where children can be sent and where they have a delightful time and enjoy it far more than wandering about with their parents. They need practically not come home at all in the summer holidays."

"But Mrs. Haymes didn't take kindly to that idea?"

"She's as obstinate as a mule, that girl. Just the time of year when I want the tennis court mowed and marked nearly every day. Old Ashe gets the lines crooked. But my convenience is never considered!"

"I presume Mrs. Haymes takes a smaller salary than is usual."

"Naturally. What else could she expect?"

"Nothing, I'm sure," said Craddock. "Good morning, Mrs. Lucas."

3

"It was dreadful," said Mrs. Swettenham happily. "Quite—quite—dreadful, and what I say is that they ought to be far more careful what advertisements they accept at the *Gazette* office. At the time, when I read it,

I thought it was very, very odd. I said so, didn't I, Edmund?"

"Do you remember just what you were doing when the lights went out, Mrs. Swettenham?" asked the Inspector.

"How that reminds me of my old Nannie! *Where was Moses when the light went out?* The answer, of course, was 'in the dark.' Just like us yesterday evening. All standing about and wondering what was going to happen. And then, you know, the thrill when it suddenly went pitch black. And the door opening—just a dim figure standing there with a revolver and that blinding light and a menacing voice saying, 'Your money or your life!' Oh, I've never enjoyed anything so much. And then, a minute later, of course, it was all dreadful. Real bullets, just whistling past our ears! It must have been just like the commandos in the war."

"Whereabouts were you standing or sitting at the time, Mrs. Swettenham?"

"Now, let me see, where was I? Who was I talking to, Edmund?"

"I really haven't the least idea, Mother."

"Was it Miss Hinchliffe I was asking about giving the hens cod-liver oil in the cold weather? Or was it Mrs. Harmon—no, she'd only just arrived. I think I was just saying to Colonel Easterbrook that I thought it was really very dangerous to have an atom research station in England. It ought to be on some lonely island in case the radioactivity gets loose."

"You don't remember if you were sitting or standing?"

"Does it really matter, Inspector? I was somewhere over by the window or near the mantelpiece, because I know I was quite near the clock when it struck. Such a thrilling moment! Waiting to see if anything might be going to happen."

"You describe the light from the flashlight as blinding. Was it turned full on you?"

"It was right in my eyes. I couldn't see a thing."

"Did the man hold it still, or did he move it about, from person to person?"

"Oh, I don't really know. Which did he do, Edmund?"

"It moved rather slowly over us all, so as to see what we were all doing, I suppose, in case we should try and rush him."

"And where exactly in the room were you, Mr. Swettenham?"

"I'd been talking to Julia Simmons. We were both standing up in the middle of the room—the long room."

"Was everyone in that room, or was there someone in the far room?"

"Phillipa Haymes had moved in there, I think. She was over by that far mantelpiece. I think she was looking for something."

"Have you any idea as to whether the third shot was suicide or an accident?"

"I've no idea at all. The man seemed to swerve round very suddenly and then crumple up and fall—but it was all very confused. You must realize that you couldn't really see anything. And then that refugee girl started yelling the place down."

"I understand it was you who unlocked the dining-room door and let her out?"

"Yes."

"The door was definitely locked on the outside?"

Edmund looked at him curiously.

"Certainly it was. Why, you don't imagine—"

"I just like to get my facts quite clear. Thank you, Mr. Swettenham."

4

Inspector Craddock was forced to spend quite a long time with Colonel and Mrs. Easterbrook. He had to listen to a long disquisition on the psychological aspect of the case.

"The psychological approach—that's the only thing nowadays," the colonel told him. "You've got to understand your criminal. Now, the whole setup here is plain as plain to a man who's had the wide experience that I have. Why does this fellow put that ad in? Psychology. He wants to advertise himself—to focus attention on himself. He's been passed over, perhaps despised as a foreigner by the other employees at the Spa Hotel. A girl has turned him down, perhaps. He wants to rivet her attention on him. Who is the idol of the movies nowadays—the gangster—the tough guy? Very well, he will be a tough guy. Robbery with violence. A mask? A revolver? But he wants an audience—he must have an audience. So he arranges for an audience. And then, at the supreme moment, his part runs away with him— he's more than a burglar. He's a killer. He shoots— blindly—"

Inspector Craddock caught gladly at a word.

"You say 'blindly,' Colonel Easterbrook. You didn't think that he was firing deliberately at one particular person—at Miss Blacklock, that is to say?"

"No, no. He just loosed off, as I say, blindly. And that's what brought him to himself. The bullet hit some-one—actually, it was only a graze, but he doesn't know that. He comes to himself with a bang. All this—this make-believe he's been indulging in—is real. He's shot at someone—perhaps killed someone. . . . It's all up with him. And so, in blind panic, he turns the revolver on himself."

Colonel Easterbrook paused, cleared his throat appreciatively and said, in a satisfied voice. "Plain as a pikestaff, that's what it is; plain as a pikestaff."

"It really is wonderful," said Mrs. Easterbrook, "the way you know exactly what happened, Archie."

Her voice was warm with admiration.

Inspector Craddock thought it was wonderful, too, but he was not quite so warmly appreciative.

"Exactly where were you in the room, Colonel Easterbrook, when the actual shooting business took place?"

"I was standing with my wife—near a center table with some flowers on it."

"I caught hold of your arm, didn't I, Archie, when it happened? I was simply scared to death. I just had to hold on to you."

"Poor little kitten," said the colonel playfully.

5

The Inspector ran Miss Hinchliffe to earth beside a pigsty.

"Nice creatures, pigs," said Miss Hinchliffe, scratching a wrinkled pink back. "Coming on well, isn't he? Good bacon round about Christmas time. Well, what do you want to see me about? I told your people last night I hadn't the least idea who the man was. Never saw him anywhere in the neighborhood snooping about or anything of that sort. Our Mrs. Mopp says he came from one of the big hotels in Medenham Wells. Why didn't he hold up someone there if he wanted to? Get a much better haul."

That was undeniable—Craddock proceeded with his inquiries.

"Where were you exactly when the incident took place?"

"Incident! Reminds me of my A.R.P. days. Saw some incidents then, I can tell you. Where was I when the shooting started? That what you want to know?"

"Yes."

"Leaning up against the mantelpiece, hoping to God someone would offer me a drink soon," replied Miss Hinchliffe promptly.

"Do you think that the shots were fired blindly, or aimed carefully at one particular person?"

"You mean aimed at Letty Blacklock? How the devil should I know? Damned hard to sort out what your impressions really were or what really happened, after it's all over. All I know is the lights went out, and that flashlight went whirling round, dazzling us all, and then the shots were fired and I thought to myself, If that damned young fool Patrick Simmons is playing his jokes with a loaded revolver, somebody will get hurt."

"You thought it was Patrick Simmons."

"Well, it seemed likely. Edmund Swettenham is intellectual and writes books and doesn't care for horseplay, and old Colonel Easterbrook wouldn't think that sort of thing funny. But Patrick's a wild boy. However, I apologize to him for the idea."

"Did your friend think it might be Patrick Simmons?"

"Murgatroyd? You'd better talk to her yourself. Not that you'll get any sense out of her. She's down in the orchard. I'll yell for her if you like."

Miss Hinchliffe raised her stentorian voice in a powerful bellow:

"Hi-youp, Murgatroyd!"

"Coming—" floated back a thin cry.

"Hurry up—poleece!" bellowed Miss Hinchliffe.

Miss Murgatroyd arrived at a brisk trot, very much out of breath. Her skirt was down at the hem and her hair was escaping from an inadequate hairnet. Her round good-natured face beamed.

"Is it Scotland Yard?" she asked breathlessly. "I'd no idea, or I wouldn't have left the house."

"We haven't called in Scotland Yard yet, Miss Murgatroyd. I'm Inspector Craddock from Milchester."

'Well, that's very nice, I'm sure," said Miss Murgatroyd vaguely. "Have you found any clues?"

"Where were you at the time of the crime, that's what he wants to know, Murgatroyd," said Miss Hinchliffe. She winked at Craddock.

"Oh, dear," gasped Miss Murgatroyd. "Of course. I ought to have been prepared. Alibis, of course. Now, let me see, I was just with everybody else."

"You weren't with me," said Miss Hinchliffe.

"Oh, dear, Hinch, wasn't I? No, of course, I'd been admiring the chrysanthemums. Very poor specimens really. And then it all happened—only I didn't really know it had happened—I mean I didn't know that anything like that had happened. I didn't imagine for a moment it was a real revolver—and all so awkward in the dark, and that dreadful screaming. I got it all wrong, you know. I thought she was being murdered—I mean the refugee girl. I thought she was having her throat cut across the hall somewhere. I didn't know it was him— I mean I didn't even know there was a man. It was really just a voice, you know, saying, 'Put them up, please!' "

" 'Stick 'em up!' " Miss Hinchliffe corrected. "And no suggestion of 'please' about it."

"It's so terrible to think that until that girl started screaming I was actually enjoying myself. Only being in the dark was very awkward and I got a knock on my corn. Agony, it was. Is there anything more you want to know, Inspector?"

"No," said Inspector Craddock, eyeing Miss Murgatroyd speculatively. "I don't really think there is."

Her friend gave a short bark of laughter.

"He's got you taped, Murgatroyd."

"I'm sure, Hinch," said Miss Murgatroyd, "that I'm only too willing to say anything I can."

"He doesn't want that," said Miss Hinchliffe.

She looked at the Inspector. "If you're doing this geographically, I suppose you'll go to the vicarage next. You might get something there. Mrs. Harmon looks as vague as they make them—but I sometimes think she's got brains. Anyway, she's got something."

As they watched the Inspector and Sergeant Fletcher stalk away, Amy Murgatroyd said breathlessly, "Oh, Hinch, was I very awful? I do get so flustered!"

"Not at all." Miss Hinchliffe smiled. "On the whole, I should say you did very well."

6

Inspector Craddock looked round the big shabby room with a sense of pleasure. It reminded him a little of his own Cumberland home. Faded chintz, big shabby chairs, flowers and books strewn about and a spaniel in a basket. Mrs. Harmon, too, with her distraught air, her general disarray and her eager face he found sympathetic.

But she said at once, frankly, "I shan't be any help to you, because I shut my eyes. I hate being dazzled. And then there were shots and I screwed them up tighter than ever. And I did wish, oh, I did wish, that it had been a quiet murder. I don't like bangs."

"So you didn't see anything." The Inspector smiled at her. "But you heard—"

"Oh, my goodness, yes, there was plenty to hear. Doors opening and shutting, and people saying silly things and gasping and old Mitzi screaming like a steam-engine—and poor Bunny squealing like a trapped pig. And everyone pushing and falling over everyone else. However, when there really didn't seem to be any more bangs coming, I opened my eyes. Everyone was out in the hall then, with candles. And then the lights came on and suddenly it was all as usual—I don't mean really as usual, but we were ourselves again, not just— people in the dark. People in the dark are quite different, aren't they?"

"I think I know what you mean, Mrs. Harmon."

Mrs. Harmon smiled at him.

"And there he was," she said. "A rather weasely looking foreigner—all pink and surprised-looking— lying there dead—with a revolver beside him. It didn't —oh, it didn't seem to make sense somehow."

It did not make sense to the Inspector either. . . .

The whole business worried him.

CHAPTER 8

Enter Miss Marple

CRADDOCK laid the typed transcript of the various interviews before the Chief Constable. The latter had just finished reading the wire received from the Swiss police.

"So he had a police record all right," said Rydesdale. "Hm—very much as one thought."

"Yes, sir."

"Jewelry . . . hm, yes . . . falsified entries . . . yes . . . check. Definitely a dishonest fellow."

"Yes, sir—in a small way."

"Quite so. And small things lead to large things."

"I wonder, sir."

The Chief Constable looked up.

"Worried, Craddock?"

"Yes, sir."

"Why? It's a straightforward story. Or isn't it? Let's see what all these people you've been talking to have to say."

He drew the report towards him and read it through rapidly.

"The usual thing—plenty of inconsistencies and contradictions. Different people's accounts of a few moments of stress never agree. But the main picture seems clear enough."

"I know, sir—but it's an unsatisfactory picture. If you know what I mean—it's the wrong picture."

"Well, let's take the facts. Rudi Scherz took the 5:20 bus from Medenham to Chipping Cleghorn, arriving there at six o'clock. Evidence of conductor and two passengers. From the bus stop he walked away in the direction of Little Paddocks. He got into the house with no particular difficulty—probably through the front door. He held up the company with a revolver, he fired two shots, one of which slightly wounded Miss Blacklock; he then killed himself with a third shot, whether accidentally or deliberately there is not sufficient evidence to show. The reasons why he did all this are profoundly unsatisfactory, I agree. But why isn't really a question we are called upon to answer. A coroner's jury may bring it in suicide—or accidental death. Whichever verdict it is, it's the same as far as we're concerned. We can write finis."

"You mean we can always fall back upon Colonel Easterbrook's psychology," said Craddock gloomily.

Rydesdale smiled.

"After all, the colonel's probably had a good deal of experience," he said. "I'm pretty sick of the psychological jargon that's used so glibly about everything nowadays—but we can't really rule it out."

"I still feel the picture's all wrong, sir."

"Any reason to believe that somebody in the setup at Chipping Cleghorn is lying to you?"

Craddock hesitated.

"I think the foreign girl knows more than she lets on. But that may be just prejudice on my part."

"You think she might possibly have been in it with this fellow? Let him into the house? Put him up to it?"

"Something of the kind. I wouldn't put it past her. But that surely indicates that there really was something valuable, money or jewelry, in the house, and that doesn't seem to have been the case. Miss Blacklock negatived it quite decidedly. So did the others. That leaves us with the proposition that there was something valuable in the house that nobody knew about—"

"Quite a best-seller plot."

"I agree it's ridiculous, sir. The only other point is Miss Bunner's certainty that it was a definite attempt by Scherz to murder Miss Blacklock."

"Well, from what you say—and from her statement— this Miss Bunner—"

"Oh, I agree, sir," Craddock put in quickly, "she's an utterly unreliable witness. Highly suggestible. Anyone could put a thing into her head—but the interesting thing is that this is quite her own theory—no one has suggested it to her. Everybody else negatives it. For once she's not swimming with the tide. It definitely is her own impression."

"And why should Rudi Scherz want to kill Miss Blacklock?"

"There you are, sir. I don't know. Miss Blacklock doesn't know—unless she's a much better liar than I think she is. Nobody knows. So presumably it isn't true."

He sighed.

"Cheer up, Craddock," said the Chief Constable. "I'm taking you off to lunch with Sir Henry and myself. The best that the Royal Spa Hotel in Medenham Wells can provide."

"Thank you, sir." Craddock looked slightly surprised.

"You see, we received a letter—" He broke off as Sir Henry Clithering entered the room. "Ah, there you are, Henry."

Sir Henry, informal this time, said, "Morning, Dermot."

"I've got something for you, Henry," said the Chief Constable.

"What's that?"

"Authentic letter from an old pussy. Staying at the

Royal Spa Hotel. Something she thinks we might like to know in connection with this Chipping Cleghorn business."

"The old pussies," said Sir Henry triumphantly. "What did I tell you? They hear everything. They see everything. And, unlike the famous adage, they speak all evil. What's this particular one got hold of?"

Rydesdale consulted the letter.

"Writes just like my old grandmother," he complained. "Spiky. Like a spider in the ink bottle, and all underlined. A good deal about how she hopes it won't be taking up our valuable time, but might possibly be of some slight assistance etc., etc. What's her name? Jane —something—Murple—no, Marple, Jane Marple."

"Ye gods and little fishes," said Sir Henry, "can it be? George, it's my own particular, one and only, four-starred pussy. The super-pussy of all old pussies. And she has managed somehow to be at Medenham Wells, instead of peacefully at home in St. Mary Mead, just at the right time to be mixed up in a murder. Once more a murder is announced—for the benefit and enjoyment of Miss Marple."

"Well, Henry," said Rydesdale sardonically. "I'll be glad to see your paragon. Come on! We'll lunch at the Royal Spa and we'll interview the lady. Craddock, here, is looking highly skeptical."

"Not at all, sir," said Craddock politely.

He thought to himself that sometimes his godfather carried things a bit far.

2

Miss Jane Marple was very nearly, if not quite, as Craddock had pictured her. She was far more benignant then he had imagined and a good deal older. Indeed she seemed very old. She had snow-white hair and a pink, crinkled face and very soft, innocent blue eyes, and she was heavily enmeshed in fleecy wool. Wool round her shoulders in the form of a lacy cape and wool that she was knitting and which turned out to be a baby's shawl.

She was all incoherent delight and pleasure at seeing Sir Henry, and became quite flustered when introduced to the Chief Constable and Detective Inspector Craddock.

"But really, Sir Henry, how fortunate . . . how very fortunate. So long since I have seen you . . . Yes, my rheumatism. Very bad of late. Of course, I couldn't have afforded this hotel (really fantasic what they charge nowadays), but Raymond—my nephew, Raymond West, you may remember him—"

"Everyone knows his name."

"Yes, the dear boy has been so successful with his clever books. The last one was the Book Society choice —quite the worst one he has written, actually, but I do think that is so often the case, don't you? The dear boy insisted on paying all my expenses. And his dear wife is making a name for herself, too, as an artist. Mostly jugs of dying flowers and broken combs on windowsills. I never dare tell her, but I still admire Blair Leighton and Alma-Tadema. Oh, but I'm chattering. And the Chief Constable himself—indeed I never expected—so afraid I shall be taking up his time—"

Completely ga-ga, thought the disgusted Detective Inspector Craddock.

"Come into the manager's private room," said Rydesdale. "We can talk better there."

When Miss Marple had been disentangled from her wool and her spare knitting-pins collected, she accompanied them, fluttering and protesting, to Mr. Rowlandson's comfortable sitting room.

"Now, Miss Marple, let's hear what you have to tell us," said the Chief Constable.

Miss Marple came to the point with unexpected brevity.

"It was a check," she said. "He altered it."

"He?"

"The young man at the desk here, the one who is supposed to have staged that holdup and shot himself."

"He altered a check, you say?"

Miss Marple nodded.

"Yes. I have it here." She extracted it from her bag and laid it on the table. "It came this morning with my others from the bank. You can see, it was for seven pounds, and he altered it to seventeen. A stroke in front of the seven, and *teen* added after the word seven with a nice artistic little blot just blurring the whole word. Really, very nicely done. A certain amount of practice, I should say. It's the same ink, because I wrote the check actually at the desk. I should think he'd done it quite often before, wouldn't you?"

"He picked the wrong person to do it to, this time," remarked Sir Henry.

Miss Marple nodded agreement.

"Yes. I'm afraid he would never have gone very far in crime. I was quite the wrong person. Some busy young married woman, or some girl having a love affair —that's the kind who write checks for all sorts of different sums and don't really look through their passbooks carefully. But an old woman who has to be careful of the pennies, and who has formed habits—that's quite the wrong person to choose. Seventeen pounds is a sum I never write a check for. Twenty pounds, a round sum, for the monthly wages and books. And for my personal expenditure I usually cash seven—it used to be five, but everything has gone up so."

"And perhaps he reminded you of someone?" prompted Sir Henry, mischief in his eye.

Miss Marple smiled and shook her head at him.

"You are very naughty, Sir Henry. As a matter of fact he did. Fred Tyler, at the fish shop. Always slipped an extra one in the shillings column. Eating so much fish as we do nowadays, it made a long bill, and lots of people never added it up. Just ten shillings in his pocket every time; not much but enough to get himself a few neckties and take Jessie Spragg (the girl in the draper's) to the pictures. Cut a splash, that's what these young fellows want to do. Well, the very first week I was here, there was a mistake in my bill. I pointed it out to the young man and he apologized very nicely and looked very much upset; but I thought to myself then, You've got a shifty eye, young man.

"What I mean by a shifty eye," continued Miss Marple, "is the kind that looks very straight at you and never looks away nor blinks."

Craddock gave a sudden movement of appreciation. He thought to himself, Jim Kelly to the life, remembering a notorious swindler he had helped to put behind bars not long ago.

"Rudi Scherz was a thoroughly unsatisfactory character," said Rydesdale. "He's got a police record in Switzerland, we find."

"Made the place too hot for him, I suppose, and came over here with forged papers?" said Miss Marple.

"Exactly," said Rydesdale.

"He was going about with the little red-haired waitress from the dining-room," said Miss Marple. "Fortunately I don't think her heart's affected at all. She just liked to have someone a bit different, and he used to give her flowers and chocolates, which the English boys don't do much. Has she told you all she knows?" she asked, turning suddenly to Craddock. "Or not quite all yet?"

"I'm not absolutely sure," said Craddock cautiously.

"I think there's a little to come," said Miss Marple. "She's looking very worried. Brought me kippers instead of herrings this morning, and forgot the milk jug. Usually she's an excellent waitress. Yes, she's worried. Afraid she might have to give evidence or something like that. But I expect"—her candid blue eyes swept over the manly proportions and handsome face of Detective Inspector Craddock with truly feminine Victorian appreciation—"that you will be able to persuade her to tell you all she knows."

Detective Inspector Craddock blushed and Sir Henry chuckled.

"It might be important," said Miss Marple. "He may have told her who it was."

Rydesdale stared at her.

"Who what was?"

"I express myself so badly. Who it was who put him up to it, I mean."

"So you think someone put him up to it?"

Miss Marple's eyes widened in surprise.

"Oh, but surely—I mean—Here's a personable young man—who filches a little bit here and a little bit there —alters a small check, perhaps helps himself to a small piece of jewelry if it's left lying around or takes a little money from the till—all sorts of small, petty thefts. Keeps himself going in ready money so that he can dress well and take a girl about—all that sort of thing. And then, suddenly, he goes off with a revolver, holds up a roomful of people and shoots at someone. He'd never have done a thing like that—not for a moment! He wasn't that kind of person. It doesn't make sense."

Craddock drew in his breath sharply. That was what Letitia Blacklock had said. What the vicar's wife had said. What he himself felt with increasing force. *It didn't make sense.* And now Sir Henry's old pussy was saying it, too, with complete certainty in her fluting old lady's voice.

"Perhaps you'll tell us, Miss Marple," he said, and his voice was suddenly aggressive, "what did happen, then?"

She turned on him in surprise.

"But how should I know what happened? There was an account in the paper—but it says so little. One can make conjectures, of course, but one has no accurate information."

"George," said Sir Henry, "would it be very unorthodox if Miss Marple were allowed to read the notes of the interviews Craddock had with these people at Chipping Cleghorn?"

"It may be unorthodox," said Rydesdale, "but I've not got where I am by being orthodox. She can read them. I'd be curious to hear what she has to say."

Miss Marple was all embarrassment.

"I'm afraid you've been listening to Sir Henry. Sir Henry is always too kind. He thinks too much of any little observations I may have made in the past. Really, I have no gifts—no gifts at all—except perhaps a certain knowledge of human nature. People, I find, are apt to be far too trustful. I'm afraid that I have a tendency always to believe the worst. Not a nice trait, but so often justified by subsequent events."

"Read these," said Rydesdale, thrusting the typewritten sheets upon her. "They won't take you long. After all, these people are your kind—you must know a lot of people like them. You may be able to spot something that we haven't. The case is just going to be closed. Let's have an amateur's opinion on it before we shut up the files. I don't mind telling you that Craddock here isn't satisfied. He says, like you, that it doesn't make sense."

There was silence whilst Miss Marple read. She put the typewritten sheets down at last.

"It's very interesting," she said with a sigh. "All the different things that people say—and think. The things they see—or think that they see. And all so complex, nearly all so trivial and if one thing isn't trivial, it's so hard to spot which one—like a needle in a haystack."

Craddock felt a twinge of disappointment. Just for a moment or two, he had wondered if Sir Henry might be right about this funny old lady. She might have put her finger on something—old people were often very sharp. He'd never, for instance, been able to conceal anything from his own great aunt Emma. She had finally told him that his nose twitched when he was about to tell a lie.

But just a few fluffy generalities, that was all that Sir Henry's famous Miss Marple could produce. He felt annoyed with her and said rather curtly, "The truth of the matter is that the facts are indisputable. Whatever conflicting details these people give, they all saw one thing. They saw a masked man with a revolver and a flashlight open the door and hold them up, and whether they think he said, 'Stick 'em up,' or 'Your money or your life,' or whatever phrase is associated with a hold-up in their minds, they saw him."

"But surely," said Miss Marple gently. "They couldn't —actually—have seen anything at all . . ."

Craddock caught his breath. She'd got it! She was sharp, after all. He was testing her by that speech of his, but she hadn't fallen for it. It didn't actually make any difference to the facts, or to what happened, but she'd realized, as he had, that those people who had seen a masked man holding them up couldn't really have seen him at all.

"If I understand rightly," Miss Marple had a pink flush on her cheeks, her eyes were bright and pleased as a child's, "there wasn't any light in the hall outside— and not on the landing upstairs either?"

"That's right," said Craddock.

"And so, if a man stood in the doorway and flashed a powerful light in the room, *nobody could see anything but that light,* could they?"

"No, they couldn't. I tried it out."

"And so when some of them say they saw a masked man, et cetera, they are really, though they don't realize it, recapitulating from what they saw afterwards—when the lights came on. So it all fits in very well, doesn't it, on the assumption that Rudi Scherz was the—I think 'fall guy' is the expression I mean?"

Rydesdale stared at her in such surprise that she grew pinker still.

"I may have got the term wrong," she murmured. "I am not very clever about Americanisms—and I understand they change very quickly. I got it from one of Mr. Dashiell Hammett's stories. (I understand from my nephew Raymond that he is considered at the top of the tree in what is called the tough style of literature.) A 'fall guy,' if I understand it rightly, means someone who will be blamed for a crime really committed by someone else. This Rudi Scherz seems to me exactly the right type for that. Rather stupid really, you know, but full of cupidity and probably extremely credulous."

Rydesdale said, smiling tolerantly, "Are you suggesting that he was persuaded by someone to go out and take pot shots at a roomful of people? Rather a tall order."

"I think he was told that it was a joke," said Miss Marple. "He was paid for doing it, of course. Paid, that is, to put an advertisement in the newspaper, to go out and spy out the household premises and then, on the night in question, he was to go there, assume a mask and a black cloak and throw open a door, brandish a flashlight and cry, 'Hands up!' "

"And fire off a revolver?"

"No, no," said Miss Marple. "He never had a revolver."

"But everyone says—" began Rydesdale, and stopped.

"Exactly," said Miss Marple. "Nobody could possibly have seen a revolver even if he had one. And I don't think he had. I think that after he'd called, 'Hands up,' somebody came up quietly behind him in the darkness and fired those two shots over his shoulder. It frightened him to death. He swung round and as he did so, that other person shot him and then let the revolver drop beside him . . ."

The three men looked at her. Sir Henry said softly, "It's a possible theory."

"But who is Mr. X who came up in the darkness?" asked the Chief Constable.

Miss Marple coughed.

"You'll have to find out from Miss Blacklock who wanted to kill her."

Good for old Dora Bunner, thought Craddock. Instinct against intelligence every time.

"So you think it was a deliberate attempt on Miss Blacklock's life?" asked Rydesdale.

"It certainly has that appearance," said Miss Marple. "Though there are one or two difficulties. But what I was really wondering about was whether there mightn't be a short cut. I've no doubt that whoever arranged this with Rudi Scherz took pains to tell him to keep his mouth shut about it, and perhaps he did keep his mouth shut; but if he talked to anybody it would probably be to that girl, Myrna Harris. And he may—he just may—

have dropped some hint as to the kind of person who'd suggested the whole thing."

"I'll see her now," said Craddock, rising.

Miss Marple nodded.

"Yes, do, Inspector Craddock. I'll feel happier when you have. Because once she's told you anything she knows she'll be much safer."

"Safer? Yes, I see."

He left the room. The Chief Constable said doubtfully, but tactfully, "Well, Miss Marple, you've certainly given us something to think about."

3

"I'm sorry about it, I am really," said Myrna Harris. "It's ever so nice of you not to be ratty about it. But you see Mum's the sort of person who fusses like anything. And it did look as though I'd—what's the phrase —been an accessory before the fact." (The words ran glibly off her tongue.) "I mean, I was afraid you'd never take my word for it that I only thought it was just a bit of fun."

Inspector Craddock repeated the reassuring phrases with which he had broken down Myrna's resistance.

"I will. I'll tell you all about it. But you will keep me out of it if you can because of Mum? It all started with Rudi breaking a date with me. We were going to the pictures that evening and then he said he wouldn't be able to come and I was a bit standoffish with him about it—because, after all, it had been his idea and I don't fancy being stood up by a foreigner. And he said it wasn't his fault, and I said that was a likely story, and then he said he'd got a bit of a lark on that night—and that he wasn't going to be out of pocket by it and how would I fancy a wristwatch? So I said what did he mean by a lark? And he said not to tell anyone, but there was to be a party somewhere and he was to stage a sham holdup. Then he showed me the advertisement he'd put in and I had to laugh. He was a bit scornful about it all. Said it was kids' stuff really—but that was just like the English. They never really grew up—and of course I said what did he mean by talking like that about us— and we had a bit of an argument, but we made it up. Only you can understand, can't you, sir, that when I read all about it, and it hadn't been a joke at all and Rudi had shot someone and then shot himself—why, I didn't know what to do. I thought if I said I knew about it beforehand, it would look as though I were in on the whole thing. But it really did seem like a joke when he told me about it. I'd have sworn he meant it that way. I didn't even know he'd got a revolver. He never said anything about taking a revolver with him."

Craddock comforted her and then asked the most important question.

"Who did he say it was who had arranged this party?"

But there he drew a blank.

"He never said who it was that was getting him to do it. I suppose nobody was, really. It was all his own doing."

"He didn't mention a name? Did he say he—or she?"

"He didn't say anything except that it was going to be a scream. 'I shall laugh to see all their faces.' That's what he said."

He hadn't had long to laugh, Craddock thought.

4

"It is only a theory," said Rydesdale as they drove back to Medenham. "Nothing to support it, nothing at all. Put it down as old maid's vaporings and let it go, eh?"

"I'd rather not do that, sir."

"It's all very improbable. A mysterious X appearing suddenly in the darkness behind our Swiss friend. Where did he come from? Who was he? Where had he been?"

"He could have come in through the side door," said Craddock, "just as Scherz came. Or," he added slowly, "he could have come from the kitchen."

"She could have come from the kitchen, you mean?"

"Yes, sir, it's a possibility. I've not been satisfied about that girl all along. She strikes me as a nasty bit of goods. All that screaming and hysterics—it could have been put on. She could have worked on this young fellow, let him in at the right moment, rigged the whole thing, shot him, bolted back into the dining-room, caught up her bit of silver and her chamois and started her screaming act."

"Against that we have the fact that—er—What's-his-name—oh, yes, Edmund Swettenham, definitely says the key was turned on the outside of the door, and that he turned it to release her. Any other door into that part of the house?"

"Yes, there's a door to the back stairs and kitchen just under the stairs, but it seems the handle came off three weeks ago and nobody's come to put it on yet. In the meantime, you can't open the door. I'm bound to say that story seems correct. The spindle and the two handles were on a shelf outside the door in the hall and they were thickly coated with dust, but, of course, a professional would have ways of opening that door all right."

"Better look up the girl's record. See if her papers are in order. But it seems to me the whole thing is very theoretical."

Again the Chief Constable looked inquiringly at his

subordinate. Craddock replied quietly, "I know, sir, and, of course, if you think the case ought to be closed, it must be. But I'd appreciate it if I could work on it for just a little longer."

Rather to his surprise the Chief Constable said quietly and approvingly, "Good lad."

"There's the revolver to work on. If this theory is correct, it wasn't Scherz's revolver and certainly nobody so far has been able to say that Scherz ever had a revolver."

"It's a German make."

"I know, sir. But this country's absolutely full of continental makes of guns. All the Americans brought them back and so did our chaps. You can't go by that."

"True enough. Any other lines of inquiry?"

"There's got to be a motive. If there's anything in this theory at all, it means that last Friday's business wasn't a mere joke and wasn't an ordinary holdup; it was a cold-blooded attempt at murder. Somebody tried to murder Miss Blacklock. Now why? It seems to me that if anyone knows the answer to that, it must be Miss Blacklock herself."

"I understand she rather poured cold water on that idea?"

"She poured cold water on the idea that Rudi Scherz wanted to murder her. And she was quite right. And there's another thing, sir."

"Yes?"

"Somebody might try again."

"That would certainly prove the truth of the theory," said the Chief Constable dryly. "By the way, look after Miss Marple, won't you?"

"Miss Marple? Why?"

"I gather she is taking up residence at the vicarage in Chipping Cleghorn and coming into Medenham Wells twice a week for her treatments. It seems that Mrs.

What's-her-name is the daughter of an old friend of Miss Marple's. Good sporting instincts, that old bean. Oh, well, I suppose she hasn't much excitement in her life and sniffing round after possible murderers gives her a kick."

"I wish she wasn't coming," said Craddock seriously.

"Going to get under your feet?"

"Not that, sir, but she's a nice old thing. I shouldn't like anything to happen to her . . . always supposing, I mean, that there's anything in this theory."

CHAPTER 9

Concerning a Door

"I'M SORRY to bother you again, Miss Blacklock—"

"Oh, it doesn't matter. I suppose, as the inquest was adjourned for a week, you're hoping to get more evidence?"

Detective Inspector Craddock nodded.

"To begin with, Miss Blacklock, Rudi Scherz was not the son of the proprietor of the Hôtel des Alpes at Montreux. He seems to have started his career as an orderly in a hospital at Berne. A good many of the patients missed small pieces of jewelry. Under another name he was a waiter at one of the small winter sports places. His specialty there was making out duplicate bills in the restaurant with items on one that didn't appear on the other. The difference, of course, went into his pocket. After that he was in a department store in Zürich. Their losses from shoplifting were rather above the average while he was with them. It seems likely that the shoplifting wasn't entirely due to customers."

"He was a picker-up of unconsidered trifles, in fact?" said Miss Blacklock dryly. "Then I was right in thinking that I had not seen him before?"

"You were quite right. No doubt you were pointed out to him at the Royal Spa Hotel and he pretended to recognize you. The Swiss police had begun to make his own country rather too hot for him, and he came over here with a very nice set of forged papers and took a job at the Royal Spa."

"Quite a good hunting ground," said Miss Blacklock dryly. "It's extremely expensive and very well off people stay there. Some of them are careless about their bills, I expect."

"Yes," said Craddock. "There were prospects of a satisfactory harvest."

Miss Blacklock was frowning.

"I see all that," she said. "But why come to Chipping Cleghorn? What does he think we've got here that could possibly be better than the rich Royal Spa Hotel?"

"You stick to your statement that there's nothing of especial value in the house?"

"Of course there isn't. I should know. I can assure you, Inspector, we've not got an unrecognized Rembrandt or anything like that."

"Then it looks, doesn't it, as though your friend Miss Bunner were right? He came here to attack you."

("There, Letty, what did I tell you!" "Oh, nonsense, Bunny.")

"But is it nonsense?" said Craddock. "I think, you know, that it's true."

Miss Blacklock stared very hard at him.

"Now let's get this straight. You really believe that this young man came out here—having previously arranged by means of an advertisement that half the village would turn up agog—at that particular time—"

"But he mayn't have meant that to happen," interrupted Miss Bunner eagerly. "It may have been just a horrid sort of warning—to you, Letty—that's how I read it at the time. *'A murder is announced.'* I felt in my bones that it was sinister—if it had all gone as planned he would have shot you and got away—and how would anyone have ever known who it was?"

"That's true enough," said Miss Blacklock. "But—"

"I knew that advertisement wasn't a joke, Letty. I said so. And look at Mitzi—she was frightened, too!"

"Ah," said Craddock, "Mitzi. I'd like to know rather more about that young woman."

"Her permit and papers are quite in order."

"I don't doubt that," said Craddock dryly. "Scherz's papers appeared to be quite correct, too."

"But why should this Rudi Scherz want to murder me? That's what you don't attempt to explain, Inspector Craddock."

"There may have been someone behind Scherz," said Craddock slowly. "Have you thought of that?"

He used the words metaphorically though it flashed across his mind that if Miss Marple's theory was correct, the words would also be true in a literal sense. In any case, they made little impression on Miss Blacklock who still looked skeptical.

"The point remains the same," she said. "Why on earth should anyone want to murder me?"

"It's the answer to that that I want you to give me, Miss Blacklock."

"Well, I can't! That's flat. I've no enemies. As far as I'm aware I've always lived on perfectly good terms with my neighbors. I don't know any guilty secrets about anyone. The whole idea is ridiculous! And if what you're hinting is that Mitzi has something to do with this, that's absurd, too. As Miss Bunner has just told you, she was frightened to death when she saw that advertisement in the *Gazette*. She actually wanted to pack up and leave the house then and there."

"That may have been a clever move on her part. She may have known you'd press her to stay."

"Of course, if you've made up your mind about it, you'll find an answer to everything. But I can assure you that if Mitzi had taken an unreasoning dislike to me, she might conceivably poison my food, but I'm sure she wouldn't go in for all this elaborate rigmarole.

"The whole idea's absurd. I believe you police have got an anti-foreigner complex. Mitzi may be a liar but she's not a cold-blooded murderer. Go and bully her if you must. But when she's departed in a whirl of indignation, or shut herself up howling in her room, I've a good mind to make you cook the dinner. Mrs. Harmon is bringing some old lady who is staying with her to tea this afternoon and I wanted Mitzi to make some little cakes—but I suppose you'll upset her completely. Can't you possibly go and suspect somebody else?"

2

Craddock went out to the kitchen. He asked Mitzi questions that he had asked her before and received the same answers.

Yes, she had locked the front door soon after four o'clock. No, she did not always do so, but that afternoon she had been nervous because of "that dreadful advertisement." It was no good locking the side door because Miss Blacklock and Miss Bunner went out that way to shut up the ducks and feed the chickens and Mrs. Haymes usually came in that way from work.

"Mrs. Haymes says she locked the door when she came in at 5:30."

"Ah, and you believe her—oh, yes, you believe her—"

"Do you think we shouldn't believe her?"

"What does it matter what I think? You will not believe me."

"Supposing you give us a chance. You think Mrs. Haymes didn't lock that door?"

"I think she was very careful not to lock it."

"What do you mean by that?" asked Craddock.

"That young man, he does not work alone. No, he knows where to come, he knows that when he comes a door will be left open for him—oh, very conveniently open!"

"What are you trying to say?"

"What is the use of what I say? You will not listen. You say I am a poor refugee girl who tell lies. You say that a fair-haired English lady, oh, no, she does not tell lies—she is so British—so honest. So you believe her and not me. But I could tell you. Oh, yes, I could tell you!"

She banged down a saucepan on the stove.

Craddock was in two minds whether to take notice of what might be only a stream of spite.

"We note everything we are told," he said.

"I shall not tell you anything at all. Why should I? You are all alike. You persecute and despise poor refugees. If I say to you that when, a week before, that young man comes to ask Miss Blacklock for money and she sends him away, as you say, with a flea in the ear —if I tell you that after that I hear him talking with Mrs. Haymes—yes, out there in the summer-house— all you say is that I make it up!"

And so you probably are making it up, thought Craddock. But he said aloud, "You couldn't hear what was said out in the summer-house."

"There you are wrong," screamed Mitzi triumphantly. "I go out to get nettles—it makes very nice vegetables, nettles. They do not think so, but I cook it and not tell them. And I hear them talking in there. He say to her, 'But where can I hide?' And she say, 'I will show you'—and then she say, 'At a quarter past six,' and I think, *Ach,* so that is how you behave, my fine lady! After you come back from work, you go out to meet a man. You bring him into the house. Miss Blacklock, I think, she will not like that. She will turn you out. I will watch, I think, and listen and then I will tell Miss Blacklock. But I understand now I was wrong. It was not love she planned with him, it was to rob and to murder. But you will say I make all this up. Wicked Mitzi, you will say. I will take her to prison."

Craddock wondered. She might be making it up. But possibly she might not. He asked cautiously, "You are sure it was this Rudi Scherz she was talking to?"

"Of course I am sure. He just leave and I see him go from the drive across to the summer-house. And presently," said Mitzi defiantly, "I go out to see if there are any nice young green nettles."

Would there, the Inspector wondered, be any nice young green nettles in October? But he appreciated that Mitzi had had to produce a hurried reason for what had undoubtedly been nothing more than plain snooping.

"You didn't hear any more than what you have told me?"

Mitzi looked aggrieved.

"That Miss Bunner, the one with the long nose, she call and call me. 'Mitzi! Mitzi!' So I have to go. Oh, she is irritating. Always interfering. Says she will teach me to cook. Her cooking! It tastes, yes, everything does, of water, water, water!"

"Why didn't you tell me this the other day?" asked Craddock sternly.

"Because I did not remember—I did not think . . . Only afterwards do I say to myself, it was planned then —planned with her."

"You are quite sure it was Mrs. Haymes?"

"Oh, yes, I am sure. Oh, yes, I am very sure, She is a thief, that Mrs. Haymes. A thief and the associate of thieves. What she gets for working in the garden, it is not enough for such a fine lady, no. She has to rob Miss

Blacklock who has been kind to her. Oh, she is bad, bad, bad, that one!"

"Supposing," said the Inspector, watching her closely, "that someone was to say that you had been seen talking to Rudi Scherz?"

The suggestion had less effect than he had hoped for. Mitzi merely snorted and tossed her head.

"If anyone they see me talking to him, that is lies, lies, lies, lies," she said contemptuously. "To tell lies about anyone, that is easy, but in England you have to prove them true. Miss Blacklock tell me that, and it is true, is it not? I do not speak with murderers and thieves. And no English policeman shall say I do. And how can I do cooking for lunch if you are here, talk, talk, talk? Go out of my kitchens, please. I want now to make a very careful sauce."

Craddock went obediently. He was a little shaken in his suspicions of Mitzi. Her story about Phillipa Haymes had been told with great conviction. Mitzi might be a liar (he thought she was), but he fancied that there might be some substratum of truth in this particular tale. He resolved to speak to Phillipa on the subject. She had seemed to him, when he questioned her, a quiet, well-bred young woman. He had had no suspicion of her.

Crossing the hall, in his abstraction he tried to open the wrong door. Miss Bunner, descending the staircase, hastily put him right.

"Not that door," she said. "It doesn't open. The next one to the left. Very confusing, isn't it? So many doors."

"There are a good many," said Craddock, looking up and down the narrow hall.

Miss Bunner amiably enumerated them for him.

"First, the door to the cloakroom, and then the cloaks cupboard door and then the dining-room—that's on that side. And on this side, the dummy door that you were trying to get through and then there's the drawing-room door proper, and then the china cupboard door and the door of the little flower room and at the end the side door. Most confusing. Especially these two being so near together. I've often tried the wrong one by mistake. We used to have the hall table against it, as a matter of fact, but then we moved it along against the wall there."

Craddock had noted, almost mechanically, a thin line horizontally across the panels of the door he had been trying to open. He realized now it was the mark where the table had been. Something stirred vaguely in his mind as he asked, "Moved? How long ago?"

In questioning Dora Bunner there was fortunately no need to give a reason for any questions. Any query on any subject seemed perfectly natural to the garrulous Miss Bunner, who delighted in the giving of information however trivial.

"Now let me see, really quite recently—ten days or a fortnight ago."

"Why was it moved?"

"I really can't remember. Something to do with the flowers. I think Phillipa did a big vase—she arranges flowers quite beautifully—all Autumn coloring and twigs and branches, and it was so big it caught your hair as you went past, and so Phillipa said, 'Why not move the table along and anyway the flowers would look much better against the bare wall than against the panels of the door.' Only we had to take down Wellington at Waterloo. Not a print I'm really very fond of. We put it under the stairs."

"It's not really a dummy, then?" Craddock asked, looking at the door.

"Oh, no, it's a real door, if that's what you mean. It's the door of the small drawing-room, but when the rooms were thrown into one, one didn't need two doors, so this one was fastened up."

"Fastened up?" Craddock tried it again gently. "You mean it's nailed up? Or just locked?"

"Oh, locked, I think, and bolted, too."

He saw the bolt at the top and tried it. The bolt slid back easily—too easily . . .

"When was it last opened?" he asked Miss Bunner.

"Oh, years and years ago, I imagine. It's never been opened since I've been here, I know that."

"You don't know where the key is?"

"There are a lot of keys in the hall table drawer. It's probably among those."

Craddock followed her and looked at a rusty assortment of old keys pushed far back in the drawer. He scanned them and selected one that looked different from the rest and went back to the door. The key fitted and turned easily. He pushed and the door slid open noiselessly.

"Oh, do be careful," cried Miss Bunner. "There may be something resting against it inside. We never open it."

"Don't you?" said the Inspector.

His face now was grim. He said with emphasis:

"This door's been opened quite recently, Miss Bunner. The lock's been oiled and the hinges."

She stared at him, her foolish face agape.

"But who could have done that?" she asked.

"That's what I mean to find out," said Craddock grimly. He thought—X from outside? No—X was here —in this house—X was in the drawing-room that night.

CHAPTER 10

Pip and Emma

MISS BLACKLOCK listened to him this time with more attention. She was an intelligent woman, as he had known, and she grasped the implications of what he had to tell her.

"Yes," she said quietly, "that does alter things . . . No one had any right to meddle with that door. Nobody has meddled with it to my knowledge."

"You see what it means," the Inspector urged. "When the lights went out, anybody in this room the other night could have slipped out of that door, come up behind Rudi Scherz and fired at you."

"Without being seen or heard or noticed?"

"Without being seen or heard or noticed. Remember, when the lights went out people moved, exclaimed, bumped into each other. And after that all that could be seen was the blinding light of the flashlight."

Miss Blacklock said slowly, "And you believe that one of those people—one of my nice commonplace neighbors—slipped out and tried to murder me? Me? But why? For goodness' sake, why?"

"I've a feeling that you must know the answer to that question, Miss Blacklock."

"But I don't, Inspector. I can assure you I don't."

"Well, let's make a start. Who gets your money if you were to die?"

Miss Blacklock said rather reluctantly, "Patrick and Julia. I've left the furniture in this house and a small annuity to Bunny. Really I've not much to leave. I had holdings in German and Italian securities which became worthless, and what with taxation and the lower percentages that are now paid on invested capital, I can assure you I'm not worth murdering—I put most of my money into an annuity about a year ago."

"Still, you have some income, Miss Blacklock, and your nephew and niece would come into it."

"And so Patrick and Julia would plan to murder me? I simply don't believe it. They're not desperately hard up or anything like that."

"Do you know that for a fact?"

"No. I suppose I only know it from what they've told me . . . But I really refuse to suspect them. Some day I might be worth murdering, but not now."

"What do you mean by some day you might be worth murdering, Miss Blacklock?" Inspector Craddock pounced on the statement.

"Simply that one day—possibly quite soon—I may be a very rich woman."

"That sounds interesting. Will you explain?"

"Certainly. You may not know it, but for more than twenty years I was secretary to, and closely associated with, Randall Goedler."

Craddock was interested. Randall Goedler had been a big name in the world of finance. His daring speculations and the rather theatrical publicity with which he surrounded himself had made him a personality not quickly forgotten. He had died, if Craddock remembered rightly, in 1937 or 1938.

"He's rather before your time, I expect," said Miss Blacklock. "But you've probably heard of him."

"Oh, yes. He was a millionaire, wasn't he?"

"Oh, several times over—though his finances fluctuated. He always risked most of what he made on some new *coup*."

She spoke with a certain animation, her eyes brightened by memory.

"Anyway, he died a very rich man. He had no children. He left his fortune in trust for his wife during her lifetime and after her death to me absolutely."

A vague memory stirred in the Inspector's mind.

IMMENSE FORTUNE TO COME TO FAITHFUL SECRETARY—something of that kind.

"For the last twelve years or so," said Miss Blacklock with a slight twinkle, "I've had an excellent motive for murdering Mrs. Goedler—but that doesn't help you, does it?"

"Did—excuse me for asking this—did Mrs. Goedler resent her husband's disposition of his fortune?"

Miss Blacklock was now looking frankly amused.

"You needn't be so very discreet. What you really mean is, was I Randall Goedler's mistress? No, I wasn't. I don't think Randall ever gave me a sentimental thought, and I certainly didn't give him one. He was in love with Belle (his wife), and remained in love with her until he died. I think in all probability it was gratitude on his part that prompted his making his will. You see, Inspector, in the very early days, when Randall was still on an insecure footing, he came very near to disaster. It was a question of just a few thousand of actual cash. It was a big *coup*, and a very exciting one; daring, as all his schemes were; but he just hadn't got that little bit of cash to tide him over. I came to the rescue. I had a little money of my own. I believed in Randall. I sold out every penny I had and gave it to him. It did the trick. A week later he was an immensely wealthy man.

"After that, he treated me more or less as a junior partner. Oh, they were exciting days!" She sighed. "I enjoyed it all thoroughly. Then my father died, and my only sister was left a hopeless invalid. I had to give it all up and go and look after her. Randall died a couple of years later. I had made quite a lot of money during our association and I didn't really expect him to leave me anything, but I was very touched, yes, and very proud, to find that if Belle predeceased me (and she was one of those delicate creatures whom everyone always says won't live long), I was to inherit his entire fortune. I really think the poor man didn't know who to leave it to. Belle's a dear, and she was delighted about it. She's really a very sweet person. She lives up in Scotland. I haven't seen her for years—we just write at Christmas. I went with my sister to a sanatorium in Switzerland just before the war. She died of consumption out there."

She was silent for a moment or two, then said, "I only came back to England just over a year ago."

"You said you might be a rich woman very soon. How soon?"

"I heard from the nurse attendant who looks after Belle Goedler that Belle is sinking rapidly. It may be—only a few weeks."

She added sadly, "The money won't mean much to me now. I've got quite enough still for my rather simple needs. Once I should have enjoyed playing the markets again—but now . . . Oh, well, one grows old. Still, you do see, Inspector, don't you, that if Patrick and Julia wanted to kill me for a financial reason they'd be crazy not to wait for another few weeks."

"Yes, Miss Blacklock, but what happens if you should predecease Mrs. Goedler? Who does the money go to them?"

"D'you know, I've never really thought. Pip and Emma, I suppose . . ."

Craddock stared and Miss Blacklock smiled.

"Does that sound rather crazy? I believe, if I pre-

decease Belle, the money would go to the legal offspring
—or whatever the term is—of Randall's only sister,
Sonia. Randall had quarreled with his sister. She married
a man whom he considered a crook and worse."

"And was he a crook?"

"Oh, definitely, I should say. But I believe a very
attractive person to women. He was a Greek or a
Romanian or something—what was his name now?—
Stamfordis, Dmitri Stamfordis."

"Randall Goedler cut his sister out of his will when
she married this man?"

"Oh, no! Sonia was a very wealthy woman in her own
right. Randall had already settled packets of money on
her, as far as possible in a way so that her husband
couldn't touch it. But I believe that when the lawyers
urged him to put in someone in case I predeceased
Belle, he reluctantly put down Sonia's offspring, simply
because he couldn't think of anyone else and he wasn't
the sort of man to leave money to charities."

"And there were children of the marriage?"

"Well, there are Pip and Emma." She laughed. "I
know it sounds ridiculous. All I know is that Sonia
wrote once to Belle after her marriage, telling her to tell
Randall that she was extremely happy and that she had
just had twins and was calling them Pip and Emma. As
far as I know she never wrote again. But Belle, of
course, may be able to tell you more."

Miss Blacklock had been amused by her own recital.
The Inspector did not look amused.

"It comes to this," he said. "If you had been killed
the other night, there are presumably at least two
people in the world who would have come into a very
large fortune. You were wrong, Miss Blacklock, when
you say that there is no one who had a motive for de-
siring your death. There are two people, at least, who

are vitally interested. How old would this brother and sister be?"

Miss Blacklock frowned.

"Let me see . . . 1922 . . . no—it's difficult to remember . . . I suppose about twenty-five or twenty-six." Her face had sobered. "But you surely don't think—"

"I think somebody shot at you with the intent to kill you. I think it possible that that same person or persons might try again. I would like you, if you will, to be very, very careful, Miss Blacklock. One murder has been arranged and did not come off. I think it possible that another murder may be arranged very soon."

2

Phillipa Haymes straightened her back and pushed back a tendril of hair from her damp forehead. She was cleaning a flower border.

"Yes, Inspector?"

She looked at him inquiringly. In return he gave her a rather closer scrutiny than he had done before. Yes, a good-looking girl, a very English type with her pale ash-blond hair and her rather long face. An obstinate chin and mouth. Something of repression—of tautness about her. The eyes were blue, very steady in their glance, and told you nothing at all. The sort of girl, he thought, who would keep a secret well.

"I'm sorry always to bother you when you're at work, Mrs. Haymes," he said, "but I didn't want to wait until you came back for lunch. Besides, I thought it might be easier to talk to you here, away from Little Paddocks."

"Yes, Inspector?"

No emotion and little interest in the voice. But was there a note of wariness—or did he imagine it?

"A certain statement has been made to me this morning. This statement concerns you."

Phillipa raised her eyebrows very slightly.

"You told me, Mrs. Haymes, that this man Rudi Scherz was quite unknown to you?"

"Yes."

"That when you saw him there, dead, it was the first time you had set eyes on him. Is that so?"

"Certainly. I had never seen him before."

"You did not, for instance, have a conversation with him in the summer-house of Little Paddiocks?"

"In the summer-house?"

He was almost sure he caught a note of fear in her voice.

"Yes, Mrs. Haymes."

"Who says so?"

"I am told that you had a conversation with this man Rudi Scherz, and that he asked you where he could hide and you replied you would show him, and that a time, a quarter past six, was definitely mentioned. It would be a quarter past six, roughly, when Scherz would get here from the bus stop on the evening of the holdup."

There was a moment's silence. Then Phillipa gave a short scornful laugh. She looked amused.

"I don't know who told you that," she said. "At least I can guess. It's a very silly clumsy story—spiteful, of course. For some reason Mitzi dislikes me even more than she dislikes the rest of us."

"You deny it?"

"Of course it's not true . . . I never met or saw Rudi Scherz in my life, and I was nowhere near the house that morning. I was over here working."

Inspector Craddock said very gently,

"Which morning?"

There was a momentary pause. Her eyelids flickered.

"Every morning. I'm here every morning. I don't get away until one o'clock."

She added scornfully, "It's no good listening to what Mitzi tells you. She tells lies all the time."

"And that's that," said Craddock, when he was walking away with Sergeant Fletcher. "Two young women whose stories flatly contradict each other. Which one am I to believe?"

"Everyone seems to agree that this foreign girl tells whoppers," said Fletcher. "It's been my experience in dealing with aliens that lying comes more easy than truth-telling. Seems to be clear she's got a spite against this Mrs. Haymes."

"So if you were me, you'd believe Mrs. Haymes?"

"Unless you've got reason to think otherwise, sir."

And Craddock hadn't, not really—only the remembrance of a pair of over-steady blue eyes and the glib enunciation of the words "that morning." For to the best of his recollection he hadn't said whether the interview in the summer-house had taken place in the morning or the afternoon.

Still, Miss Blacklock, or if not Miss Blacklock, certainly Miss Bunner, might have mentioned the visit of the young foreigner who had come to cadge his fare back to Switzerland. And Phillipa Haymes might have therefore assumed that the conversation was supposed to have taken place on that particular morning.

But Craddock still thought that there had been a note of fear in her voice as she asked, "In the summer-house?"

He decided to keep an open mind on the subject.

3

It was very pleasant in the vicarage garden. One of those sudden spells of Autumn warmth had descended upon England. Inspector Craddock could never remember if it was St. Martin's or St. Luke's Summer, but he knew that it was very pleasant—and also very enervating. He sat in a deck chair provided for him by an energetic Bunch, just on her way to a Mothers' Meeting, and, well protected with shawls and a large rug round her knees, Miss Marple sat knitting beside him. The sunshine, the peace, the steady click of Miss Marple's knitting-needles, all combined to produce a soporific feeling in the Inspector. And yet, at the same time, there was a nightmarish feeling at the back of his mind. It was like the familiar dream where an undertone of menace grows and finally turns ease into terror . . .

He said abruptly, "You oughtn't to be here."

Miss Marple's needles stopped clicking for a moment. Her placid china-blue eyes regarded him thoughtfully.

She said, "I know what you mean. You're a very conscientious boy. But it's perfectly all right. Bunch's father (he was rector of our parish, a very fine scholar) and her mother (who is a most remarkable woman— real spiritual power) are very old friends of mine. It's the most natural thing in the world that when I'm at Medenham I should come on here to stay with Bunch for a little."

"Oh, perhaps," said Craddock. "But—but don't snoop around . . . I've a feeling—I have really—that it isn't safe."

Miss Marple smiled a little.

"But I'm afraid," she said, "that we old women always do snoop. It would be very odd and much more noticeable if I didn't. Questions about mutual friends in different parts of the world and whether they remember so and so, and do they remember who it was that Lady Somebody's daughter married? All that helps, doesn't it?"

"Helps?" said the Inspector rather stupidly.

"Helps to find out if people are who they say they are," said Miss Marple.

She went on:

"Because that's what's worrying you, isn't it? And that's really the particular way the world has changed since the war. Take this place, Chipping Cleghorn, for instance. It's very much like St. Mary Mead where I live. Fifteen years ago one knew who everybody was. The Bantrys in the big house—and the Hartnells and the Price Ridleys and the Weatherbys . . . They were people whose fathers and mothers and grandfathers and grandmothers, or whose aunts and uncles, had lived there before them. If somebody new came to live there, they brought letters of introduction, or they'd been in the same regiment or served on the same ship as someone already there. If anybody new—really new—really a stranger—came, well, they stuck out—everybody wondered about them and didn't rest till they found out."

She nodded her head gently.

"But it's not like that any more. Every village and small country place is full of people who've just come and settled there without any ties to bring them. The big houses have been sold, and the cottages have been converted and changed. And people just come—and all you know about them is what they say of themselves. They've come, you see, from all over the world. People from India and Hong Kong and China, and people who used to live in France and Italy in little cheap places and odd islands. And people who've made a little money and can afford to retire. But nobody knows any more who anyone is. You can have Benares brassware in your house and talk about tiffin and *chota Hazri* —and you can have pictures of Taormina and talk about the English church and the library—like Miss Hinchliffe and Miss Murgatroyd. You can come from the South of France, or have spent your life in the East. People take you at your own valuation. They don't wait to call until they've had a letter from a friend saying that the So-and-So's are delightful people and she's known them all their lives."

And that, thought Craddock, was exactly what was oppressing him. He didn't know. There were just faces and personalities and they were backed up by ration books and identity cards—nice neat identity cards with numbers on them, without photographs or fingerprints. Anybody who took the trouble could have a suitable identity card—and partly because of that, the subtler links that had held English social rural life together had fallen apart. In a town nobody expected to know his neighbor. In the country now nobody knew his neighbor either, though possibly he still thought he did . . .

Because of the oiled door, Craddock knew that there had been somebody in Letitia Blacklock's drawing-room who was not the pleasant friendly country neighbor he or she pretended to be . . .

And because of that he was afraid for Miss Marple who was frail and old and who noticed things . . .

He said: "We can, to a certain extent, check up on these people . . ." But he knew that that wasn't so easy. India and China and Hong Kong and the South of France . . . It wasn't as easy as it would have been fifteen years ago. There were people, as he knew only too well, who were going about the country with borrowed identities—borrowed from people who had met sudden death by "incidents" in the cities. There were organizations who bought up identities, who faked identity cards and ration books—there were a hundred small rackets springing into being. You could check up—but it would take time—and time was what he hadn't got, because Randall Goedler's widow was very near death.

It was then that, worried and tired, lulled by the sunshine, he told Miss Marple about Randall Goedler and Pip and Emma.

"Just a couple of names," he said. "Nicknames at that! They mayn't exist. They may be respectable citizens living in Europe somewhere. On the other hand, one, or both, of them may be here in Chipping Cleghorn . . ."

Twenty-five years old approximately—who filled that description? He said, thinking aloud:

"That nephew and niece of hers—or cousins, or whatever they are . . . I wonder when she saw them last—"

Miss Marple said gently, "I'll find out for you, shall I?"

"Now, please, Miss Marple, don't—"

"It will be quite simple, Inspector; you really need not worry. And it won't be noticeable if I do it, because, you see, it won't be official. If there is anything wrong you don't want to put them on their guard."

Pip and Emma, thought Craddock, Pip and Emma? He was getting obsessed by Pip and Emma. That attractive dare-devil young man, the good-looking girl with the cool stare . . .

He said: "I may find out more about them in the next forty-eight hours. I'm going up to Scotland. Mrs. Goedler, if she's able to talk, may know a good deal more about them."

"I think that's a very wise move." Miss Marple hesitated. "I hope," she murmured, "that you have warned Miss Blacklock to be careful?"

"I've warned her, yes. And I shall leave a man here to keep an unobstrusive eye on things."

He avoided Miss Marple's eye which said plainly enough that a policeman keeping an eye on things would be little good if the danger was in the family circle . . .

"And remember," said Craddock, looking squarely at her, "I've warned you."

"I assure you, Inspector," said Miss Marple, "that I can take care of myself."

CHAPTER 11

Miss Marple Comes to Tea

IF LETITIA BLACKLOCK seemed slightly absent-minded when Mrs. Harmon came to tea and brought a guest who was staying with her, Miss Marple, the guest in question, was hardly likely to notice the fact since it was the first time she had met her hostess.

The old lady was very charming in her gentle gossipy fashion. She revealed herself almost at once to be one of those old ladies who have a constant preoccupation with burglars.

"They can get in anywhere, my dear," she assured her hostess, "absolutely anywhere nowadays. So many new American methods. I myself pin my faith to a very old-fashioned device. A cabin hook and eye. They can pick locks and draw back bolts but a brass hook and eye defeats them. Have you ever tried that?"

"I'm afraid we're not very good at bolts and bars," said Miss Blacklock cheerfully. "There's really nothing much to burgle."

"A chain on the front door," Miss Marple advised. "Then the maid need only open it a crack and see who is there and they can't force their way in."

"I expect Mitzi, our Mittel European, would love that."

"The holdup you had must have been very, very

121

frightening," said Miss Marple. "Bunch has been telling me all about it."

"I was scared stiff," said Bunch.

"It was an alarming experience," admitted Miss Blacklock.

"It really seems like Providence that the man tripped himself up and shot himself. These burglars are so violent nowadays. How did he get in?"

"Well, I'm afraid we don't lock our doors much."

"Oh, Letty," exclaimed Miss Bunner. "I forgot to tell you the Inspector was most peculiar this morning. He insisted on opening the second door—you know, the one that's never been opened—the one over there. He hunted for the key and everything and said the door had been oiled. But I can't see why because—"

Too late she got Miss Blacklock's signal to be quiet, and paused open-mouthed.

"Oh, Lotty, I'm so—sorry—I mean, I do beg your pardon, Letty—Oh, dear, how stupid I am."

"It doesn't matter," said Miss Blacklock, but she was annoyed. "Only I don't think Inspector Craddock wants that talked about. I didn't know you had been there when he was experimenting, Dora. You do understand, don't you, Mrs. Harmon?"

"Oh, yes," said Bunch. "We won't breathe a word, will we, Aunt Jane? But I wonder why he—"

She relapsed into thought. Miss Bunner fidgeted and looked miserable, bursting out at last: "I always say the wrong thing. Oh, dear, I'm nothing but a trial to you, Letty."

Miss Blacklock said quickly, "You're my great comfort, Dora. And, anyway, in a small place like Chipping Cleghorn, there aren't really any secrets."

"Now that is very true," said Miss Marple. "I'm afraid, you know, that things do get round in the most extraordinary way. Servants, of course, and yet it can't only be that, because one has so few servants nowadays. Still, there are the daily women and perhaps they are worse, because they go to everybody in turn and pass the news round."

"Oh," said Bunch Harmon suddenly. "I've got it! Of course, if that door could open, too, someone might have gone out of here in the dark and done the holdup —only, of course, they didn't—because it was the man from the Royal Spa Hotel. Or wasn't it? . . . No, I don't see after all . . ." she frowned.

"Did it all happen in this room then?" asked Miss Marple, adding apologetically, "I'm afraid you must think me sadly curious, Miss Blacklock—but it really is so very exciting—just like something one reads about in the paper—and actually to have happened to some-one one knows . . . I'm just longing to hear all about it and to picture it all, if you know what I mean—"

Immediately Miss Marple received a confused and voluble account from Bunch and Miss Bunner—with occasional emendations and corrections from Miss Blacklock.

In the middle of it Patrick came in and good-natured-ly entered into the spirit of the recital—going so far as to enact himself the part of Rudi Scherz.

"And Aunt Letty was there—in the corner by the archway—Go and stand there, Aunt Letty."

Miss Blacklock obeyed, and then Miss Marple was shown the actual bullet holes.

"What a marvelous—what a providential escape," she gasped.

"I was just going to offer my guests cigarettes—" Miss Blacklock indicated the big silver box on the table.

"People are so careless when they smoke," said Miss Bunner disapprovingly. "Nobody really respects good furniture as they used to do. Look at the horrid burn somebody made on this beautiful table by putting a cigarette down on it. Disgraceful."

Miss Blacklock sighed.

"Sometimes, I'm afraid, one thinks too much of one's possessions."

"But it's such a lovely table, Letty."

Miss Bunner loved her friend's possessions with as much fervor as though they had been her own. Bunch Harmon had always thought it was a very endearing trait in her. She showed no sign of envy.

"It is a lovely table," said Miss Marple politely. "And what a very pretty china lamp on it."

Again it was Miss Bunner who accepted the compliment as though she and not Miss Blacklock was the owner of the lamp.

"Isn't it delightful? Dresden. There is a pair of them. The other's in the spare room, I think."

"You know where everything in this house is, Dora —or you think you do," said Miss Blacklock good-humoredly. "You care far more about my things than I do."

Miss Bunner flushed.

"I do like nice things," she said. Her voice was half defiant—half wistful.

"I must confess," said Miss Marple, "that my own few possessions are very dear to me, too—so many memories, you know. It's the same with photographs. People nowadays have so few photographs about. Now I like to keep all the pictures of my nephews and nieces as babies—and then as children—and so on."

"You've got a horrible one of me, aged three," said Bunch. "Holding a fox terrier and squinting."

"I expect your aunt has many photographs of you," said Miss Marple, turning to Patrick.

"Oh, we're only distant cousins," said Patrick.

"I believe Elinor did send me one of you as a baby,

Pat," said Miss Blacklock. "But I'm afraid I didn't keep it. I'd really forogotten how many children she had or what their names were until she wrote me about you two being over here."

"Another sign of the times," said Miss Marple. "Nowadays one so often doesn't know one's younger relations at all. In the old days, with all the big family reunions, that would have been impossible."

"I last saw Pat's and Julia's mother at a wedding thirty years ago," said Miss Blacklock. "She was a very pretty girl."

"That's why she has such handsome children," said Patrick with a grin.

"You've got a marvelous old album," said Julia. "Do you remember, Aunt Letty, we looked through it the other day. The hats!"

"And how smart we thought ourselves," said Miss Blacklock with a sigh.

"Never mind, Aunt Letty," said Patrick. "Julia will come across a snapshot of herself in about thirty years' time—and won't she think she looks a guy!"

"Did you do that on purpose?" said Bunch, as she and Miss Marple were walking home. "Talk about photographs I mean?"

"Well, my dear, it is interesting to know that Miss Blacklock didn't know either of her two young relatives by sight. Yes—I think Inspector Craddock will be interested to hear that."

CHAPTER 12

Morning Activities in Chipping Cleghorn

EDMUND SWETTENHAM sat down rather precariously on a garden roller.

"Good morning, Phillipa," he said.

"Hullo."

"Are you very busy?"

"Moderately."

"What are you doing?"

"Can't you see?"

"No. I'm not a gardener. You seem to be playing with earth in some fashion."

"I'm pricking out winter lettuce."

"Pricking out? What a curious term! Like pinking. Do you know what pinking is? I only learned the other day. I always thought it was a term for professional dueling."

"Do you want anything particular?" asked Phillipa coldly.

"Yes. I want to see you."

Phillipa gave him a quick glance.

"I wish you wouldn't come here like this. Mrs. Lucas won't like it."

"Doesn't she allow you to have followers?"

"Don't be absurd."

"Followers. That's another nice word. It describes

my attitude perfectly. Respectful—at a distance—but firmly pursuing."

"Please go away, Edmund. You've no business to come here."

"You're wrong," said Edmund triumphantly. "I have business here. Mrs. Lucas rang up my mama this morning and said she had a good many vegetable marrows."

"Masses of them."

"And would we like to exchange a pot of honey for a vegetable marrow or so?"

"That's not a fair exchange at all! Vegetable marrows are quite unsalable at the moment—everybody has such a lot."

"Naturally. That's why Mrs. Lucas rang up. Last time, if I remember rightly, the exchange suggested was some skim milk—skim milk, mark you—in exchange for some lettuces. It was then very early in the season for lettuces. They were about a shilling each."

Phillipa did not speak.

Edmund tugged at his pocket and extracted a pot of honey.

"So here," he said, "is my alibi. Used in a loose and quite indefensible meaning of the term. If Mrs. Lucas pops her bust round the door of the potting shed, I'm here in quest of vegetable marrows. There is absolutely no question of dalliance."

"I see."

"Do you ever read Tennyson?" inquired Edmund conversationally.

"Not very often."

"You should. Tennyson is shortly going to make a comeback in a big way. When you turn on your radio in the evening it will be the *Idylls of the King* you will hear and not interminable Trollope. I always thought the Trollope pose was the most unbearable affectation.

Perhaps a little of Trollope, but not to drown in him. But speaking of Tennyson, have you read *Maud?*"

"Once, long ago."

"It's got some points about it." He quoted softly. " 'Faultily faultless, icily regular, splendidly null.' That's you, Phillipa."

"Hardly a compliment!"

"No, it wasn't meant to be. I gather Maud got under the poor fellow's skin just like you've got under mine."

"Don't be absurd, Edmund."

"Oh, hell, Phillipa, why are you like you are? What goes on behind your splendidly regular features? What do you think? What do you feel? Are you happy, or miserable, or frightened or what? There must be something."

Phillipa said quietly, "What I feel is my own business."

"It's mine, too. I want to make you talk. I want to know what goes on in that quiet head of yours. I've a right to know. I have really. I didn't want to fall in love with you. I wanted to sit quietly and write my book. Such a nice book, all about how miserable the world is. It's frightfully easy to be clever about how miserable everybody is. And it's all a habit, really. Yes, I've suddenly become convinced of that. After reading a life of Burne-Jones."

Phillipa had stopped pricking out. She was staring at him with a puzzled frown.

"What has Burne-Jones got to do with it?"

"Everything. When you've read all about the Pre-Raphaelites you realize just what fashion is. They were all terrifically hearty and slangy and jolly, and laughed and joked, and everything was fine and wonderful. That was fashion, too. They weren't any happier or heartier than we are. And we're not any more miserable than they were. It's all fashion, I tell you. After the last war, we went in for sex. Now it's all frustration. None of it matters. Why are we talking about all this? I started out to talk about us. Only I got cold feet and shied off. Because you won't help me."

"What do you want me to do?"

"Talk! Tell me things. Is it your husband? Did you adore him and he's dead and so you've shut up like a clam? Is that it? All right, you adored him, and he's dead. Well, other girls' husbands are dead—lots of them—and some of the girls loved their husbands. They tell you so in bars, and cry a bit when they're drunk enough, and then want to go to bed with you so that they'll feel better. It's one way of getting over it, I suppose. You've got to get over it, Phillipa. You're young—and you're extremely lovely—and I love you like hell. Talk about your damned husband, tell me about him."

"There's nothing to tell. We met and got married."

"You must have been very young."

"Too young."

"Then you weren't happy with him? Go on, Phillipa."

"There's nothing to go on about. We were married. We were as happy as most people are, I suppose. Harry was born. Ronald went overseas. He—he was killed in Italy."

"And now there's Harry?"

"And now there's Harry."

"I like Harry. He's a really nice kid. He likes me. We'd get on. What about it, Phillipa? Shall we get married? You can go on gardening and I can go on writing my book and in the holidays we'll leave off working and enjoy ourselves. We can manage, with tact, not to have to live with mother. She can fork out a bit to support her adored son. I sponge, I write tripey books. I have defective eyesight and I talk too much. That's the worst. Will you try it?"

Phillipa looked at him. She saw a tall, rather solemn young man with an anxious face and large spectacles. His sandy head was rumpled and he was regarding her with a reassuring friendliness.

"No," said Phillipa.

"Definitely no?"

"Definitely no."

"Why?"

"You don't know anything about me."

"Is that all?"

"No, you don't know anything about anything."

Edmund considered.

"Perhaps not," he admitted. "But who does? Phillipa, my adored one—" He broke off.

A shrill and prolonged yapping was rapidly approaching.

"Pekes in the high hall garden," said Edmund *"When twilight was falling* (only it's eleven A.M.); *Phil, Phil, Phil, Phil, They were crying and calling . . .*

"Your name doesn't lend itself to the rhythm, does it? Sounds like an Ode to a Fountain Pen. Have you got another name?"

"Joan. Please go away. That's Mrs. Lucas."

"Joan, Joan, Joan, Joan. Better, but still not good. *When greasy Joan the pot doth keel*—that's not a nice picture of married life, either."

"Mrs. Lucas is—"

"Oh, hell," said Edmund. "Get me a blasted vegetable marrow."

2

Sergeant Fletcher had the house at Little Paddocks
to himself.

It was Mitzi's day off. She always went by the eleven
o'clock bus into Medenham Wells. By arrangement with
Miss Blacklock, Sergeant Fletcher had the run of the
house. She and Dora Bunner had gone down to the
village.

Fletcher worked fast. Someone in the house had oiled
and prepared that door, and whoever had done it, had
done it in order to be able to leave the drawing-room
unnoticed as soon as the lights went out. That ruled
out Mitzi who wouldn't have needed to use the door.

Who was left? The neighbors, Fletcher thought, might
also be ruled out. He didn't see how they could have
found an opportunity to oil and prepare the door. That
left Patrick and Julia Simmons, Phillipa Haymes and
possibly Dora Bunner. The young Simmonses were in
Milchester. Phillipa Haymes was at work. Sergeant
Fletcher was free to search out any secrets he could.
But the house was disappointingly innocent. Fletcher,
who was an expert on electricity, could find nothing sug-
gestive in the wiring or appurtenances of the electric
fixtures to show how the lights had been turned off.
Making a rapid survey of the household bedrooms, he
found an irritating normality. In Phillipa Haymes' room
were photographs of a small boy with serious eyes, an
earlier photo of the same child, a pile of schoolboy letters, a theater program or two. In Julia's room there
was a drawer full of snapshots of the south of France.
Bathing photos, a village set amidst mimosa. Patrick's
held some souvenirs of Naval days. Dora Bunner's held
few personal possessions and they seemed innocent
enough.

And yet, thought Fletcher, someone in the house must have oiled that door.

His thoughts broke off at a sound below stairs. He went quickly to the top of the staircase and looked down.

Mrs. Swettenham was crossing the hall. She had a basket on her arm. She looked into the drawing-room, crossed the hall and went into the dining-room. She came out again without the basket.

Some faint sound that Fletcher made, a board that creaked unexpectedly under his feet, made her turn her head. She called up, "Is that you, Miss Blacklock?"

"No, Mrs. Swettenham, it's me," said Fletcher.

Mrs. Swettenham gave a faint scream.

"Oh! How you startled me. I thought it might be another burglar."

Fletcher came down the stairs.

"This house doesn't seem very well protected against burglars," he said. "Can anybody always walk in and out just as they like?"

"I just brought up some of my quinces," explained Mrs. Swettenham. "Miss Blacklock wants to make quince jelly and she hasn't got a quince tree here. I left them in the dining-room."

Then she smiled.

"Oh, I see, you mean how did I get in? Well, I just came in through the side door. We all walk in and out of each other's houses, Sergeant. Nobody dreams of locking a door until it's dark. I mean it would be so awkward, wouldn't it, if you brought things and couldn't get in to leave them? It's not like the old days when you rang a bell and a servant always came to answer it." Mrs. Swettenham sighed. "In India, I remember," she said mournfully, "we had eighteen servants—eighteen. Not counting the ayah. Just as a matter of course. And at home, when I was a girl, we always had three—although mother always felt it was terribly poverty stricken not to be able to afford a kitchen maid. I must say that I find life very odd nowadays, Sergeant, though I know one mustn't complain. So much worse for the miners always getting psittacosis (or is that parrot disease?) and having to come out of the mines and try to be gardeners though they don't know weeds from spinach."

She added, as she tripped towards the door, "I mustn't keep you. I expect you're very busy. Nothing else is going to happen, is it?"

"Why should it, Mrs. Swettenham?"

"I just wondered, seeing you here. I thought it might be a gang. You'll tell Miss Blacklock about the quinces, won't you?"

Mrs. Swettenham departed. Fletcher felt like a man who has received an unexpected jolt. He had been assuming—erroneously, he now perceived—that it must have been someone in the house who had done the oiling of the door He saw now that he was wrong. An outsider had only to wait until Mitzi had departed by bus and Letitia Blacklock and Dora Bunner were both out of the house. Such an opportunity must have been simplicity itself. That meant that he couldn't rule out anybody who had been in the drawing-room that night.

3

"Murgatroyd."

"Yes, Hinch?"

"I've been doing a bit of thinking."

"Have you, Hinch?"

"Yes, the great brain has been working. You know, Murgatroyd, the whole setup the other evening was decidedly fishy."

"Fishy?"

"Yes. Tuck your hair up, Murgatroyd, and take this trowel. Pretend it's a revolver."

"Oh," said Miss Murgatroyd nervously.

"All right. It won't bite you. Now come along to the kitchen door. You're going to be the burglar. You stand here. Now you're going into the kitchen to hold up a lot of nitwits. Take the flashlight. Switch it on."

"But it's broad daylight!"

"Use your imagination, Murgatroyd. Switch it on."

Miss Murgatroyd did so, rather clumsily, shifting the trowel under one arm while she did so.

"Now then," said Miss Hinchliffe, "off you go. Remember the time you played Hermia in *A Midsummer Night's Dream* at the Women's Institute? Act. Give it all you've got. 'Stick 'em up!' Those are your lines—and don't ruin them by saying 'Please.' "

Obediently, Miss Murgatroyd raised her flashlight, flourished the trowel and advanced on the kitchen door.

Transferring the torch to her right hand, she swiftly turned the handle and stepped forward, resuming the flashlight in her left hand.

"Stick 'em up!" she fluted, adding vexedly: "Dear me, this is very difficult, Hinch."

"Why?"

"The door. It's a swing door, it keeps coming back and I've got both hands full."

"Exactly," boomed Miss Hinchliffe. "And the drawing-room door at Little Paddocks always swings too. It isn't a swing door like this, but it won't stay open. That's why Letty Blacklock bought that absolutely delectable heavy glass doorstop from Elliot's in the High Street. I don't mind saying I've never forgiven her for getting in ahead of me there. I was beating the old brute down most successfully. He'd come down from eight guineas to six pound ten, and then Blacklock comes along and buys the damned thing. I'd never seen as attractive a doorstop; you don't often get those glass bubbles in that big size."

"Perhaps the burglar put the doorstop against the door to keep it open," suggested Miss Murgatroyd.

"Use your common sense, Murgatroyd. What does he do? Throw the door open, say, 'Excuse me a moment,' stoop and put the stop into position and then resume business by saying, 'Hands up'? Try holding the door with your shoulder."

"It's still very awkward," complained Miss Murgatroyd.

"Exactly," said Miss Hinchliffe. "A revolver, a flashlight and a door to hold open—a bit too much, isn't it? So what's the answer?"

Miss Murgatroyd did not attempt to supply an answer. She looked inquiringly and admiringly at her masterful friend and waited to be enlightened.

"We know he'd got a revolver, because he fired it," said Miss Hinchliffe. "And we know he had a flashlight because we all saw it—that is, unless we're all the victims of mass hypnotism, like explanations of the Indian rope trick—(what a bore that old Easterbrook is with his Indian stories)—so the question is, did someone hold that door open for him?"

"But who could have done that?"

"Well, you could have for one, Murgatroyd. As far as I remember, you were standing directly behind it when the lights went out." Miss Hinchliffe laughed heartily. "Highly suspicious character, aren't you, Murgatroyd? But who'd think it to look at you? Here, give me that trowel—thank heavens it isn't really a revolver. You'd have shot yourself by now!"

4

"It's a most extraordinary thing," muttered Colonel Easterbrook. "Most extraordinary. Laura."

"Yes, darling?"

"Come into my dressing room a moment."

"What is it, darling?"

Mrs. Easterbrook appeared through the open door.

"Remember my showing you that revolver of mine?"

"Oh, yes, Archie, a nasty horrid black thing."

"Yes. Hun souvenir. Was in this drawer, wasn't it?"

"Yes, it was."

"Well, it's not there now."

"Archie, how extraordinary!"

"You haven't moved it or anything?"

"Oh, no, I'd never dare to touch the horrid thing."

"Think old Mother What's-her-name did?"

"Oh, I shouldn't think so, for a minute. Mrs. Butt would never do a thing like that. Shall I ask her?"

"No—no, better not. Don't want to start a lot of talk. Tell me, do you remember when it was I showed it to you?"

"Oh, about a week ago. You were grumbling about your collars and the laundry and you opened this drawer wide and there it was at the back and I asked you what it was."

"Yes, that's right. About a week ago. You don't remember the date?"

Mrs. Easterbrook considered, eyelids down over her eyes, a shrewd brain working.

"Of course," she said. "It was Saturday. The day we were to have gone in to the pictures, but we didn't."

"Hm—sure it wasn't before that? Wednesday? Thursday, or even the week before that?"

"No, dear," said Mrs. Easterbrook. "I remember

quite distinctly. It was Saturday, the 30th. It just seems a long time because of all the trouble there's been. And I can tell you how I remember. It's because it was the day after the holdup at Miss Blacklock's. Because when I saw your revolver it reminded me of the shooting the night before."

"Ah," said Colonel Easterbrook, "then that's a great load off my mind."

"Oh, Archie, why?"

"Just because if that revolver had disappeared before the shooting—well, it might possibly have been my revolver that was pinched by that Swiss fellow."

"But how would he have known you had one?"

"These gangs have a most extraordinary communication service. They get to know everything about a place and who lives there."

"What a lot you do know, Archie."

"Ha! Yes. Seen a thing or two in my time. Still, as you definitely remember seeing my revolver after the holdup—well, that settles it. The revolver that Swiss fellow used can't have been mine, can it?"

"Of course it can't."

"A great relief. I should have had to go to the police about it. And they ask a lot of awkward questions. Bound to. As a matter of fact, I never took out a license for it. Somehow, after a war, one forgets these peace-time regulations. I looked on it as a war souvenir, not as a firearm."

"Yes, I see. Of course."

"But all the same—where on earth can the damned thing be?"

"Perhaps Mrs. Butt took it. She's always seemed quite honest but perhaps she felt nervous after the holdup and thought she'd like to—to have a revolver in the house. Of course, she'll never admit doing that. I shan't even ask her. She might get offended. And what should we do then? This is such a big house—I simply couldn't."

"Quite so," said Colonel Easterbrook. "Better not say anything."

CHAPTER 13

Morning Activities in Chipping Cleghorn
(Continued)

Miss Marple came out of the vicarage gate and walked
down the little lane that led into the main street.

She walked fairly briskly with the aid of the Rev.
Julian Harmon's stout ashplant stick.

She passed the Red Cow and the butcher's and
stopped for a brief moment to look into the window
of Mr. Elliot's antique shop. This was cunningly situ-
ated next door to the Bluebird Tea Room and Café so
that rich motorists, after stopping for a nice cup of tea
and the somewhat euphemistically named "Home made
Cakes" of a bright saffron color, could be tempted by
Mr. Elliot's judiciously planned shop window.

In this antique bow frame, Mr. Elliot catered for
all tastes. Two pieces of Waterford glass reposed on an
impeccable wine cooler. A walnut bureau, made up of
various bits and pieces proclaimed itself a genuine bar-
gain and on a table, in the window itself, was a nice
assortment of cheap doorknockers and quaint pixies, a
few chipped bits of Dresden, a couple of sad-looking
bead necklaces, a mug with "A Present from Tunbridge
Wells" on it and some tidbits of Victorian silver.

Miss Marple gave the window her rapt attention, and
Mr. Elliot, an elderly obese spider, peeped out of his
web to appraise the possibilities of this new fly.

But just as he decided that the charms of the "Present from Tunbridge Wells" were about to be too much for the lady who was staying at the vicarage (for, of course, Mr. Elliot, like everybody else, knew exactly who she was), Miss Marple saw out of the corner of her eye Miss Dora Bunner entering the Bluebird Café, and immediately decided that what she needed to counteract the cold wind was a nice cup of morning coffee.

Four or five ladies were already engaged in sweetening their morning shopping by a pause for refreshments. Miss Marple, blinking a little in the gloom of the interior of the Bluebird, and hovering artistically, was greeted by the voice of Dora Bunner at her elbow.

"Oh, good morning, Miss Marple. Do sit down here. I'm all alone."

"Thank you."

Miss Marple subsided gratefully onto the rather angular little blue painted armchair which the Bluebird affected.

"Such a sharp wind," she complained. "And I can't walk very fast because of my rheumatic leg."

"Oh, I know. I had sciatica one year—and really most of the time I was in agony."

The two ladies talked rheumatism, sciatica and neuritis for some moments with avidity. A sulky-looking girl in a pink overall with a flight of bluebirds down the front of it took their order for coffee and cakes with a yawn and an air of weary patience.

"The cakes," Miss Bunner said in a conspiratorial whisper, "are really quite good here."

"I was so interested in that very pretty girl I met as we were coming away from Miss Blacklock's the other day," said Miss Marple. "I think she said she does gardening. Or is she on the land? Hynes—was that her name?"

"Oh, yes, Phillipa Haymes. Our Lodger, as we call

her." Miss Bunner laughed at her own humor. "Such a nice quiet girl. A lady, if you know what I mean."

"I wonder now. I knew a Colonel Haymes—in the Indian cavalry. Her father perhaps?"

"She's Mrs. Haymes. A widow. Her husband was killed in Sicily or Italy. Of course it might have been his father."

"I wondered, perhaps, if there might be a little romance on the way," Miss Marple suggested roguishly. "With that tall young man?"

"With Patrick, do you mean? Oh, I don't—"

"No, I meant a young man with spectacles. I've seen him about."

"Oh, of course, Edmund Swettenham. Sh! That's his mother, Mrs. Swettenham, over in the corner. I don't know, I'm sure. You think he admires her? He's such an odd young man—says the most disturbing things sometimes. He's supposed to be clever, you know," said Miss Bunner with frank disapproval.

"Cleverness isn't everything," said Miss Marple, shaking her head. "Ah, here is our coffee."

The sulky girl deposited it with a clatter. Miss Marple and Miss Bunner pressed cakes on each other.

"I was so interested to hear you were at school with Miss Blacklock. Yours is indeed an old friendship."

"Yes, indeed." Miss Bunner sighed. "Very few people would be as loyal to their old friends as dear Miss Blacklock is. Oh, dear, those days seem a long time ago. Such a pretty girl and enjoyed life so much. It all seemed so sad."

Miss Marple, though with no idea of what had seemed so sad, sighed and shook her head.

"Life is indeed hard," she murmured.

" 'And sad affliction bravely borne,' " murmured Miss Bunner, her eyes suffusing with tears. "I always think of that verse. True patience, true resignation. Such courage and patience ought to be rewarded, that is what I say. What I feel is that nothing is too good for dear Miss Blacklock, and whatever good things come to her, she truly deserves them."

"Money," said Miss Marple, "can do a lot to ease one's path in life."

She felt herself safe in this observation since she judged that it must be Miss Blacklock's prospects of future affluence to which her friend referred.

The remark, however, started Miss Bunner on another train of thought.

"Money!" she exclaimed with bitterness. "I don't believe, you know, that until one has really experienced it, one can know what money, or rather the lack of it, means."

Miss Marple nodded her white head sympathetically.

Miss Bunner went on rapidly, working herself up, and speaking with a flushed face.

"I've heard people say so often, 'I'd rather have flowers on the table, than a meal without them.' But how many meals have those people ever missed? They don't know what it is—nobody knows who hasn't been through it—to be really hungry. Bread, you know, and a jar of meat paste, and a scrape of margarine. Day after day and how one longs for a good plate of meat and two vegetables. And the shabbiness. Darning one's clothes and hoping it won't show. And applying for jobs and always being told you're too old. And then perhaps getting a job and after all one isn't strong enough. One faints. And you're back again. It's the rent—always the rent—that's got to be paid—otherwise you're out in the street. And in these days it leaves so little over. One's old-age pension doesn't go far—indeed it doesn't."

"I know," said Miss Marple gently. She looked with compassion at Miss Bunner's twitching face.

"I wrote to Letty. I just happened to see her name

in the paper. It was a luncheon in aid of Milchester Hospital. There is was in black and white, Miss Letitia Blacklock. It brought the past back to me. I hadn't heard of her for years and years. She's been secretary, you know, to that very rich man, Goedler. She was always a clever girl—the kind that gets on in the world. Not so much looks as character. I thought—well, I thought—perhaps she'll remember me—and she's one of the people I could ask for a little help. I mean someone you've known as a girl—been at school with—well, they do know about you—they know you're not just a —a begging letter writer—"

Tears came into Dora Bunner's eyes.

"And then Lotty came and took me away—said she needed someone to help her. Of course, I was very surprised—very surprised—but then newspapers do get things wrong. How kind she was—and how sympathetic. And remembering all the old days so well . . . I'd do anything for her—I really would. And I try very hard, but I'm afraid sometimes I muddle things—my head's not what it was. I make mistakes. And I forget and say foolish things. She's very patient. What's so nice about her is that she always pretends that I am useful to her. That's real kindness, isn't it?"

Miss Marple said gently, "Yes, that's real kindness."

"I used to worry, you know, even after I came to Little Paddocks—about what would become of me if —if anything were to happen to Miss Blacklock. After all, there are so many accidents—these motors dashing about—one never knows, does one? But naturally I never said anything—but she must have guessed. Suddenly one day she told me that she'd left me a small annuity in her will—and—what I value far more—all her beautiful furniture. I was quite overcome— But she said nobody else would value it as I should—and that is quite true—I can't bear to see some lovely piece of china smashed—or wet glasses put down on a table and leaving a mark. I do really look after her things. Some people—some people especially, are so terribly careless —and sometimes worse than careless!

"I'm not really as stupid as I look," Miss Bunner continued with simplicity. "I can see, you know, when Letty's being imposed upon. Some people—I won't name names—but they take advantage. Dear Miss Blacklock is, perhaps, just a shade too trusting."

Miss Marple shook her head.

"That's a mistake."

"Yes, it is. You and I, Miss Marple, know the world. Dear Miss Blacklock—" she shook her head.

Miss Marple thought that as the secretary of a big financier Miss Blacklock might be presumed to know the world, too. But probably what Dora Bunner meant was that Letty Blacklock had always been comfortably off, and that the comfortably off do not know the deeper abysses of human nature.

"That Patrick!" said Miss Bunner with a suddenness and an asperity that made Miss Marple jump. "Twice, at least, to my knowledge, he's got money out of her. Pretending he's hard up. Run into debt. All that sort of thing. She's far too generous. All she said to me was when I remonstrated with her, 'The boy's young, Dora. Youth is the time to have your fling.' "

"Well, that's true enough," said Miss Marple. "Such a handsome young man, too."

"Handsome is as handsome does," said Dora Bunner. "Much too fond of poking fun at people. And a lot of goings on with girls, I expect. I'm just a figure of fun to him—that's all. He doesn't seem to realize that people have their feelings."

"Young people are rather careless that way," said Miss Marple.

Miss Bunner leaned forward suddenly with a mysterious air.

"You won't breathe a word, will you, my dear?" she demanded. "But I can't help feeling that he was mixed up in this dreadful business. I think he knew that young man—or else Julia did. I daren't hint at such a thing to dear Miss Blacklock—at least I did, and she just snapped my head off. And, of course, it's awkward—because he's her nephew—or at any rate her consin—and if the Swiss young man shot himself Patrick might be held morally responsible, mightn't he? If he'd put him up to it, I mean. I'm really terribly confused about the whole thing. Everyone making such a fuss about that other door into the drawing-room. That's another thing that worries me—the detective saying it had been oiled. Because you see, I saw—"

She came to an abrupt stop.

Miss Marple paused to select a phrase.

"Most difficult for you," she said sympathetically. "Naturally you wouldn't want anything to get round to the police."

"That's just it," Dora Bunner cried. "I lie awake at nights and worry . . . because, you see, I came upon Patrick in the shrubbery the other day. I was looking for eggs—one hen hides out—and there he was holding a feather and a cup—an oily cup. And he jumped most guiltily when he saw me and he said: 'I was just wondering what this was doing here.' Well, of course, he's a quick thinker. I should say he thought that up quickly when I startled him. And how did he come to find a thing like that in the shrubbery unless he was looking for it, knowing perfectly well it was there? Of course, I didn't say anything."

"No, no, of course not."

"But I gave him a look, if you know what I mean."

Dora Bunner stretched out her hand and bit abstractedly into a lurid salmon-colored cake.

"And then another day I happened to overhear him having a very curious conversation with Julia. They seemed to be having a kind of quarrel. He was saying, 'If I thought you had anything to do with a thing like that!' And Julia (she's always so calm, you know) said: 'Well, little brother, what would you do about it?' And then, most unfortunately, I trod on that board that always squeaks, and they saw me. So I said, quite gaily: 'You two having a quarrel?' And Patrick said, 'I'm warning Julia not to go in for these black market clothes coupons deals.' Oh, it was all very slick, but I don't believe they were talking about anything of the sort! And, if you ask me, I believe Patrick had tampered with that lamp in the drawing-room—to make the lights go out, because I remember distinctly that it was the shepherdess—not the shepherd. And the next day—"

She stopped and her face grew pink. Miss Marple turned her head to see Miss Blacklock standing behind them—she must have just come in.

"Coffee and gossip, Bunny?" said Miss Blacklock with quite a shade of reproach in her voice. "Good morning, Miss Marple. Cold, isn't it?"

"We were just talking about clothes coupons," said Miss Bunner hurriedly. "They really don't give us enough, do they? A little better now shoes have come off. But fifteen still for a winter coat is too much."

The doors flew open with a clang and Bunch Harmon came into the Bluebird with a rush.

"Hullo," she said, "am I too late for coffee?"

"No, dear," said Miss Marple. "Sit down and have a cup."

"We must get home," said Miss Blacklock. "Done your shopping, Bunny?"

Her tone was indulgent once more, but her eyes still held a slight reproach.

"Yes—yes, thank you, Letty. I must just pop into the chemist's in passing and get some aspirin and some corn plasters."

As the door of the Bluebird swung to behind them, Bunch asked, "What were you talking about?"

Miss Marple did not reply at once. She waited whilst Bunch gave the order, then she said, "Family solidarity is a very strong thing. Very strong. Do you remember some famous case—I really can't remember what it was. They said the husband poisoned his wife. In a glass of wine. Then, at the trial, the daughter said she'd drunk half her mother's glass—so that knocked the case against her father to pieces. They do say—but it may be just rumor—that she never spoke to her father or lived with him again. Of course, a father is one thing—and a nephew or a distant cousin is another. But, still, there it is—no one wants a member of their own family hanged, do they?"

"No," said Bunch considering. "I shouldn't think they would."

Miss Marple leaned back in her chair. She murmured under her breath, "People are really very alike, everywhere."

"Who am I like?"

"Well, really, dear, you are very much like yourself. I don't know that you remind me of anyone in particular. Except perhaps—"

"Here it comes," said Bunch.

"I was just thinking of a parlormaid of mine, dear."

"A parlormaid? I should make a terrible parlormaid."

"Yes, dear, so did she. She was no good at all at waiting at table. Put everything on the table crooked, mixed up the kitchen knives with the dining room ones and her cap (this was a long time ago, dear)—her cap was never straight."

Bunch adjusted her hat automatically.

"Anything else?" she demanded anxiously.

"I kept her because she was so pleasant to have about the house—and because she used to make me laugh. I liked the way she said things straight out. Came to me one day, 'Of course I don't know, m'am,' she says, 'but Florrie, the way she sits down, it's just like a married woman.' And sure enough poor Florrie was in trouble—the gentlemanly assistant at the hairdresser's. Fortunately it was in good time, and I was able to have a little talk with him, and they had a very nice wedding and settled down quite happily. She was a good girl, Florrie, but inclined to be taken in by a gentlemanly appearance."

"She didn't do a murder, did she?" asked Bunch. "The parlormaid, I mean."

"No, indeed," said Miss Marple. "She married a Baptist minister and they had a family of five."

"Just like me," said Bunch. "Though I've only got as far as Edward and Susan up to date."

She added after a minute or two, "Who are you thinking about now, Aunt Jane?"

"Quite a lot of people, dear, quite a lot of people," said Miss Marple vaguely.

"In St. Mary Mead?"

"Mostly . . . I was really thinking about Nurse Ellerton—really an excellent, kindly woman. Took care of that old lady, seemed really fond of her. Then the old lady died. And another came and she died. Morphia. It all came out. Done in the kindest way, and the shocking thing was that the woman herself really couldn't see that she'd done anything wrong. They hadn't long to live in any case, she said, and one of them had cancer and quite a lot of pain."

"You mean—it was a mercy killing?"

"No, no. They signed their money away to her. She liked money, you know . . .

"And then there was that young man on the liner—Mrs. Pusey at the paper shop, her nephew. Brought stuff home he'd stolen and got her to dispose of it. Said it was things that he'd bought abroad. She was quite taken in. And then when the police came round and started asking questions, he tried to bash her on the head, so that she shouldn't be able to give him away. . . . Not a nice young man—but very good-looking. Had two girls in love with him. He spent a lot of money on one of them."

"The nastiest one, I suppose," said Bunch.

"Yes, dear. And there was Mrs. Cray at the wool shop. Devoted to her son, spoilt him, of course. He got in with a very queer lot. Do you remember Joan Croft, Bunch?"

"N—no, I don't think so."

"I thought you might have seen her when you were with me on a visit. Used to stalk about smoking a cigar or a pipe. We had a bank holdup once, and Joan Croft was in the bank at the time. She knocked the man down and took his revolver away from him. She was congratulated on her courage by the Bench."

Bunch listened attentively. She seemed to be learning by heart.

"And—" she prompted.

"That girl at St. Jean des Collines that summer. Such a quiet girl—not so much quiet as silent. Everybody liked her, but they never got to know her much better. . . . We heard afterwards that her husband was a forger. It made her feel cut off from people. It made her, in the end, a little queer. Brooding does, you know."

"Any Anglo-Indian colonels in your reminiscences, darling?"

"Naturally, dear. There was Major Vaughan at The Larches and Colonel Wright at Simla Lodge. Nothing wrong with either of them. But I do remember Mr.

Hodgson, the bank manager who went on a cruise and married a woman young enough to be his daughter. No idea of where she came from—except what she told him, of course."

"And that wasn't true?"

"No, dear, it definitely wasn't."

"Not bad," said Bunch nodding, and ticking people off of her fingers. "We've had devoted Dora, and handsome Patrick, and Mrs. Swettenham and Edmund, and Phillipa Haymes, and Colonel Easterbrook and Mrs. Easterbrook—and, if you ask me, I should say you're absolutely right about her. But there wouldn't be any reason for her murdering Letty Blacklock."

"Miss Blacklock, of course, might know something about her that she didn't want known."

"Oh, darling, that old Tanqueray stuff? Surely that's dead as the hills."

"It might not be. You see, Bunch, you are not the kind that minds much about what people think of you."

"I see what you mean," said Bunch suddenly. "If you'd been up against it, and then, rather like a shivering stray cat, you'd found a home and cream and a warm stroking hand and you were called Pretty Pussy and somebody thought the world of you. . . You'd do a lot to keep that . . . Well, I must say, you've presented me with a very complete gallery of people."

"You didn't get them all right, you know," said Miss Marple mildly.

"Didn't I? Where did I slip up? Julia, *pretty Juliar is peculiar.*"

"Three and sixpence," said the sulky waitress, materializing out of the gloom.

"And," she added, her bosom heaving beneath the bluebirds, "I'd like to know, Mrs. Harmon, why you call me peculiar. I had an aunt who joined the Peculiar

People, but I've always been good Church of England myself, as the late Rev. Hopkinson can tell you."

"I'm terribly sorry," said Bunch. "I was just quoting a song. I didn't mean you at all. I didn't know your name was Julia."

"Quite a coincidence," said the sulky waitress cheering up. "No offense, I'm sure, but hearing my name, as I thought—well, naturally, if you think someone's talking about you, it's only human nature to listen. Thank you."

She departed with her tip.

"Aunt Jane," said Bunch, "don't look so upset. What is it?"

"But surely," murmured Miss Marple. "That couldn't be so. There's no reason—"

"Aunt Jane!"

Miss Marple sighed and then smiled brightly.

"It's nothing, dear," she said.

"Did you think you knew who did the murder?" asked Bunch. "Who was it?"

"I don't know at all," said Miss Marple. "I got an idea for a moment—but it's gone. I wish I did know. Time's so short. So terribly short."

"What do you mean short?"

"That old lady up in Scotland may die any moment."

Bunch said staring, "Then you really do believe in Pip and Emma. You think it was them—and that they'll try again?"

"Of course they'll try again," said Miss Marple almost absent-mindedly. "If they tried once, they'll try again. If you've made up your mind to murder someone, you don't stop because it didn't come off the first time. Especially if you're fairly sure you're not suspected."

"But if it's Pip and Emma," said Bunch, "there are only two people it could be. It must be Patrick and

Julia. They're brother and sister and they're the only ones who are the right age."

"My dear, it isn't nearly as simple as that. There are all sorts of ramifications and combinations. There's Pip's wife if he's married, or Emma's husband. There's their mother—she's an interested party even if she doesn't inherit direct. If Letty Blacklock hasn't seen her for thirty years, she'd probably not recognize her now. One elderly woman is very like another. You remember Mrs. Wotherspoon drew her own and Mrs. Bartlett's old-age pension although Mrs. Bartlett had been dead for years. Anyway, Miss Blacklock's shortsighted. Haven't you noticed how she peers at people? And then there's the father. Apparently he was a real bad lot."

"Yes, but he's a foreigner."

"By birth. But there's no reason to believe he speaks broken English and gesticulates wth his hands. I daresay he could play the part of—of an Anglo-Indian colonel as well as anybody else."

"Is that what you think?"

"No, I don't. I don't indeed, dear. I just think that there's a great deal of money at stake, a great deal of money. And I'm afraid I know only too well the really terrible things that people will do to lay their hands on a lot of money."

"I suppose they will," said Bunch. "It doesn't really do them any good, does it? Not in the end?"

"No—but they don't usually know that."

"I can understand it." Bunch smiled suddenly, her sweet rather crooked smile. "One feels it would be different for oneself . . . Even I feel that." She considered, You pretend to yourself that you'd do a lot of good with all that money. Schemes. . . . Homes for unwanted children. . . . Tired mothers . . . . A lovely rest abroad somewhere for elderly women who have worked too hard . . . .

Her face grew somber. Her eyes were suddenly dark and tragic.

"I know what you're thinking," she said to Miss Marple. "You're thinking that I'd be the worst kind. Because I'd kid myself. If you just wanted the money for selfish reasons you'd at any rate see what you were like. But once you began to pretend about doing good with it, you'd be able to persuade yourself, perhaps, that it wouldn't very much matter killing someone."

Then her eyes cleared.

"But I shouldn't," she said. "I shouldn't really kill anyone. Not even if they were old, or ill or doing a lot of harm in the world. Not even if they were blackmailers or—or absolute beasts." She fished a fly carefully out of the dregs of the coffee and arranged it on the table to dry. "Because people like living, don't they? So do flies. Even if you're old and in pain and can just crawl out in the sun. Julian says those people like living even more than strong young people do. It's harder, he says, for them to die, the struggle's greater. I like living myself—not just being happy and enjoying myself and having a good time. I mean living—waking up and feeling, all over me, that I'm there—tickling over."

She blew on the fly gently; it waved its legs and flew rather drunkenly away.

"Cheer up, darling Aunt Jane," said Bunch. "I'd never kill anybody."

CHAPTER 14

Excursion into the Past

AFTER a night in the train Inspector Craddock alighted at a small station in the Highlands.

It struck him for a moment as strange that the wealthy Mrs. Goedler—an invalid—with a choice of a London house in a fashionable Square, an estate in Hampshire and a villa in the South of France, should have selected this remote Scottish home as her residence. Surely she was cut off here from many friends and distractions. It must be a lonely life—or was she too ill to notice or care about her surroundings?

A car was waiting to meet him. A big old-fashioned Daimler with an elderly chauffeur driving it. It was a sunny morning and the Inspector enjoyed the twenty-mile drive, though he marveled anew at this preference for isolation. A tentative remark to the chauffeur brought partial enlightenment.

"It's her own home as a girl. Ay, she's the last of the family. And she and Mr. Goedler were always happier here than anywhere, though it wasn't often he could get away from London. But when he did they enjoyed themselves like a couple of bairns."

When the gray walls of the old keep came in sight, Craddock felt that time was slipping backwards. An elderly butler received him, and after a wash and a shave he was shown into a room with a huge fire burning in the grate, and breakfast was served to him.

After breakfast, a tall middle-aged woman in nurse's dress, with a pleasant and competent manner, came in and introduced herself as Sister McClelland.

"I have my patient all ready for you, Mr. Craddock. She is, indeed, looking forward to seeing you."

"I'll do my best not to excite her," Craddock promised.

"I had better warn you of what will happen. You will find Mrs. Goedler apparently quite normal. She will talk and enjoy talking and then—quite suddenly—her powers will fail. Come away at once, then, and send for me. She is, you see, kept almost entirely under the influence of morphia. She drowses most of the time. In preparation for your visit, I have given her a strong stimulant. As soon as the effect of the stimulant wears off, she will relapse into semiconsciousness."

"I quite understand, Miss McClelland. Would it be in order for you to tell me exactly what the state of Mrs. Goedler's health is?"

"Well, Mr. Craddock, she is a dying woman. Her life cannot be prolonged for more than a few weeks. To say that she should have been dead years ago would strike you as odd, yet it is the truth. What has kept Mrs. Goedler alive is her intense enjoyment and love of being alive. That sounds, perhaps, an odd thing to say of someone who has lived the life of an invalid for many years and has not left her home here for fifteen years, but it is true. Mrs. Goedler has never been a strong woman—but she has retained to an astonishing degree the will to live." She added with a smile, "She is a very charming woman, too, as you will find."

Craddock was shown into a large bedroom where a fire was burning and where an old lady lay in a large canopied bed. Though she was only about seven or eight years older than Letitia Blacklock, her fragility made her seem older than her years.

Her white hair was carefully arranged, a froth of pale blue wool enveloped her neck and shoulders. There were lines of pain on the face, but lines of sweetness, too. And there was, strangely enough, what Craddock could only describe as a roguish twinkle in her faded blue eyes.

"Well, this is interesting," she said. "It's not often I receive a visit from the police. I hear Letitia Blacklock wasn't much hurt by this attempt on her? How is my dear Blackie?"

"She's very well, Mr. Goedler. She sent you her love."

"It's a long time since I've seen her . . . For many years now, it's been just a card at Christmas. I asked her to come up here when she came back to England after Charlotte's death, but she said it would be painful after so long and perhaps she was right . . . Blackie always had a lot of sense. I had an old school friend to see me about a year ago and, Lor' "—she smiled—"we bored each other to death. After we'd finished all the 'Do you remembers?' there wasn't anything to say. Most embarrassing."

Craddock was content to let her talk before pressing his questions. He wanted, as it were, to get back into the past, to get the feel of the Goedler-Blacklock ménage.

"I suppose," said Belle shrewdly, "that you want to ask about the money? Randall left it all to go to Blackie after my death. Really, of course, Randall never dreamed that I'd outlive him. He was a big strong man, never a day's illness, and I was always a mass of aches and pains and complaints and doctors coming and pulling long faces over me."

"I don't think complaints would be the right word, Mrs. Goedler."

The old lady chuckled.

"I didn't mean it in the complaining sense. I've never been too sorry for myself. But it was always taken for granted that I, being the weakly one, would go first. It didn't work out that way. No—it didn't work out that way . . ."

"Why, exactly, did your husband leave his money the way he did?"

"You mean, why did he leave it to Blackie? Not for the reason you've probably been thinking." The roguish twinkle was very apparent. "What minds you policemen have! Randall was never in the least in love with her and she wasn't with him. Letitia, you know, has really got a man's mind. She hasn't any feminine feelings or weaknesses. I don't believe she was ever in love with any man. She used a little make-up in deference to prevailing custom, but not to make herself look prettier." There was pity in the old voice as she went on: "She never knew any of the fun of being a woman."

Craddock looked with interest at the frail little figure in the big bed. Belle Goedler, he realized, had enjoyed—still enjoyed—being a woman. She twinkled at him.

"I've always thought," she said, "it must be terribly dull to be a man."

Then she said thoughtfully, "I think Randall looked on Blackie very much as a kind of younger brother. He relied on her judgment which was always excellent. She kept him out of trouble more than once, you know."

"She told me that she came to his rescue once with money."

"That, yes, but I meant more than that. One can speak the truth after all these years. Randall couldn't really distinguish between what was crooked and what wasn't. His conscience wasn't sensitive. The poor dear really didn't know what was just smart—and what was dishonest. Blackie kept him straight. That's one thing about Letitia Blacklock, she's absolutely dead straight. She would never do anything that was dishonest. She's a very fine character, you know. I've always admired her. They had a terrible girlhood, those girls. The father was an old country doctor—terrifically pigheaded and narrowminded—the complete family tyrant. Letitia broke away, came to London and trained herself as a chartered accountant. The other sister was an invalid, there was a deformity of kinds and she never saw people or went out. That's why, when the old man died, Letitia gave up everything to go home and look after her sister. Randall was wild with her—but it made no difference. If Letitia thought a thing was her duty, she'd do it. And you couldn't move her."

"How long was that before your husband died?"

"A couple of years, I think. Randall made his will before she left the firm, and he didn't alter it. He said to me: 'We've no one of our own.' (Our little boy died, you know, when he was two years old.) 'After you and I are gone, Blackie had better have the money. She'll play the markets and make 'em sit up.'

"You see," Belle went on, "Randall enjoyed the whole money-making game so much—it wasn't just the money—it was the adventure, the risks, the excitement of it all. And Blackie liked it, too. She had the same adventurous spirit and the same judgment. Poor darling, she'd never had any of the usual fun—being in love, and leading men on and teasing them—and having a home and children and all the real fun of life."

Craddock thought it was odd, the real pity and indulgent contempt felt by this woman, a woman whose life had been hampered by illness, whose only child had died, whose husband had died, leaving her to a lonely widowhood, and who had been a hopeless invalid for years.

She nodded her head at him.

"I know what you're thinking. But I've had all the things that make life worth while—they may have been taken from me—but I have had them. I was pretty and gay as a girl, I married the man I loved, and he never stopped loving me. My child died, but I had him for two precious years. I've had a lot of physical pain—but if you have pain, you know how to enjoy the exquisite pleasure of the times when pain stops. And everyone's been kind to me, always . . . I'm a lucky woman, really."

Craddock seized upon an opening in her former remarks.

"You said just now, Mrs. Goedler, that your husband left his fortune to Miss Blacklock because he had no one else to leave it to. But that's not strictly true, is it? He had a sister."

"Oh, Sonia. But they'd quarreled years ago and made a clean break of it."

"He disapproved of her marriage?"

"Yes, she married a man called—now what was his name—?"

"Stamfordis."

"That's it. Dmitri Stamfordis. Randall always said he was a crook. The two men didn't like each other from the first. But Sonia was wildly in love with him and quite determined to marry him. And I really never saw why she shouldn't. Men have such odd ideas about these things. Sonia wasn't a mere girl—she was twenty-five, and she knew exactly what she was doing. He was a crook, I daresay—I mean really a crook, I believe he had a criminal record—and Randall always suspected the name he was passing under wasn't his own. Sonia knew all that. The point was, which, of course, Randall couldn't appreciate, that Dmitri was really a wildly attractive person to women. And he was just as much in love with Sonia as she was with him. Randall insisted that he was just marrying her for her money—but that wasn't true. Sonia was very handsome, you know. And she had plenty of spirit. If the marriage had turned out badly, if Dmitri had been unkind to her or unfaithful to her, she would just have cut her losses and walked out on him. She was a rich woman and could do as she chose with her life."

"The quarrel was never made up?"

"No. Randall and Sonia never had got on very well. She resented his trying to prevent the marriage. She said, 'Very well. You're quite impossible! This is the last you hear of me!' "

"But it was not the last you heard of her?"

Belle smiled.

"No, I got a letter from her about eighteen months afterwards. She wrote from Budapest, I remember, but she didn't give an address. She told me to tell Randall that she was extremely happy and that she'd just had twins."

"And she told you their names?"

Again Belle smiled. "She said they were born just after midday and she intended to call them Pip and Emma. That may have been just a joke, of course."

"Didn't you hear from her again?"

"No. She said she and her husband and the babies were going to America on a short stay. I never heard any more . . . ."

"You don't happen, I suppose, to have kept that letter?"

"No, I'm afraid not . . . I read it to Randall and he just grunted: 'She'll regret marrying that fellow one of these days.' That's all he ever said about it. We really forgot about her. She went right out of our lives. . . ."

"Nevertheless, Mr. Goedler left his estate to her children in the event of Miss Blacklock predeceasing you?"

"Oh, that was my doing. I said to him, when he told

me about the will, 'And suppose Blackie dies before I do?' He was quite surprised. I said, 'Oh, I know Blackie is as strong as a horse and I'm a delicate creature—but there's such a thing as accidents, you know, and there's such a thing as creaking gates . . .' And he said, 'There's no one—absolutely no one.' I said, 'There's Sonia.' And he said at once, 'And let that fellow get hold of my money? No—indeed!' I said, 'Well, her children then. Pip and Emma, and there may be lots more by now'—and so he grumbled, but he did put it in."

"And from that day to this," Craddock said slowly, "you've heard nothing of your sister-in-law or her children?"

"Nothing—They may be dead—they may be—anywhere."

They may be in Chipping Cleghorn, thought Craddock.

As though she read his thoughts, a look of alarm came into Belle Goedler's eyes. She said, "Don't let them hurt Blackie. Blackie's good—really good—you mustn't let harm come to—"

Her voice trailed off suddenly. Craddock saw the sudden gray shadows round her mouth and eyes.

"You're tired," he said. "I'll go."

She nodded.

"Send Mac to me," she whispered. "Yes, tired . . ." She made a feeble motion of her hand. "Look after Blackie . . . nothing must happen to Blackie . . . look after her . . ."

"I'll do my very best, Mrs. Goedler." He rose and went to the door.

Her voice, a thin thread of sound, followed him.

"Not long now—until I'm dead—dangerous for her —take care . . ."

Sister McClelland passed him as he went out. He said uneasily, "I hope I haven't done her harm."

"Oh, I don't think so, Mr. Craddock. I told you she would tire quite suddenly."

Later, he asked the nurse, "The only thing I hadn't time to ask Mrs. Goedler was whether she had any old photographs. If so, I wonder—"

She interrupted him.

"I'm afraid there's nothing of that kind. All her personal papers and things were stored with their furniutre from the London house at the beginning of the war. Mrs. Goedler was desperately ill at the time. Then the storage depository was blitzed. Mrs. Goedler was very upset at losing so many personal souvenirs and family papers. I'm afraid there's nothing of that kind."

So that was that, Craddock thought.

Yet he felt his journey had not been in vain. Pip and Emma, those twin wraiths, were not quite wraiths.

Craddock thought, Here's a brother and sister brought up somewhere in Europe. Sonia Goedler was a rich woman at the time of her marriage, but money in Europe hasn't remained money. Queer things have happened to money during these war years. And so there are two young people, the son and daughter of a man who had a criminal record. Suppose they came to England, more or less penniless? What would they do? Find out about any rich relatives. Their uncle, a man of vast fortune, is dead. Possibly the first thing they'd do would be to look up that uncle's will. See if by any chance money had been left to them or to their mother. So they go to Somerset House and learn the contents of his will, and then, perhaps, they learn of the existence of Miss Letitia Blacklock. Then they make inquiries about Randall Goedler's widow. She's an invalid, living up in Scotland, and they find out she hasn't long to live.

If this Letitia Blacklock dies before her, they will come into a vast fortune. What then?

Craddock thought, They wouldn't go to Scotland. They'd find out where Letitia Blacklock is living now. And they'd go there—but not as themselves . . . They'd go together—or separately? Emma . . . I wonder . . . Pip and Emma. . . . I'll eat my hat if Pip, or Emma, or both of them, aren't in Chipping Cleghorn now.

CHAPTER 15

Delicious Death

IN THE kitchen at Little Paddocks, Miss Blacklock was giving instructions to Mitzi.

"Sardine sandwiches as well as the tomato ones. And some of those little scones you make so nicely. And I'd like you to make that special cake of yours."

"It is a party, then, that you want all these things?"

"It's Miss Bunner's birthday, and some people will be coming to tea."

"At her age one does not have birthdays. It is better to forget."

"Well, she doesn't want to forget. Several people are bringing her presents—and it will be nice to make a little party of it."

"That is what you say last time—and see what happened!"

Miss Blacklock controlled her temper.

"Well, it won't happen this time."

"How do you know what may happen in this house? All day long I shiver and at night I lock my door and I look in the wardrobe to see no one is hidden there."

"That ought to keep you nice and safe," said Miss Blacklock coldly.

"The cake that you want me to make, it is the—" Mitzi uttered a sound that to Miss Blacklock's English

164

ear sounded like *Schwitzebzr,* or, alternatively, like cats spitting at each other.

"That's the one. The rich one."

"Yes. It is rich. For it I have nothing! Impossible to make such a cake. I need for it chocolate and much butter, and sugar and raisins."

"You can use this tin of butter that was sent us from America. And some of the raisins we were keeping for Christmas, and here is a slab of chocolate and a pound of sugar."

Mitzi's face suddenly burst into radiant smiles.

"So, I make him for you good—good!" she cried, in an ecstasy. "It will be rich, rich, of a melting richness! And on top I will put the icing—chocolate icing—I make him so nice—and write on it *Good Wishes.* These English people with their cakes that taste of sand, never, never will they have tasted such a cake. Delicious, they will say—delicious—"

Her face clouded again.

"Mr. Patrick. He called it Delicious Death. My cake! I will not have my cake called that!"

"It was a compliment really," said Miss Blacklock. "He meant it was worth dying to eat such a cake."

Mitzi looked at her doubtfully.

"Well, I do not like that word—death. They are not dying because they eat my cake, no, they feel much much better."

"I'm sure we all shall."

Miss Blacklock turned away and left the kitchen with a sigh of relief at the successful ending of the interview. With Mitzi one never knew.

She ran into Dora Bunner outside.

"Oh, Letty, shall I run in and tell Mitzi just how to cut the sandwiches?"

"No," said Miss Blacklock, steering her friend firmly

into the hall. "She's in a good mood now and I don't want her disturbed."

"But I could just show her——"

"Please don't show her anything, Dora. These central Europeans don't like being shown. They hate it."

Dora looked at her doubtfully. Then she suddenly broke into smiles.

"Edmund Swettenham just rang up. He wished me many happy returns of the day and said he was bringing me a pot of honey as a present this afternoon. Isn't it kind? I can't imagine how he knew it was my birthday."

"Everybody seems to know. You must have been talking about it, Dora."

"Well, I did just happen to mention that today I should be fifty-nine——"

"You're sixty-four," said Miss Blacklock with a twinkle.

"And Miss Hinchliffe said, 'You don't look it. What age do you think I am?' Which was rather awkward because Miss Hinchliffe always looks so peculiar that she might be any age. She said she was bringing me some eggs, by the way. I said our hens hadn't been laying very well lately."

"We're not doing so badly out of your birthay," said Miss Blacklock. "Honey, eggs——a magnificent box of chocolates from Julia——"

"I don't know where she gets such things."

"Better not ask. Her methods are probably strictly illegal."

"And your lovely brooch." Miss Bunner looked down proudly at her bosom on which was pinned a small diamond leaf.

"Do you like it? I'm glad. I never cared for jewelry."

"I love it."

"Good. Let's go and feed the ducks."

2

"Ha!" cried Patrick dramatically, as the party took their places round the dining room table. "What do I see before me? Delicious Death."

"Hush," said Miss Blacklock. "Don't let Mitzi hear you. She objects to your name for her cake very much."

"Nevertheless, Delicious Death it is! Is it Bunny's birthday cake?"

"Yes, it is," said Miss Bunner. "I really am having the most wonderful birthday."

Her cheeks were flushed with excitement and had been ever since Colonel Easterbrook had handed her a small box of sweets and declaimed with a bow, "Sweets to the Sweet!"

Julia had turned her head away hurriedly, and had been frowned at by Miss Blacklock.

Full justice was done to the good things on the tea table and they rose from their seats after a round of crackers.

"I feel slightly sick," said Julia. "It's that cake. I remember I felt just the same last time."

"It's worth it," said Patrick.

"These foreigners certainly understand confectionery," said Miss Hinchliffe. "What they can't make is a plain boiled pudding."

Everybody was respectfully silent, though it seemed to be hovering on Patrick's lips to ask if anyone really wanted a plain boiled pudding.

"Got a new gardener?" asked Miss Hinchliffe of Miss Blacklock as they returned to the drawing-room.

"No, why?"

"Saw a man snooping round the henhouse. Quite a decent looking Army type."

"Oh that," said Julia. "That's our detective."

Mrs. Easterbrook dropped her handbag.

"Detective?" she exclaimed. "But—but—why?"

"I don't know," said Julia. "He prowls about and keeps an eye on the house. He's protecting Aunt Letty, I suppose."

"Absolute nonsense," said Miss Blacklock. "I can protect myself, thank you."

"But surely it's all over now," cried Mrs. Easterbrook. "Though I meant to ask you, why did they adjourn the inquest?"

"Police aren't satisfied," said her husband. "That's what that means."

"But aren't satisfied of what?"

Colonel Easterbrook shook his head with the air of a man who could say a good deal more if he chose. Edmund Swettenham, who disliked the colonel, said, "The truth of it is, we're all under suspicion."

"But suspicion of what?" repeated Mrs. Easterbrook.

"Loitering with intent," said Edmund. "The intent being to commit murder upon the first opportunity."

"Oh, don't, please don't, Mr. Swettenham." Dora Bunner began to cry. "I'm sure nobody here could possibly want to kill dear, dear Letty."

There was a moment of horrible embarrassment. Edmund turned scarlet, murmured, "Just a joke." Phillipa suggested in a high clear voice that they might listen to the six o'clock news and the suggestion was received with enthusiastic assent.

Patrick murmured to Julia: "We need Mrs. Harmon here. She'd be sure to say in that high clear voice of hers, 'But I suppose somebody is still waiting for a good chance to murder you, Miss Blacklock?' "

"I'm glad she and that old Miss Marple couldn't come," said Julia. "That old woman is the prying kind. And a mind like a sink, I should think. Real Victorian type."

Listening to the news led easily into a pleasant discussion on the horrors of atomic warfare. Colonel Easterbrook said that the real menace to civilization was undoubtedly Russia, and Edmund said that he had several charming Russian friends—which announcement was coldly received.

The party broke up with renewed thanks to the hostess.

"Enjoy yourself, Bunny?" asked Miss Blacklock, as the last guest was sped.

"Oh, I did. But I've got a terrible headache. It's the excitement, I think."

"It's the cake," said Patrick. "I feel a bit livery myself. And you've been nibbling chocolates all the morning."

"I'll go and lie down, I think," said Miss Bunner. "I'll take a couple of aspirin and try and have a nice sleep."

"That would be a very good plan," said Miss Blacklock.

Miss Bunner departed upstairs.

"Shall I shut up the ducks for you, Aunt Letty?"

Miss Blacklock looked at Patrick severely.

"If you'll be sure to latch that door properly."

"I will. I swear I will."

"Have a glass of sherry, Aunt Letty," said Julia. "As my old nurse used to say, 'It will settle your stomach.' A revolting phrase—but curiously apposite at this moment."

"Well, I daresay it might be a good thing. The truth is, one isn't used to rich things. Oh, Bunny, how you made me jump. What is it?"

"I can't find my aspirin," said Miss Bunner disconsolately.

"Well, take some of mine, dear; they're by my bed."

"There's a bottle on my dressing table," said Phillipa.

"Thank you—thank you very much. If I can't find mine—but I know I've got it somewhere. A new bottle. Now where could I have put it?"

"There's heaps in the bathroom," said Julia impatiently. "This house is chock full of aspirin."

"It vexes me to be so careless and mislay things," replied Miss Bunner, retreating up the stairs again.

"Poor old Bunny," said Julia, holding up her glass. "Do you think we ought to have given her some sherry?"

"Better not, I think," said Miss Blacklock. "She's had a lot of excitement today, and it isn't really good for her. I'm afraid she'll be the worse for it tomorrow. Still, I really do think she has enjoyed herself!"

"She's loved it," said Phillipa.

"Let's give Mitzi a glass of sherry," suggested Julia. "Hi, Pat," she called as she heard him entering the side door, "fetch Mitzi."

So Mitzi was brought in and Julia poured her out a glass of sherry.

"Here's to the best cook in the world," said Patrick raising his glass.

Mitzi was gratified—but felt nevertheless that a protest was due.

"That is not so. I am not really a cook. In my country I do intellectual work."

"Then you're wasted," said Patrick. "What's intellectual work compared to a chef-d'oeuvre like Delicious Death?"

"Oo—I say to you I do not like—"

"Never mind what you like, my girl," said Patrick. "That's my name for it and here's to it. Let's all drink to Delicious Death and to hell with the aftereffects."

3

"Phillipa, my dear, I want to talk to you."

"Yes, Miss Blacklock?"

Phillipa Haymes looked up in slight surprise.

"You're not worrying about anything, are you?"

"Worrying?"

"I've noticed that you've looked worried lately. There isn't anything wrong, is there?"

"Oh, no, Miss Blacklock. What should there be?"

"Well—I wondered. I thought, perhaps that you and Patrick—"

"Patrick?" Phillipa looked really surprised.

"It's not so, then. Please forgive me if I've been impertinent. But you've been thrown together a lot—and although Patrick is a relation, I don't think he's the type to make a satisfactory husband. Not for some time to come, at all events."

Phillipa's face had frozen into a hard immobility.

"I shan't marry again," she said.

"Oh, yes, you will some day, my child. You're young. But we needn't discuss that. There's no other trouble? You're not worried about—money, for instance?"

"No, I'm quite all right."

"I know you get anxious sometimes about your boy's education. That's why I want to tell you something. I drove into Milchester this afternoon to see Mr. Beddingfeld, my lawyer. Things haven't been very settled lately and I thought I would like to make a new will—in view of certain eventualities. Apart from Bunny's legacy, everything goes to you, Phillipa."

"What?" Phillipa spun round. Her eyes stared. She looked dismayed, almost frightened.

"But I don't want it—really, I don't . . . Oh I'd rather not . . . And, anyway, why? Why to me?"

"Perhaps," said Miss Blacklock in a peculiar voice, "because there's no one else."

"But there's Patrick and Julia."

"Yes, there's Patrick and Julia." The odd note in Miss Blacklock's voice was still there.

"They are your relations."

"Very distant ones. They have no claim on me."

"But I—I haven't either—I don't know what you think—Oh, I don't want it."

Her gaze held more hostility than gratitude. There was something almost like fear in her manner.

"I know what I'm doing, Phillipa. I've become fond of you—and there's the boy . . . You won't get very much if I should die now—but in a few weeks' time it might be different."

Her eyes met Phillipa's steadily.

"But you're not going to die!" Phillipa protested.

"Not if I can avoid it by taking due precautions."

"Precautions?"

"Yes. Think it over . . . And don't worry any more."

She left the room abruptly. Phillipa heard her speaking to Julia in the hall.

Julia entered the drawing-room a few moments later. There was a slightly steely glitter in her eyes.

"Played your cards rather well, haven't you, Phillipa? I see you're one of those quiet ones . . . a dark horse . . ."

"So you heard—"

"Yes, I heard. I rather think I was meant to hear."

"What do you mean?"

"Our Letty's no fool . . . Well, anyway, you're all right, Phillipa. Sitting pretty, aren't you?"

"Oh, Julia—I didn't mean—I never meant—"

"Didn't you? Of course you did. You're fairly up against things, aren't you? Hard up for money. But just remember this—if anyone bumps off Aunt Letty now, you'll be suspect Number 1."

"But I shan't be. It would be idiotic if I killed her now when—if I waited—"

"So you do know about old Mrs. What's-her-name dying up in Scotland? I wondered . . . Phillipa, I'm beginning to believe you're a very dark horse indeed."

"I don't want to do you and Patrick out of anything."

"Don't you, my dear? I'm sorry—but I don't believe you."

CHAPTER 16

Inspector Craddock Returns

INSPECTOR CRADDOCK had had a bad night on his journey home. His dreams had been less dreams than nightmares. Again and again he was racing through the gray corridors of an old-world castle in a desperate attempt to get somewhere, or to prevent something in time. Finally, he dreamed that he awoke. An enormous relief surged over him. Then the door of his compartment slid slowly open, and Letitia Blacklock looked in at him with blood running down her face, and said reproachfully: "Why didn't you save me? You could have if you'd tried."

This time he really awoke.

Altogether, the Inspector was thankful finally to reach Milchester. He went straight away to make his report to Rydesdale who listened carefully.

"It doesn't take us much further," he said. "But it confirms what Miss Blacklock told you. Pip and Emma —hm, I wonder."

"Patrick and Julia Simmons are the right age, sir. If we could establish that Miss Blacklock hadn't seen them since they were children—"

With a very faint chuckle, Rydesdale said: "Our ally, Miss Marple, has established that for us. Actually, Miss Blacklock had never seen either of them at all until two months ago."

"Then surely, sir—"

"It's not so easy as all that, Craddock. We've been checking up. On what we've got, Patrick and Julia seem definitely to be out of it. His Naval record is genuine—quite a good record barring a tendency to 'insubordination.' We've checked with Cannes, and an indignant Mrs. Simmons says of course her son and daughter are at Chipping Cleghorn with her cousin Letitia Blacklock. So that's that!"

"And Mrs. Simmons *is* Mrs. Simmons?"

"She's been Mrs. Simmons for a very long time, that's all I can say," said Rydesdale dryly.

"That seems clear enough. Only—those two fitted. Right age. Not known to Miss Blacklock personally. If we wanted a Pip and Emma—well, there they were."

The Chief Constable nodded thoughtfully, then he pushed a paper across to Craddock.

"Here's a little something we've dug up on Mrs. Easterbrook."

The Inspector read with lifted eyebrows.

"Very interesting," he remarked. "Hoodwinked that old ass pretty well, hasn't she? It doesn't tie in with this business though, as far as I can see."

"Apparently not."

"And here's an item that concerns Mrs. Haymes."

Again Craddock's eyebrows rose.

"I think I'll have to have another talk with the lady," he said.

"You think this information might be relevant?"

"I think it might be. It would be a long shot, of course . . ."

The two men were silent for a moment or two.

"How has Fletcher got on, sir?"

"Fletcher has been exceedingly active. He's made a routine search of the house by agreement with Miss

Blacklock—but he didn't find anything significant. Then
he's been checking up on who could have had the opportunity of oiling that door. Checking who was up at
the house on the days that that foreign girl was out. A
little more complicated than we thought, because it
appears she goes for a walk most afternoons. Usually
down to the village where she has a cup of coffee at the
Bluebird. So that when Miss Blacklock and Miss Bunner are out—which is most afternoons—they go black-
berrying—the coast is clear."

"And the doors are always left unlocked?"

"They used to be. I don't suppose they are now."

"What are Fletcher's results? Who's known to have
been in the house when it was left empty?"

"Practically the whole lot of them."

Rydesdale consulted a page in front of him.

"Miss Murgatroyd was there with a hen to sit on
some eggs. (Sounds complicated but that's what she
says.) Very flustered about it all and contradicts herself, but Fletcher thinks that's temperamental and not a
sign of guilt."

"Might be," Craddock admitted. "She flaps."

"Then Mrs. Swettenham came up to fetch some horse
meat that Miss Blacklock had left for her on the kitchen
table because Miss Blacklock had been in to Milchester
in the car that day and always gets Mrs. Swettenham's
horse meat for her. That makes sense to you?"

Craddock considered.

"Why didn't Miss Blacklock leave the horse meat
when she passed Mrs. Swettenham's house on her way
back from Milchester?"

"I don't know, but she didn't. Mrs. Swettenham says
she (Miss B.) always leaves it on the kitchen table, and
she (Mrs. S.) likes to fetch it when Mitzi isn't there
because Mitzi is sometimes so rude."

"Hangs together quite well. And the next?"

"Miss Hinchliffe. Says she wasn't there at all lately. But she was. Because Mitzi saw her coming out of the side door one day and so did a Mrs. Butt (she's one of the locals). Miss H. then admitted she might have been there but had forgotten. Can't remember what she went for. Says she probably just dropped in."

"That's rather odd."

"So was her manner, apparently. Then there's Mrs. Easterbrook. She was exercising the dear dogs out that way and she just popped in to see if Miss Blacklock would lend her a knitting pattern but Miss Blacklock wasn't in. She says she waited a little."

"Just so. Might be snooping round. Or might be oiling a door. And the colonel?"

"Went there one day with a book on India that Miss Blacklock had expressed a desire to read."

"Had she?"

"Her account is that she tried to get out of having to read it, but it was no use."

"And that's fair enough," sighed Craddock. "If anyone is really determined to lend you a book, you never can get out of it!"

"We don't know if Edmund Swettenham was up there. He's extremely vague. Said he did drop in occasionally on errands for his mother, but thinks not lately."

"In fact, it's all inconclusive."

"Yes."

Rydesdale said, with a slight grin, "Miss Marple has also been active. Fletcher reports she had morning coffee at the Bluebird. She's been to sherry at Boulders and to tea at Little Paddocks. She's admired Mrs. Swettenham's garden—and dropped in to see Colonel Easterbrook's Indian curios."

"She may be able to tell us if Colonel Easterbrook's a pukka colonel or not."

"She'd know, I agree—he seems all right. We'd have to check with the Far East authorities to get certain identification."

"And in the meantime—" Craddock broke off. "Do you think Miss Blacklock would consent to go away?"

"Go away from Chipping Cleghorn?"

"Yes. Take the faithful Bunner with her, perhaps, and leave for an unknown destination. Why shouldn't she go up to Scotland and stay with Belle Goedler? It's a pretty un-get-at-able place."

"Stop there and wait for her to die? I don't think she'd do that. I don't think any nice-natured woman would like that suggestion."

"It it's a matter of saving her life—"

"Come now, Craddock, it isn't quite so easy to bump someone off as you seem to think."

"Isn't is, sir?"

"Well—in one way—it's easy enough, I agree. Plenty of methods. Weed-killer. A bash on the head when she's out shutting up the poultry, a pot shot from behind a hedge. All quite simple. But to bump someone off and not be suspected of bumping them off—that's not quite so easy. And they must realize by now that they're all under observation. The original carefully planned scheme failed. Our unknown murderer has got to think up something else."

"I know that, sir. But there's the time element to consider. Mrs. Goedler's a dying woman—she might pop off any minute. That means that our murderer can't afford to wait."

"True."

"And another thing, sir. He—or she—must know that we're checking up on everybody."

"And that takes time," said Rydesdale with a sigh.

"It means checking with the East, with India. Yes, it's a long, tedious business."

"So that's another reason for—hurry. I'm sure, sir, that the danger is very real. It's a very large sum that's at stake. If Belle Goedler dies—"

He broke off as a constable entered.

"Constable Legg on the line from Chipping Cleghorn, sir."

"Put him through here."

Inspector Craddock, watching the Chief Constable, saw his features harden and stiffen.

"Very good," barked Rydesdale. "Detective Inspector Craddock will be coming out immediately."

He put the receiver down.

"Is it—" Craddock broke off.

Rydesdale shook his head.

"No," he said. "It's Dora Bunner. She wanted some aspirin. Apparently she took some from a bottle beside Letitia Blacklock's bed. There were only a few tablets left in the bottle. She took two and left one. The doctor's got that one and is sending it to be analyzed. He says it's definitely not aspirin."

"She's dead?"

"Yes, found dead in her bed this morning. Died in her sleep. Doctor says he doesn't think it was natural, though her health was in a bad state. Narcotic poisoning, that's his guess. Autopsy's fixed for tonight."

"Aspirin tablets by Letitia Blacklock's bed. The clever, clever devil. Patrick told me Miss Blacklock threw away a half bottle of sherry—opened a new one. I don't suppose she'd have thought of doing that with an open bottle of aspirin. Who had been in the house this time—within the last day or two? The tablets can't have been there long."

Rydesdale looked at him.

"All our lot were there yesterday," he said. "Birthday party for Miss Bunner. Any of them could have nipped upstairs and done a neat little substitution. Or, of course, anyone living in the house could have done it any time."

CHAPTER 17

The Album

Standing by the vicarage gate, well wrapped up, Miss Marple took the note from Bunch's hand.

"Tell Miss Blacklock," said Bunch, "that Julian is terribly sorry he can't come up himself. He's got a parishioner dying out at Locke Hamlet. He'll come up after lunch if Miss Blacklock would like to see him. The note's about the arrangements for the funeral. He suggests Wednesday if the inquest's on Tuesday. Poor old Bunny. It's so typical of her, somehow, to get hold of poisoned aspirin meant for someone else. Good-by, darling. I hope the walk won't be too much for you. But I've simply got to get that child to hospital at once."

Miss Marple said the walk wouldn't be too much for her, and Bunch rushed off.

Whilst waiting for Miss Blacklock, Miss Marple looked round the drawing-room, and wondered just exactly what Dora Bunner had meant that morning in the Bluebird by saying that she believed Patrick had "tampered with the lamp" to "make the lights go out." What lamp? And how had he "tampered" with it?

She must, Miss Marple decided, have meant the small lamp that stood on the table by the archway. She had said something about a shepherdess or a shepherd —and this was actually a delicate piece of Dresden china, a shepherd in a blue coat and pink breeches, holding what had originally been a candlestick and had now been adapted to electricity. The shade was a plain vellum and a little too big so that it almost masked the figure. What else was it that Dora Bunner had said? "I remember distinctly that it was the shepherdess. And the next day—" Certainly it was a shepherd now.

Miss Marple remembered that when she and Bunch had come to tea, Dora Bunner had said something about the lamp being one of a pair. Of course—a shepherd and shepherdess. And it had been the shepherdess on the day of the holdup—and the next morning it had been the other lamp—the lamp that was here now, the shepherd. The lamps had been changed over during the night. And Dora Bunner had had reason to believe (or had believed without reason) that it was Patrick who had changed them.

Why? Because, if the original lamp were examined, it would show just how Patrick had managed to "make the lights go out." How had he managed? Miss Marple looked earnestly at the lamp in front of her. The cord ran along the table over the edge and was plugged into the wall. There was a small pear-shaped switch halfway along the cord. None of it suggested anything to Miss Marple because she knew very little about electricity.

Where was the shepherdess lamp, she wondered. In the "spare room" or thrown away, or—where was it Dora Bunner had come upon Patrick Simmons with a feather and an oily cup? In the shrubbery? Miss Marple made up her mind to put all these points to Inspector Craddock.

At the very beginning Miss Blacklock had leaped to the conclusion that her nephew Patrick had been behind the insertion of that advertisement. That kind of instinctive belief was often justified, or so Miss Marple believed. Because, if you knew people fairly well, you knew the kind of things they thought of . . .

Patrick Simmons . . .

A handsome young man. An engaging young man. A young man whom women liked, both young women and old women. The kind of man, perhaps, that Randall Goedler's sister had married. Could Patrick Simmons be Pip? But he'd been in the Navy during the war. The police could soon check up on that.

Only—sometimes—the most amazing impersonations did happen.

You could get away with a great deal if you had enough audacity . . .

The door opened and Miss Blacklock came in. She looked, Miss Marple thought, many years older. All the life and energy had gone out of her.

"I'm very sorry, disturbing you like this," said Miss Marple. "But the vicar had a dying parishioner and Bunch had to rush a sick child to hospital. The vicar wrote you a note."

She held it out and Miss Blacklock took it and opened it.

"Do sit down, Miss Marple," she said. "It's very kind of you to have brought this."

She read the note through.

"The vicar's a very understanding man," she said quietly. "He doesn't offer one fatuous consolations . . . Tell him that these arrangements will do very well. Her —her favorite hymn was *Lead, Kindly Light*."

Her voice broke suddenly.

Miss Marple said gently, "I am only a stranger, but I am so very, very sorry."

And suddenly, uncontrollably, Letitia Blacklock wept. It was a piteous, overmastering grief, with a kind of hopelessness about it. Miss Marple sat quite still.

Miss Blacklock sat up at last. Her face was swollen and blotched with tears.

"I'm sorry," she said. "It—it just came over me. What I've lost. She—she was the only link with the past, you see. The only one who—remembered. Now that she's gone I'm quite alone."

"I know what you mean," said Miss Marple. "One is alone when the last one who remembers is gone. I have nephews and nieces and kind friends—but there's no one who knew me as a young girl—no one who belongs to the old days. I've been alone for quite a long time now."

Both women sat silent for some moments.

"You understand very well," said Letitia Blacklock. She rose and went over to her desk. "I must write a few words to the vicar." She held the pen rather awkwardly and wrote slowly.

"Arthritic," she explained. "Sometimes I can hardly write at all."

She sealed up the envelope and addressed it.

"If you wouldn't mind taking it, it would be very kind."

Hearing a man's voice in the hall, she said quickly, "That's Inspector Craddock."

She went to the mirror over the fireplace and applied a small powder puff to her face.

Craddock came in with a grim angry face.

He looked at Miss Marple with disapprobation.

"Oh," he said. "So you're here."

Miss Blacklock turned from the mantelpiece.

"Miss Marple kindly came up with a note from the vicar."

Miss Marple said in a flurried manner, "I am going at once—at once. Please don't let me hamper you in any way."

"Were you at the tea party here yesterday afternoon?"

Miss Marple said, nervously, "No—no, I wasn't. Bunch drove me over to call on some friends."

"Then there's nothing you can tell me." Craddock held the door open in a pointed manner, and Miss Marple scuttled out in a somewhat abashed fashion.

"Nosy Parkers, these old women," said Craddock.

"I think you're being unfair to her," said Miss Blacklock. "She really did come with a note from the vicar."

"I bet she did."

"I don't think it was idle curiosity."

"Well, perhaps, you're right, Miss Blacklock, but my own diagnosis would be a severe attack of Nosy Parkeritis ..."

"She's a very harmless old creature," said Miss Blacklock.

Dangerous as a rattlesnake if you only knew, the Inspector thought grimly. But he had no intention of taking anyone into his confidence unnecessarily. Now that he knew definitely there was a killer at large, he felt that the less said the better. He didn't want the next person bumped off to be Jane Marple.

Somewhere—a killer ... Where?

"I won't waste time offering sympathy, Miss Blacklock," he said. "As a matter of fact, I feel pretty bad about Miss Bunner's death. We ought to have been able to prevent it."

"I don't see what you could have done."

"No—well, it wouldn't have been easy. But now we've got to work fast. Who's doing this, Miss Blacklock? Who's had two shots at killing you, and will probably, if we don't work fast enough, soon have another?"

Letitia Blacklock shivered. "I don't know, Inspector —I don't know at all!"

"I've checked up with Mrs. Goedler. She's given me

all the help she can. It wasn't very much. There are just a few people who would definitely profit by your death. First: Pip and Emma. Patrick and Julia Simmons are the right age, but their background seems clear enough. Anyway, we can't concentrate on those two alone. Tell me, Miss Blacklock, would you recognize Sonia Goedler if you saw her?"

"Recognize Sonia? Why, of course—" She stopped suddenly. "No," she said slowly, "I don't know that I would. It's a long time. Thirty years . . . She'd be an elderly woman now."

"What was she like as you remember her?"

"Sonia?" Miss Blacklock considered for some moments. "She was rather small, dark . . ."

"Any special peculiarities? Mannerisms?"

"No—no, I don't think so. She was gay—very gay."

"She mayn't be so gay now," said the Inspector. "Have you got a photograph of her?"

"Of Sonia? Let me see—not a proper photograph. I've got some old snapshots—in an album somewhere —at least I think there's one of her."

"Ah. Can I have a look at it?"

"Yes, of course. Now where did I put that album?"

"Tell me, Miss Blacklock, do you consider it remotely possible that Mrs. Swettenham might be Sonia Goedler?"

"Mrs. Swettenham?" Miss Blacklock looked at him in lively astonishment. "But her husband was in the Government Service—in India first, I think, and then in Hong Kong."

"What you mean is, that that's the story she's told you. You don't, as we say in the Courts, know it of your own knowledge, do you?"

"No," said Miss Blacklock slowly. "When you put it like that, I don't . . . But Mrs. Swettenham? Oh, its absurd!"

"Did Sonia Goedler ever do any acting? Amateur theatricals?"

"Oh, yes. She was good."

"There you are! Another thing, Mrs. Swettenham wears a wig. At least," the Inspector corrected himself, "Mrs. Harmon says she does."

"Yes—yes, I suppose it might be a wig. All those little gray curls. But I still think it's absurd. She's really very nice end exceedingly funny sometimes."

"Then there's Miss Hinchliffe and Miss Murgatroyd. Could either of them be Sonia Goedler?"

"Miss Hinchliffe is too tall. She's as tall as a man."

"Miss Murgatroyd then?"

"Oh, but—oh, no, I'm sure Miss Murgatroyd couldn't be Sonia."

"You don't see very well, do you, Miss Blacklock?"

"I'm nearsighted; is that what you mean?"

"Yes. What I'd like to see is a snapshot of this Sonia Goedler, even if it's a long time ago and not a good likeness. We're trained, you know, to pick out resemblances, in a way no amateur can ever do."

"I'll try and find it for you."

"Now."

"What, at once?"

"I'd prefer it."

"Very well. Now, let me see. I saw that album when we were tidying a lot of books out of the cupboard. Julia was helping me. She laughed, I remember, at the clothes we used to wear in those days ... The books we put in the shelf in the drawing-room. Where did we put the albums and the big bound volumes of the *Art Journal?* What a wretched memory I have! Perhaps Julia will remember. She's at home today."

"I'll find her."

The Inspector departed on his quest. He did not find Julia in any of the downstairs rooms. Mitzi, asked where

Miss Simmons was, said crossly that it was not her affair.

"Me! I stay in my kitchen and concern myself with the lunch. And nothing do I eat that I have not cooked myself. Nothing, do you hear?"

The Inspector called up the stairs, "Miss Simmons," and getting no response, went up.

He met Julia face to face just as he turned the corner of the landing. She had just emerged from a door that showed behind it a small twisty staircase.

"I was up in the attic," she explained. "What is it?"

Inspector Craddock explained.

"Those old photograph albums? Yes, I remember them quite well. We put them in the big cupboard in the study, I think. I'll find them for you."

She led the way downstairs and pushed open the study door. Near the window there was a large cupboard. Julia pulled it open and disclosed a heterogeneous mass of objects.

"Junk," said Julia. "All junk. But elderly people simply will not throw things away."

The Inspector knelt down and took a couple of old-fashioned albums from the bottom shelf.

"Are these they?"

"Yes."

Miss Blacklock came in and joined them.

"Oh, so that's where we put them. I couldn't remember."

Craddock had the books on the table and was turning the pages.

Women in large cartwheel hats, women with dresses tapering down to their feet so that they could hardly walk. The photos had captions neatly printed underneath them, but the ink was old and faded.

"It would be in this one," said Miss Blacklock. "On about the second or third page. The other book is after

Sonia had married and gone away." She turned a page. "It ought to be here." She stopped.

There were several empty spaces on the page. Craddock bent down and deciphered the faded writing: "Sonia . . . Self . . . R.G." A little further along, "Sonia and Belle on beach." And again on the opposite page, "Picnic at Skeyne." He turned over another page: "Charlotte, Self, Sonia, R.G."

Craddock stood up. His lips were grim.

"Somebody has removed these photographs—not long ago, I should say."

"There weren't any blank spaces when we looked at them the other day. Were there, Julia?"

"I didn't look very closely—only at some of the dresses. But no, you're right, Aunt Letty, there weren't any blank spaces."

Craddock looked grimmer still.

"Somebody," he said, "has removed every photo of Sonia Goedler from this album."

CHAPTER 18

The Letters

"SORRY to worry you again, Mrs. Haymes."

"It doesn't matter," said Phillipa coldly.

"Shall we go into this room here?"

"The study? Yes, if you like, Inspector. It's very cold. There's no fire."

"It doesn't matter. It's not for long. And we're not so likely to be overheard here."

"Does that matter?"

"Not to me, Mrs. Haymes. It might to you."

"What do you mean?"

"I think you told me, Mrs. Haymes, that your husband was killed fighting in Italy?"

"Well?"

"Wouldn't it have been simpler to have told me the truth—that he was a deserter from his regiment."

He saw her face grow white, and her hands close and unclose themselves.

She said bitterly, "Do you have to rake up everything?"

Craddock said dryly, "We expect people to tell us the truth about themselves."

She was silent. Then she said, "Well?"

"What do you mean by 'Well,' Mrs. Haymes?"

"I mean, what are you gong to do about it? Tell everybody? Is that necessary—or fair—or kind?"

"Does nobody know?"

"Nobody here. Harry—" Her voice changed. "My son, he doesn't know. I don't want him to know. I don't want him to know—ever."

"Then let me tell you that you're taking a very big risk, Mrs. Haymes. When the boy is old enough to understand, tell him the truth. If he finds out by himself some day—it won't be good for him. If you go on stuffing him up with tales of his father dying like a hero—"

"I don't do that. I'm not completely dishonest. I just don't talk about it. His father was—killed in the war. After all, that's what it amounts to—for us."

"But your husband is still alive?"

"Perhaps. How should I know?"

"When did you see him last, Mrs. Haymes?"

Phillipa said quickly, "I haven't seen him for years."

"Are you quite sure that's true? You didn't, for instance, see him about a fortnight ago?"

"What are you suggesting?"

"It never seemed to me very likely that you met Rudi Scherz in the summer-house here. But Mitzi's story was very emphatic. I suggest, Mrs. Haymes, that the man you came back from work to meet that morning was your husband."

"I didn't meet anybody in the summer-house."

"He was hard up for money, perhaps, and you supplied him with some?"

"I've not seen him, I tell you. I didn't meet anybody in the summer-house."

"Deserters are often rather desperate men. They often take part in robberies, you know. Holdups. Things of that kind. And they have foreign revolvers very often that they've brought back from abroad."

"I don't know where my husband is. I haven't seen him for years."

"Is that your last word, Mrs. Haymes?"

"I've nothing else to say."

2

Craddock came away from his interview with Phillipa Haymes feeling angry and baffled.

"Obstinate as a mule," he said to himself angrily.

He was fairly sure that Phillipa was lying, but he hadn't succeeded in breaking down her obstinate denials.

He wished he knew a little more about ex-Captain Haymes. His information was meager. An unsatisfactory Army record, but nothing to suggest that Haymes was likely to turn criminal.

And, anyway, Haymes didn't fit in with the oiled door.

Someone in the house had done that, or someone with easy access to it.

He stood looking up the staircase, and suddenly he wondered what Julia had been doing up in the attic. An attic, he thought, was an unlikely place for the fastidious Julia to visit.

What had she been doing up there?

He ran lightly up to the first floor. There was no one about. He opened the door out of which Julia had come and went up the narrow stairs to the attic.

There were trunks there, old suitcases, various broken articles of furniture, a chair with a leg off, a broken china lamp, part of an old dinner service.

He turned to the trunks and opened the lid of one.

Clothes. Old-fashioned, quite good quality women's clothes. Clothes belonging, he supposed, to Miss Blacklock, or to her sister who had died.

He opened another trunk.

Curtains.

He passed to a small attaché case. It had papers in it and letters. Very old letters, yellowed with time.

He looked at the outside of the case which had the initials CLB on it. He deduced correctly that it had belonged to Letitia's sister Charlotte. He unfolded one of the letters. It began, *Dearest Charlotte: Yesterday Belle felt well enough to go for a picnic. R. G. also took a day off. The Asvogel flotation has gone splendidly; R. G. is terribly pleased about it. The preference shares are at a premium.*

He skipped the rest and looked at the signature:

Your loving sister, Letitia.

He picked up another.

Darling Charlotte: I wish you would sometimes make up your mind to see people. You do exaggerate, you know. It isn't nearly as bad as you think. And people really don't mind things like that. It's not the disfigurement you think it is.

He nodded his head. He remembered Belle Goedler saying that Charlotte Blacklock had a disfigurement or deformity of some kind. Letitia had, in the end, resigned her job to go and look after her sister. These letters all breathed the anxious spirit of her affection and love for an invalid. She had written her sister, apparently, long accounts of everyday happenings, of any little detail that she thought might interest the sick girl. And Charlotte had kept these letters. Occasionally odd snapshots had been enclosed.

Excitement suddenly flooded Craddock's mind. Here, it might be, he would find a clue. In these letters there would be written down things that Letitia Blacklock herself had long forgotten. Here was a faithful picture of the past and somewhere amongst it there might be a clue that would help him to identify the unknown. Photographs, too. There might, just possibly, be a photograph of Sonia Goedler here that the person who had taken the other photos out of the album did not know about.

Inspector Craddock packed the letters up again carefully, closed the case and started down the stairs.

Letitia Blacklock, standing on the landing below, looked at him in amazement.

"Was that you up in the attic? I heard footsteps. I couldn't imagine who—"

"Miss Blacklock, I have found some letters here, written by you to your sister Charlotte many years ago. Will you allow me to take them away and read them?"

She flushed angrily.

"Must you do a thing like that? Why? What good can they be to you?"

"They might give me a picture of Sonia Goedler, of her character—there may be some allusion—some incident—that will help."

"They are private letters, Inspector."

"I know."

"I suppose you will take them anyway . . . You have the power to do so, I suppose, or you can easily get it. Take them—take them! But you'll find very little about Sonia. She married and went away only a year or two after I began to work for Randall Goedler."

Craddock said obstinately, "There may be something." He added, "We've got to try everything. I assure you the danger is very real."

She said, biting her lips:

"I know. Bunny is dead—from taking an aspirin tablet that was meant for me. It may be Patrick, or Julia, or Phillipa or Mitzi next—somebody young with their life in front of them. Somebody who drinks a glass of wine that is poured out for me, or eats a chocolate that is sent to me. Oh, take the letters—take them away. And afterwards burn them. They don't mean anything to anyone but me and Charlotte. It's all over—gone—past. Nobody remembers now . . ."

Her hand went up to the choker of false pearls she was wearing. Craddock thought how incongruous it looked with her tweed coat and skirt.

She said again, "Take the letters."

3

It was the following afternoon that the Inspector called at the vicarage.

It was a dark gusty day.

Miss Marple had her chair pulled close to the fire and was knitting. Bunch was on hands and knees, crawling about the floor, cutting out material to a pattern.

She sat back and pushed a mop of hair out of her eyes, looking up expectantly at Craddock.

"I don't know if it's a breach of confidence," said the Inspector, addressing himself to Miss Marple, "but I'd like you to look at this letter."

He explained the circumstances of his discovery in the attic.

"It's rather a touching collection of letters," he said. "Miss Blacklock poured out everything in the hopes of sustaining her sister's interest in life and keeping her health good. There's a very clear picture of an old father in the background—old Dr. Blacklock. A real old pigheaded bully, absolutely set in his ways, and convinced that everything he thought and said was right. Probably killed thousands of patients through obstinacy. He wouldn't stand for any new ideas or methods."

"I don't really know that I blame him there," said Miss Marple. "I always feel that the young doctors are only too anxious to experiment. After they've whipped out all our teeth, and administered quantities of very peculiar glands, and removed bits of our insides, they then confess that nothing can be done for us. I really prefer the old-fashioned remedy of big black bottles of medicine. After all, one can always pour those down the sink."

She took the letter that Craddock handed her.

He said:

"I want you to read it because I think that that generation is more easily understood by you than by me. I don't know really quite how these people's minds worked."

Miss Marple unfolded the fragile paper.

Dearest Charlotte,

I've not written for two days because we've been having the most terrible domestic complications. Randall's sister Sonia—(you remember her? She came to take you out in the car that day? How I wish you would go out more)—Sonia has declared her intention of marrying one Dmitri Stamfordis. I've only seen him once. Very attractive—not to be trusted, I should say. R.G. raves against him and says he is a crook and a swindler. Belle, bless her, just smiles and lies on her sofa. Sonia, who though she looks so impassive has really a terrific temper, is simply wild with R.G. I really thought yesterday she was going to murder him!

I've done my best. I've talked to Sonia and I've talked to R.G. and I've got them both in a more reasonable frame of mind and then they come together and it all starts over again! You've no idea how *tiring* it is. R.G. has been making enquiries—and it does really seem as though this Stamfordis man is thoroughly undesirable.

In the meantime, business is being neglected.

I carry on at the office and in a way it's rather fun because R.G. gives me a free hand. He said to me yesterday: "Thank heaven, there's one sane person in the world. You're never likely to fall in love with a crook, Blackie, are you?" I said I didn't think I was likely to fall in love with anybody. R.G. said: "Let's start a few new hares in the city." He's really rather a mischievous devil sometimes and he sails terribly near the wind. "You're quite determined to keep me on the straight and narrow path, aren't you, Blackie?" he said the other day. And I shall, too! I can't understand how people can't *see* when a thing's dishonest—but R.G. really and truly *doesn't*. He only knows what is actually against the law.

Belle only laughs at all this. She thinks the fuss about Sonia is all nonsense. "Sonia has her own money," she said. "Why shouldn't she marry this man if she wants to?" I said it might turn out to be a terrible mistake and Belle said, "It's never a mistake to marry a man you want to marry—even if you regret it." And then she said, "I suppose Sonia doesn't want to break with Randall because of money. Sonia's very fond of money."

No more now. How is Father? I won't say give him my love. But you can if you think it's better to do so. Have you seen more people? You really must not be morbid, darling.

Sonia asks to be remembered to you. She has just come in and is closing and unclosing her hands like an angry cat sharpening its claws. I think she and R.G. have had another row. Of course Sonia can be very irritating. She stares you down with that cool stare of hers.

Lots of love, darling, and buck up. This iodine treatment may make a lot of difference. I've been enquiring about it and it really does seem to have good results.

> Your loving sister,
> Letitia

Miss Marple folded the letter and handed it back. She looked abstracted.

"Well, what do you think about her?" Craddock urged. "What picture do you get of her?"

"Of Sonia? It's difficult, you know, to see anyone through another person's mind . . . Determined to get her own way—that, definitely. I think. And wanting the best of two worlds . . ."

"Closing and unclosing her hands like an angry cat," murmured Craddock. "You know, that reminds me of someone . . ."

He frowned.

"Making enquiries . . ." murmured Miss Marple.

"If we could get hold of the result of those enquiries—" said Craddock.

"Does that letter remind you of anything in St. Mary Mead?" asked Bunch, rather indistinctly since her mouth was full of pins.

"I really can't say it does, dear . . . Dr. Blacklock was, perhaps, a little like Mr. Curtiss the Wesleyan minister. He wouldn't let his child wear a plate on her teeth. Said it was the Lord's will if her teeth stuck out. 'After all,' I said to him, 'you do trim your beard and cut your hair. It might be the Lord's will that your hair should grow out.' He said that was quite different. So like a man. But that doesn't help us with our present problem."

"We've never traced that revolver, you know. It wasn't Rudi Scherz's. If I knew who had had a revolver in Chipping Cleghorn."

"Colonel Easterbrook has one," said Bunch. "He keeps it in his collar drawer."

"How do you know, Mrs. Harmon?"

"Mrs. Butt told me. She's my daily. Or rather, my twice weekly. Being a military gentleman, she said, he'd naturally have a revolver and very handy it would be if burglars were to come along."

"When did she tell you this?"

"Ages ago. About six months ago, I should think."

"Colonel Easterbrook?" murmured Craddock.

"It's like those pointer things at fairs, isn't it?" said Bunch, still speaking through a mouthful of pins. "Go round and round and stop at something different every time."

"You're telling me!" said Craddock and groaned.

"Colonel Easterbrook was up at Little Paddocks to leave a book there one day. He could have oiled that door then. He was quite straightforward about being there, though. Not like Miss Hinchliffe."

Miss Marple coughed gently.

"You must make allowances for the times we live in, Inspector," she said. Craddock looked at her uncomprehendingly.

"After all," said Miss Marple, "you *are* the police, aren't you? People can't say everything they'd like to say to the police, can they?"

"I don't see why not," said Craddock. "Unless they've got some criminal matter to conceal."

"She means butter," said Bunch, crawling actively round a table leg to anchor a floating bit of paper. "Butter and corn for hens and sometimes cream—and sometimes even a side of bacon."

"Show him that note from Miss Blacklock," said Miss Marple. "It's some time ago now, but it reads like a first-class mystery story."

"What have I done with it? Is this the one you mean, Aunt Jane?"

Miss Marple took it and looked at it.

"Yes," she said with satisfaction. "That's the one."

She handed it to the Inspector.

I have made inquiries—Thursday is the day, Miss Blacklock had written. *Any time after three. If there is any for me leave it in the usual place.*

Bunch spat out her pins and laughed. Miss Marple was watching the Inspector's face.

The vicar's wife took upon herself to explain.

"Thursday is the day one of the farms round here makes butter. They let anybody they like have a bit. It's usually Miss Hinchliffe who collects it. She's very much in with all the farmers—because of her pigs, I think. But it's all a bit hush-hush, you know; a kind of local scheme of barter. One person gets butter and sends along cucumbers, or something like that—and a little something when a pig's killed. And now and then an animal has an 'accident' and has to be destroyed. Oh, you know the sort of thing. Only one can't very well say it right out to the police. Because I suppose quite a lot of this barter is illegal—only nobody really knows because it's all so complicated. But I expect Hinch had slipped into Little Paddocks with a pound of butter or something and had put it in the 'usual place.' That's a flour bin under the cupboard, by the way. It doesn't have flour in it."

Craddock sighed.

"I'm glad I came here to you ladies," he said.

"There are clothing coupons, too," said Bunch. "Not usually bought—that's not considered honest. No money passes. But people like Mrs. Butt or Mrs. Finch or Mrs. Huggins like a nice woolen dress or a winter coat that hasn't seen too much wear and they pay for it with coupons instead of money."

"You'd better not tell me any more," said Craddock. "It's all against the law."

"Then there oughtn't to be such silly laws," said Bunch, filling her mouth up with pins again. "I don't do it, of course, because Julian doesn't like me to, so I don't. But I know what's going on, of course."

A kind of despair was coming over the Inspector.

"It all sounds so pleasant and ordinary," he said. "Funny and petty and simple. And yet one woman and a man have been killed, and another woman may be killed before I can get anything definite to go on. I've left off worrying about Pip and Emma for the moment. I'm concentrating on Sonia. I wish I knew what she looked like. There was a snapshot or two in with these letters, but not one that could have been her."

"How do you know it couldn't have been her? Do you know what she looked like?"

"She was small and dark, Miss Blacklock said."

"Really," said Miss Marple, "that's very interesting."

"There was one snap that reminded me vaguely of someone. A tall fair girl with her hair all done up on top of her head. I don't know who she could have been. Anyway, it can't have been Sonia. Do you think Mrs. Swettenham could have been dark when she was a girl?"

"Not very dark," said Bunch. "She's got blue eyes."

"I hoped there might be a photo of Dmitri Stamfordis—but I suppose that was too much to hope for—Well"—he took up the letter—"I'm sorry this doesn't suggest anything to you, Miss Marple."

"Oh, but it does," said Miss Marple. "It suggests a good deal—Just read it through again, Inspector—especially where it says that Randall Goedler was making inquiries about Dmitri Stamfordis."

Craddock stared at her.

The telephone rang.

Bunch got up from the floor and went out into the hall where, in accordance with the best Victorian traditions, the telephone had originally been placed and where it still was.

She re-entered the room to say to Craddock, "It's for you."

Slightly surprised, the Inspector went out to the instrument—carefully shutting the door of the living room behind him.

"Craddock? Rydesdale here."

"Yes, sir."

"I've been looking through your report. In the interview you had with Phillipa Haymes I see she states positively that she hasn't seen her husband since his desertion from the Army."

"That's right, sir—she was most emphatic. But in my opinion she wasn't speaking the truth."

"I agree with you. Do you remember a case about ten days ago—man run over by a lorry—taken to Milchester General with concussion and a fractured pelvis?"

"The fellow who snatched a child practically from under the wheels of a lorry, and got run down himself?"

"That's the one. No papers of any kind on him and nobody came forward to identify him. Looked as though he might be on the run. He died last night without regaining consciousness. But he's been identified—deserter from the Army—Ronald Haymes, ex-Captain in the South Loamshires."

"Phillipa Haymes' husband?"

"Yes. He had an old Chipping Cleghorn bus ticket on him, by the way—and quite a reasonable amount of money."

"So he did get money from his wife? I always thought he was the man Mitzi overheard talking to her in the summer-house. She denied it flatly, of course. But surely, sir, that lorry accident was before—"

Rydesdale took the words out of his mouth.

"Yes, he was taken to Milchester General on the 28th. The holdup at Little Paddocks was on the 29th. That lets him out of any possible connection with it. But his wife, of course, knew nothing about the accident. She may have been thinking all along that he was concerned in it. She'd hold her tongue—naturally— after all he was her husband."

"It was a fairly gallant bit of work, wasn't it, sir?" said Craddock slowly.

"Rescuing that child from the lorry? Yes. Plucky. Don't suppose it was cowardice that made Haymes desert. Well, all that's past history. For a man who'd blotted his copybook, it was a good death."

"I'm glad for her sake," said the Inspector. "And for that boy of theirs."

"Yes, he needn't be too ashamed of his father. And the young woman will be able to marry again now."

Craddock said slowly, "I was thinking of that, sir . . . It opens up—possibilities."

"You'd better break the news to her since you're on the spot."

"I will, sir. I'll push along there now. Or perhaps I'd better wait until she's back at Little Paddocks. It may be rather a shock—and there's someone else I rather want to have a word with first."

CHAPTER 19

Reconstruction of the Crime

"I'LL PUT on a lamp by you before I go," said Bunch. "It's so dark in here. There's going to be a storm, I think."

She lifted the small reading lamp to the other side of the table where it would throw light on Miss Marple's knitting as she sat in a wide high-backed chair.

As the cord pulled across the table, Tiglath-Pileser, the cat, leapt upon it and bit and clawed it violently.

"No, Tiglath-Pileser, you mustn't. He really is awful. Look, he's nearly bitten it through—it's all frayed. Don't you understand, you idiotic puss, that you may get a nasty electric shock if you do that?"

"Thank you, dear," said Miss Marple, and put out a hand to turn on the lamp.

"It doesn't turn on there. You have to press that silly little switch halfway along the cord. Wait a minute. I'll take these flowers out of the way."

She lifted a bowl of Christmas roses across the table. Tiglath-Pileser, his tail switching, put out a mischievous paw and clawed Bunch's arm. She spilled some of the water out of the vase. It fell on the frayed area of cord and on Tiglath-Pileser himself, who leapt to the floor with an indignant hiss.

Miss Marple pressed the small pear-shaped switch.

204

Where the water had soaked the frayed cord there was a flash and a crackle.

"Oh, dear," said Bunch. "It's blown out. Now I suppose all the lights in here are off." She tried them. "Yes, they are. So stupid being all on the same thingumabob. And it's made a burn on the table, too. Naughty Tiglath-Pileser—it's all his fault. Aunt Jane—what's the matter? Did it startle you?"

"It's nothing, dear. Just something I saw quite suddenly which I ought to have seen before. . . ."

"I'll go and fix the fuse and get the lamp from Julian's study."

"No, dear, don't bother. You'll miss your bus. I don't want any more light. I just want to sit quietly and—think about something. Hurry, dear, or you won't catch your bus."

When Bunch had gone, Miss Marple sat quite still for about two minutes. The air of the room was heavy and menacing with the gathering storm outside.

Miss Marple drew a sheet of paper towards her.

She wrote first: *Lamp?* and underlined it heavily.

After a moment or two, she wrote another word.

Her pencil traveled down the paper, making brief monosyllabic notes. . . .

2

In the rather dark living room of Boulders with its low ceiling and latticed windowpanes, Miss Hinchliffe and Miss Murgatroyd were having an argument.

"The trouble with you, Murgatroyd," said Miss Hinchliffe, "is that you won't try."

"But I tell you, Hinch, I can't remember a thing."

"Now look here, Amy Murgatroyd, we're going to do some constructive thinking. So far we haven't shone on the detective angle. I was quite wrong over that door business. You didn't hold the door open for the murderer after all. You're cleared, Murgatroyd!"

Miss Murgatroyd gave a rather watery smile.

"It's just our luck to have the only silent cleaning woman in Chipping Cleghorn," continued Miss Hinchliffe. "Usually I'm thankful for it, but this time it means we've got off to a bad start. Everybody else in the place knows about that second door in the drawing-room being used—and we only heard about it yesterday—"

"I still don't quite understand how—"

"It's perfectly simple. Our original premises were quite right. You can't hold open a door, wave a flashlight and shoot with a revolver all at the same time. We kept in the revolver and the flashlight and cut out the door. Well, we were wrong. It was the revolver we ought to have cut out."

"But he did have a revolver," said Miss Murgatroyd. "I saw it. It was there on the floor beside him."

"When he was dead, yes. It's all quite clear. He didn't fire that revolver—"

"Then who did?"

"That's what we're going to find out. But whoever did it, the same person put a couple of poisoned aspirin tablets by Letty Blacklock's bed—and thereby bumped off poor Dora Bunner. And that couldn't have been Rudi Scherz, because he's as dead as a doornail. It was someone who was in the room that night of the holdup and probably someone who was at the birthday party, too. And the only person that lets out is Mrs. Harmon."

"You think someone put those aspirins there the day of the birthday party?"

"Why not?"

"But how could they?"

"Well, we all went to the loo, didn't we?" said Miss

Hinchliffe coarsely. "And I washed my hands in the bathroom because of that sticky cake. And little Sweetie Easterbrook powdered her grubby little face in Blacklock's bedroom, didn't she?"

"Hinch! Do you think she—"

"I don't know yet. Rather obvious, if she did. I don't think, if you were going to plant some tablets, that you'd want to be seen in the bedroom at all. Oh, yes there were plenty of opportunities."

"The men didn't go upstairs."

"There are back stairs. After all, if a man leaves the room, you don't follow him to see if he really is going where you think he is going. It wouldn't be delicate! Anyway, don't argue, Murgatroyd. I want to get back to the original attempt on Letty Blacklock. Now, to begin with, get the facts firmly into your head, because it's all going to depend upon you."

Miss Murgatroyd looked alarmed.

"Oh, dear, Hinch, you know what a muddle I get into!"

"It's not a question of your brains, or the gray fluff that passes for brains with you. It's a question of eyes. It's a question of what you saw."

"But I didn't see anything."

"The trouble with you is, Murgatroyd, as I said just now, that you won't try. Now pay attention. This is what happened: Whoever it is that's got it in for Letty Blacklock was there in that room that evening. He (I say he because it's easier, but there's no reason why it should be a man more than a woman except, of course, that men are dirty dogs), well, he has previously oiled that second door that leads out of the drawing-room and which is supposed to be nailed up or something. Don't ask me when he did it, because that confuses things. Actually, by choosing my time, I could walk into any house in Chipping Cleghorn and do anything

I liked there for half an hour or so with no one being
the wiser. It's just a question of working out where the
daily women are and when the occupiers are out and
exactly where they've gone and how long they'll be.
Just good staff work. Now to continue: He's oiled that
second door. It will open without a sound. Here's the
setup: Lights go out, door A (the front door) opens
with a flourish. Business with flashlight and holdup lines.
In the meantime, while we're all goggling, X (that's the
best term to use) slips quietly out by door B into the
dark hall, comes up behind that Swiss idiot, takes a
couple of shots at Letty Blacklock and then shoots the
Swiss. Drops the revolver, where lazy thinkers like you
will assume it's evidence that the Swiss did the shooting,
and nips back into the room again by the time that
someone gets a lighter going. Got it?"

"Yes—ye-es, but who was it?"

"Well, if you don't know, Murgatroyd, nobody does!"

"Me?" Miss Murgatroyd fairly twittered in alarm.
"But I don't know anything at all. I don't really, Hinch!"

"Use that fluff of yours you call a brain. To begin
with, where was everybody when the lights went out?"

"I don't know."

"Yes, you do. You're maddening, Murgatroyd. You
know where you were, don't you? You were behind
the door."

"Yes—yes, I was. It knocked against my corn when
it flew open."

"Why don't you go to a proper chiropodist instead
of messing about yourself with your feet? You'll give
yourself blood poisoning one of these days. Come on
now—you're behind the door. I'm standing against the
mantelpiece with my tongue hanging out for a drink.
Letty Blacklock is by the table near the archway, getting
the cigarettes. Patrick Simmons has gone through the

archway into the small room where Letty Blacklock has had the drinks put. Agreed?"

"Yes, yes, I remember all that."

"Good; now somebody else followed Patrick into that room or was just starting to follow him. One of the men. The annoying thing is that I can't remember whether it was Easterbrook or Edmund Swettenham. Do you remember?"

"No, I don't."

"You wouldn't! And there was someone else who went through to the small room: Phillipa Haymes. I remember that distinctly because I remember noticing what a nice flat back she has, and I thought to myself that girl would look well on a horse. I was watching her and thinking just that. She went over to the mantelpiece in the other room. I don't know what it was she wanted there, because at that moment the lights went out.

"So that's the position. In the far drawing-room are Patrick Simmons, Phillipa Haymes and either Colonel Easterbrook or Edmund Swettenham—we don't know which. Now, Murgatroyd, pay attention. The most probable thing is that it was one of those three who did it. If anyone wanted to get out of that far door, they'd naturally take care to put themselves in a convenient place when the lights went out. So, as I say, in all probability, it's one of those three. And in that case, Murgatroyd, there's not a thing you can do about it!"

Miss Murgatroyd brightened perceptibly.

"On the other hand," continued Miss Hinchliffe, "there's the possibility that it wasn't one of those three. And that's where you come in, Murgatroyd."

"But how should I know anything about it?"

"As I said before, if you don't nobody does."

"But I don't! I really don't! I couldn't see anything at all!"

"Oh, yes, you could. You're the only person who could see. You were standing behind the door. You couldn't look at the flashlight—because the door was between you and it. You were facing the other way, the same way as the flashlight was pointing. The rest of us were just dazzled. But you weren't dazzled."

"No—no, perhaps not, but I didn't see anything, the flashlight went round and round—"

"Showing you what? It rested on faces, didn't it? And on tables? And on chairs?"

"Yes—yes, it did . . . Miss Bunner, her mouth wide open and her eyes popping out of her head, staring and blinking."

"That's the stuff!" Miss Hinchliffe gave a sigh of relief. "The difficulty there is in making you use that gray fluff of yours! Now then, keep it up."

"But I didn't see any more. I didn't really."

"You mean you saw an empty room? Nobody standing about? Nobody sitting down?"

"No, of course not that. Mrs. Harmon was sitting on the arm of a chair. She had her eyes tight shut and her knuckles all doubled up to her face—like a child."

"Good, that's Mrs. Harmon and Miss Bunner. Don't you see yet what I'm getting at? The difficulty is that I don't want to put ideas into your head. But when we've eliminated who you did see—we can get on to the important point which is, was there anyone you didn't see? Got it? Besides the tables and the chairs and the chrysanthemums and the rest of it, there were certain people: Julia Simmons, Mrs. Swettenham, Mrs. Easterbrook—either Colonel Easterbrook or Edmund Swettenham—Dora Bunner and Bunch Harmon. All right, you saw Bunch Harmon and Dora Bunner. Cross them off. Now think, Murgatroyd, *think,* was there one of those people who definitely *wasn't* there?"

Miss Murgatroyd jumped slightly as a branch knocked against the open window. She shut her eyes. She murmured to herself . . .

"The flowers . . . on the table . . . the big armchair . . . the flashlight didn't come round as far as you, Hinch —Mrs. Harmon, yes. . . ."

The telephone rang sharply. Miss Hinchliffe went to it.

"Hullo, yes? The station?"

The obedient Miss Murgatroyd, her eyes closed, was reliving the night of the 29th. The flashlight sweeping slowly round . . . a group of people . . . the windows . . . the sofa . . . Dora Bunner . . . the wall . . . the table with the lamp . . . the archway . . . the sudden spat of the revolver . . .

". . . but that's extraordinary!" said Miss Murgatroyd.

"What?" Miss Hinchliffe was barking angrily into the telephone. "Been there since this morning? What time? Damn and blast you, and you only ring me up now? I'll set the S.P.C.A. after you. An oversight? Is that all you've got to say?"

She banged down the receiver.

"It's that dog," she said. "The red setter. Been at the station since this morning—since this morning at eight o'clock! Without a drop of water! And the idiots only ring me up now. I'm going to get her right away."

She plunged out of the room, Miss Murgatroyd squeaking shrilly in her wake.

"But listen, Hinch, a most extraordinary thing . . . I don't understand it . . ."

Miss Hinchliffe had dashed out of the door and across to the shed which served as a garage.

"We'll go on with it when I come back," she called. "I can't wait for you to come with me. You've got your bedroom slippers on as usual."

She pressed the starter of the car and backed out of the garage with a jerk. Miss Murgatroyd skipped nimbly sideways.

"But listen, Hinch, I must tell you—"

"When I come back . . ."

The car jerked and shot forwards. Miss Murgatroyd's voice came faintly after it on a high excited note:

"But, Hinch, she wasn't there . . ."

3

Overhead, the clouds had been gathering thick and dark. Miss Murgatroyd plunged across to a line of string on which she had, some hours previously, hung out a couple of jumpers and a pair of woolen combinations to dry.

She was murmuring under her breath:

"Really most extraordinary . . . Oh, dear, I shall never get these down in time . . . and they were nearly dry. . . ."

She struggled with a recalcitrant clothespeg, then turned her head, as she heard someone approaching.

Then she smiled a pleased welcome.

"Hullo—do go inside; you'll get wet."

"Let me help you."

"Oh, if you don't mind . . . so annoying if they all get soaked again. I really ought to let down the line, but I think I can just reach."

"Here's your scarf. Shall I put it round your neck?"

"Oh, thank you . . . Yes, perhaps . . . If I could just reach this peg. . . ."

The woolen scarf was slipped round her neck and then, suddenly, pulled tight . . .

Miss Murgatroyd's mouth opened, but no sound came except a small choking gurgle.

And the scarf was pulled tighter still . . .

4

On her way back from the station, Miss Hinchliffe stopped the car to pick up Miss Marple who was hurrying along the street.

"Hullo," she shouted. "You'll get very wet. Come and have tea with us. I saw Bunch waiting for the bus. You'll be all alone at the vicarage. Come and join us. Murgatroyd and I are doing a bit of reconstruction of the crime. I rather think we're just getting somewhere. Mind the dog. She's rather nervous."

"What a beauty."

"Yes, lovely bitch, isn't she? Those fools kept her at the station since this morning without letting me know. I told them off, the lazy devils. Oh! Excuse my language, I was brought up by grooms at home in Ireland."

The little car turned with a jerk into the small back yard of Boulders.

A crowd of eager ducks and fowls encircled the two ladies as they descended.

"Curse Murgatroyd," said Miss Hinchliffe, "she hasn't given 'em their corn."

"Is it difficult to get corn?" Miss Marple inquired.

Miss Hinchliffe winked.

"I'm in with most of the farmers," she said.

Shooing away the hens, she escorted Miss Marple towards the cottage.

"Hope you're not too wet?"

"No, this is a very good mackintosh."

"I'll light the fire if Murgatroyd hasn't lit it. Hiyah,

Murgatroyd? Where is the woman? Murgatroyd! Where's that dog? She's disappeared now."

A slow dismal howl came from outside.

"Curse the silly bitch." Miss Hinchliffe tramped to the door and called:

"Hyoup, Cutie—Cutie! Damn silly name but that's what they called her apparently. We must find her another name. Hiyah, Cutie!"

The red setter was sniffing at something lying below the taut line where a row of garments swirled in the wind.

"Murgatroyd's not even had the sense to bring the washing in. Where is she?"

Again the red setter nosed at what seemed to be a pile of clothes, and raised her nose high in the air and howled again.

"What's the matter with the dog?"

Miss Hinchliffe strode across the grass.

And quickly, apprehensively, Miss Marple ran after her. They stood there, side by side, the rain beating down on them and the older woman's arm went round the younger one's shoulders.

She felt the muscles go stiff and taut as Miss Hinchliffe stood looking down on the thing lying there, with the blue congested face and the protruding tongue.

"I'll kill whoever did this," said Miss Hinchliffe in a low quiet voice, "if I once get my hands on her. . . ."

Miss Marple said questioningly:

"Her?"

Miss Hinchliffe turned a ravaged face towards her.

"Yes. I know who it is—near enough . . . That is, it's one of three possibles."

She stood for another moment, looking down at her dead friend, and then turned towards the house. Her voice was dry and hard.

"We must ring up the police," she said. "And while

we're waiting for them, I'll tell you. My fault, in a way, that Murgatroyd's lying out there. I made a game of it . . . Murder isn't a game . . ."

"No," said Miss Marple. "Murder isn't a game."

"You know something about it, don't you?" said Miss Hinchliffe as she lifted the receiver and dialed.

She made a brief report and hung up.

"They'll be here in a few minutes . . . Yes, I heard that you'd been mixed up in this sort of business before . . . I think it was Edmund Swettenham told me so . . . Do you want to hear what we were doing, Murgatroyd and I?"

Succinctly she described the conversation held before her departure for the station.

"She called after me, you know, just as I was leaving . . . That's how I know it's a woman and not a man . . . If I'd waited—if I'd only listened! God dammit, the dog could have stopped where she was for another quarter of an hour."

"Don't blame yourself, my dear. That does no good. One can't foresee."

"No, one can't. . . . Something tapped against the window, I remember. Perhaps she was outside there then—yes, of course, she must have been . . . coming to the house . . . and there were Murgatroyd and I shouting at each other. Top of our voices . . . She heard . . . She heard it all . . ."

"You haven't told me yet what your friend said."

"Just one sentence! *'She wasn't there.'* "

She paused. "You see? There were three women we hadn't eliminated. Mrs. Swettenham, Mrs. Easterbrook, Julia Simmons. And one of those three—*wasn't there* . . . She wasn't there in the drawing-room because she had slipped out through the other door and was out in the hall."

"Yes," said Miss Marple, "I see."

"It's one of those three women. I don't know which. But I'll find out!"

"Excuse me," said Miss Marple. "But did she—did Miss Murgatroyd, I mean—say it exactly as you said it?"

"How d'you mean—as I said it?"

"Oh, dear, how can I explain? You said it like this. *She wasn't there.* An equal emphasis on every word. You see, there are three ways you could say it. You could say, '*She* wasn't there.' Very personal. Or again, 'She *wasn't* there.' Confirming some suspicion already held. Or else you could say (and this is nearer to the way you said it just now), 'She wasn't *there.*' Quite blankly—with the emphasis, if there was emphasis—on the *there.*"

"I don't know," Miss Hinchliffe shook her head. "I can't remember . . . How the hell can I remember? I think, yes, surely she'd say, '*She* wasn't there.' That would be the natural way, I should think. But I simply don't know. Does it make any difference?"

"Yes," said Miss Marple thoughtfully. "I think so. It's a very *slight* indication, of course, but I think it *is* an indication. Yes, I should think it makes a lot of difference."

CHAPTER 20

Miss Marple Is Missing

THE POSTMAN, rather to his disgust, had lately been given orders to make an afternoon delivery of letters in Chipping Cleghorn as well as a morning one.

On this particular afternoon he left three letters at Little Paddocks at exactly ten minutes to five.

One was addressed to Phillipa Haymes in a schoolboy's hand; the other two were for Miss Blacklock. She opened them as she and Phillipa sat down at the tea table. The torrential rain had enabled Phillipa to leave Dayas Hall early today, since once she had shut up the greenhouses there was nothing more to do.

Miss Blacklock tore open her first letter which was a bill for repairing the kitchen boiler. She snorted angrily.

"Dymond's prices are preposterous—quite preposterous. Still, I suppose all the other people are just as bad."

She opened the second letter which was in a handwriting quite unknown t › her.

Dear Cousin Letty (it said),
I hope it will be all right for me to come to you on Tuesday? I wrote to Patrick two days ago but he hasn't answered. So I presume it's all right. Mother is coming to England next month and hopes to see you then.

217

My train arrives at Chipping Cleghorn at 6:15 if that's convenient?

Yours affectionately,
Julia Simmons

Miss Blacklock read the letter once with astonishment pure and simple, and then again with a certain grimness. She looked up at Phillipa who was smiling over her son's letter.

"Are Julia and Patrick back, do you know?"

Phillipa looked up.

"Yes, they came in just after I did. They went upstairs to change. They were wet."

"Perhaps you'd not mind going and calling them."

"Of course I will."

"Wait a moment—I'd like you to read this."

She handed Phillipa the letter she had received.

Phillipa read it and frowned. "I don't understand . . ."

"Nor do I, quite . . . I think it's about time I did. Call Patrick and Julia, Phillipa."

Phillipa called from the bottom of the stairs, "Patrick! Julia! Miss Blacklock wants you."

Patrick came running down the stairs and entered the room.

"Don't go, Phillipa," said Miss Blacklock.

"Hullo, Aunt Letty," said Patrick cheerfully. "Want me?"

"Yes, I do. Perhaps you'll give me an explanation of this?"

Patrick's face showed an almost comical dismay as he read.

"I meant to telegraph her! What an ass I am!"

"This letter, I presume, is from your sister Julia?"

"Yes—Yes, it is."

Miss Blacklock said grimly, *"Then who, may I ask, is the young woman whom you brought here as Julia*

Simmons, and who I was given to understand was your sister and my cousin?"

"Well—you see—Aunt Letty—the fact of the matter is—I can explain it all—I know I oughtn't to have done it—but it really seemed more of a lark than anything else. If you'll just let me explain—"

"I am waiting for you to explain. *Who is this young woman?"*

"Well, I met her at a cocktail party soon after I got demobbed. We got talking and I said I was coming here and then—well, we thought it might be rather a good wheeze if I brought her along . . . You see Julia, the real Julia, was mad to go on the stage and mother had seven fits at the idea—however, Julia got a chance to join a jolly good repertory company up in Perth or somewhere and she thought she'd give it a try—but she thought she'd keep Mum calm by letting Mum think that she was here with me, studying to be a dispenser like a good little girl."

"I still want to know who this other young woman is."

Patrick turned with relief as Julia, cool and aloof, came into the room.

"The balloon's gone up," he said.

Julia raised her eyebrows. Then, still cool, she came forward and sat down.

"O.K." she said. "That's that. I suppose you're very angry?" She studied Miss Blacklock's face with almost dispassionate interest. "I should be if I were you."

"Who are you?"

Julia sighed.

"I think the moment's come when I make a clean breast of things. Here we go. I'm one-half of the Pip and Emma combination. To be exact, my christened name is Emma Jocelyn Stamfordis—only father soon dropped the Stamfordis. I think he called himself De Courcy next.

"My father and mother, let me tell you, split up about three years after Pip and I were born. Each of them went their own way. And they split us up. I was father's part of the loot. He was a bad parent on the whole, though quite a charming one. I had various desert spells of being educated in convents—when father hadn't any money, or was preparing to engage in some particularly nefarious deal. He used to pay the first term with every sign of affluence and then depart and leave me on the nuns' hands for a year or two. In the intervals, he and I had some very good times together, moving in cosmopolitan society. However, the war separated us completely. I've no idea of what's happened to him. I had a few adventures myself. I was with the French Resistance for a time. Quite exciting. To cut a long story short, I landed up in London and began to think about my future. I knew that mother's brother with whom she'd had a frightful row, had died a very rich man. I looked up his will to see if there was anything for me. There wasn't—not directly, that is to say. I made a few inquiries about his widow—it seemed she was quite gaga and kept under drugs and was dying by inches. Frankly, it looked as though *you* were my best bet. You were going to come into a hell of a lot of money and from all I could find out, you didn't seem to have anyone much to spend it on. I'll be quite frank. It occurred to me that if I could get to know you in a friendly kind of way, and if you took a fancy to me— well, after all, conditions have changed a bit, haven't they, since Uncle Randall died? I mean, any money we ever had has been swept away in the cataclysm of Europe. I thought you might pity a poor orphan girl, all alone in the world, and make her, perhaps, a small allowance."

"Oh, you did, did you?" said Miss Blacklock grimly.

"Yes. Of course, I hadn't seen you then . . . I visualized a kind of sob stuff approach . . . Then, by a marvelous stroke of luck, I met Patrick here—and he turned out to be your nephew or your cousin, or something. Well, that struck me as a marvelous chance. I went bullheaded for Patrick and he fell for me in a most gratifying way. The real Julia was all wet about this acting stuff and I soon persuaded her it was her duty to Art to go and fix herself up in some uncomfortable lodgings in Perth and train to be the new Sarah Bernhardt.

"You mustn't blame Patrick too much. He felt awfully sorry for me, all alone in the world— and he soon thought it would be a really marvelous idea for me to come here as his sister and do my stuff."

"And he also approved of your continuing to tell a tissue of lies to the police?"

"Have a heart, Letty. Don't you see that when that ridiculous holdup business happened—or rather after it happened—I began to feel I was in a bit of a spot? Let's face it; I've got a perfectly good motive for putting you out of the way. You've only got my word for it now that I wasn't the one who tried to do it. You can't expect me deliberately to go and incriminate myself. Even Patrick got nasty ideas about me from time to time, and if even *he* could think things like that, what on earth would the police think? That Detective Inspector struck me as a man of singularly skeptical mind. No; I figured out the only thing for me to do was to sit tight as Julia and just fade away when term came to an end.

"How was I to know that fool Julia, the real Julia, would go and have a row with the producer, and fling the whole thing up in a fit of temperament? She writes to Patrick and asks if she can come here, and instead of wiring to her 'Keep away,' he goes and forgets to

do anything at all!" She cast an angry glance at Patrick.
"Of all the utter idiots!"

She sighed.

"You don't know the straits I've been put to in Milchester! Of course, I haven't been to the hospital at all.
But I had to go somewhere. Hours and hours I've spent
in the pictures, seeing the most frightful films over and
over again."

"Pip and Emma," murmured Miss Blacklock. "I
never believed, somehow, in spite of what the Inspector
said, that they were real—"

She looked searchingly at Julia.

"You're Emma," she said. "Where's Pip?"

Julia's eyes, limpid and innocent, met hers.

"I don't know," she said. "I haven't the least idea."

"I think you're lying, Julia. When did you see him
last?"

Was there a momentary hesitation before Julia
spoke?

She said clearly and deliberately, "I haven't seen him
since we were both three years old—when my mother
took him away. I haven't seen either him or my mother.
I don't know where they are."

"And that's all you have to say?"

Julia sighed.

"I could say I was sorry. But it wouldn't really be
true; because actually I'd do the same thing again—
though not if I'd known about this murder business, of
course."

"Julia," said Miss Blacklock, "I call you that because
I'm used to it. You were with the French Resistance,
you say?"

"Yes. For eighteen months."

"Then I suppose you learned to shoot?"

Again those cool blue eyes met hers.

"I can shoot all right. I'm a first-class shot. I didn't

shoot at you, Letitia Blacklock, though you've only got my word for that. But I can tell you this, that if *I* had shot at you, I wouldn't have been likely to miss."

2

The sound of a car driving up to the door broke through the tenseness of the moment.

"Who can that be?" asked Miss Blacklock.

Mitzi put a tousled head in. She was showing the whites of her eyes.

"It is the police come again," she said. "This, it is persecution! Why will they not leave us alone? I will not bear it. I will write to the Prime Minister. I will write to your King."

Craddock's hand put her firmly and not too kindly aside. He came in with such a grim set to his lips that they all looked at him apprehensively. This was a new Inspector Craddock.

He said sternly, "Miss Murgatroyd has been murdered. She was strangled—not more than an hour ago." His eyes singled out Julia. "You—Miss Simmons—where have you been all day?"

Julia said warily, "In Milchester. I've just got in."

"And you?" The eyes went on to Patrick.

"Yes."

"Did you both come back here together?"

"Yes—yes, we did," said Patrick.

"No," said Julia. "It's no good, Patrick. That's the kind of lie that will be found out at once. The bus people know us well. I came back on the earlier bus, Inspector—the one that gets here at four o'clock."

"And what did you do then?"

"I went for a walk."

"In the direction of Boulders?"

"No, I went across the fields."

He stared at her. Julia, her face pale, her lips tense, stared back.

Before anyone could speak, the telephone rang.

Miss Blacklock, with an inquiring glance at Craddock, picked up the receiver.

"Yes, Who? Oh, Bunch. What? No. No, she hasn't. I've no idea . . . Yes, he's here now."

She lowered the instrument and said:

"Mrs. Harmon would like to speak to you, Inspector. Miss Marple has not come back to the vicarage and Mrs. Harmon is worried about her."

Craddock took two strides forward and gripped the telephone.

"Craddock speaking."

"I'm worried, Inspector." Bunch's voice came through with a childish tremor in it. "Aunt Jane's out somewhere—and I don't know where. And they say that Miss Murgatroyd's been killed. Is it true?"

"Yes, it's true, Mrs. Harmon. Miss Marple was there, with Miss Hinchliffe, when they found the body."

"Oh, so that's where she is." Bunch sounded relieved.

"No—no, I'm afraid she isn't. Not now. She left there about—let me see—half an hour ago. She hasn't got home?"

"No—she hasn't. It's only ten minutes' walk. Where can she be?"

"Perhaps she's called in on one of your neighbors?"

"I've rung them up—all of them. She's not there. I'm frightened, Inspector."

So am I, thought Craddock.

He said quickly, "I'll come round to you—at once."

"Oh, do—there's a piece of paper. She was writing on it before she went out. I don't know if it means anything . . . It just seems gibberish to me."

Craddock replaced the receiver.

Miss Blacklock said anxiously, "Has something happened to Miss Marple? Oh, I hope not."

"I hope not, too." His mouth was grim.

"She's so old—and frail."

"I know."

Miss Blacklock, standing with her hand pulling at the choker of pearls round her neck, said in a hoarse voice, "It's getting worse and worse. Whoever's doing these things must be mad, Inspector—quite mad . . ."

"I wonder."

The choker of pearls round Miss Blacklock's neck broke under the clutch of her nervous fingers. The smooth white globules rolled all over the room.

Letitia cried out in an anguished tone, "My pearls— my *pearls*—" The agony in her voice was so acute that they all looked at her in astonishment. She turned, her hand to her throat, and rushed sobbing out of the room.

Phillipa began picking up the pearls.

"I've never seen her so upset over anything," she said. "Of course—she always wears them. Do you think, perhaps, that someone special gave them to her? Randall Goedler, perhaps?"

"It's possible," said the Inspector slowly.

"They're not—they couldn't be—real by any chance?" Phillipa asked from where, on her knees, she was still collecting the shining white globes.

Taking one in his hand, Craddock was just about to reply contemptuously. "Real? Of course not!" when he suddenly stifled the words.

After all, *could* the pearls be real?

They were so large, so even, so white that their falseness seemed palpable, but Craddock remembered suddenly a police case where a string of real pearls had been bought for a few shillings in a pawnbroker's shop.

Letitia Blacklock had assured him that there was no

jewelry of value in the house. If these pearls were, by any chance, genuine, they must be worth a fabulous sum. And if Randall Goedler had given them to her—then they might be worth any sum you cared to name.

They looked false—they *must* be false, but—if they were real?

Why not? She might herself be unaware of their value. Or she might choose to protect her treasure by treating it as though it were a cheap ornament worth a couple of guineas at most. What would they be worth if real? A fabulous sum . . . Worth doing murder for—*if anybody knew about them . . .*

With a start, the Inspector wrenched himself away from his speculations. Miss Marple was missing. He must go to the vicarage.

3

He found Bunch and her husband waiting for him, their faces anxious and drawn.

"She hasn't come back," said Bunch.

"Did she say she was coming back here when she left Boulders?" asked Julian.

"She didn't actually say so," said Craddock slowly, throwing his mind back to the last time he had seen Jane Marple.

He remembered the grimness of her lips and the severe frosty light in those usually gentle blue eyes.

Grimness, an inexorable determination . . . to do what? To go where?

"She was talking to Sergeant Fletcher when I last saw her," he said. "Just by the gate. And then she went through it and out. I took it she was going straight home to the vicarage. I would have sent her in the car—but there was so much to attend to, and she slipped away very quietly. Fletcher may know something! Where's Fletcher?"

But Sergeant Fletcher, it seemed, as Craddock learned when he rang up Boulders, was neither to be found there nor had he left any message where he had gone. There was some idea that he had returned to Milchester for some reason.

The Inspector rang up headquarters in Milchester, but no news of Fletcher was to be found there.

Then Craddock turned to Bunch as he remembered what she had told him over the telephone.

"Where's that paper? You said she'd been writing something on a bit of paper."

Bunch brought it to him. He spread it out on the table and looked down on it. Bunch leant over his shoulder and spelled it out as he read. The writing was shaky and not easy to read:

Lamp.

Then came the word *Violets.*

Then, after a space:

Where is bottle of aspirin?

The next item in this curious list was more difficult to make out. "Delicious Death," Bunch read. "That's Mitzi's cake."

"Making enquiries," read Craddock.

"Inquiries? What about, I wonder? What's this? *Severe affliction bravely borne* . . . What on earth—!"

"Iodine," read the Inspector. "Pearls. Ah, pearls."

"And then *Lotty*—no, *Letty.* Her *e's* look like *o's.* And then *Berne.* And what's this? *Old-Age Pension . . .*"

They looked at each other in bewilderment.

Craddock recapitulated swiftly.

"Lamp. Violets. Where is bottle of aspirin? Delicious Death. Making enquiries. Severe affliction bravely borne. Iodine. Pearls. Letty. Berne. Old-Age Pension."

Bunch asked: "Does it mean anything? Anything at all? I can't see any connection."

Craddock said slowly: "I've just a glimmer—but I don't see. It's odd that she should have put that down about pearls."

"What about pearls? What does it mean?"

"Does Miss Blacklock always wear that three-tier choker of pearls?"

"Yes, she does. We laugh about it sometimes. They're so dreadfully pale-looking, aren't they. But I suppose she thinks it's fashionable."

"There might be another reason," said Craddock slowly.

"You don't mean that they're *real?* Oh, they *couldn't* be!"

"How often have you had an opportunity of seeing real pearls of that size, Mrs. Harmon?"

"But they're so glassy."

Craddock shrugged his shoulders.

"Anyway, they don't matter now. It's Miss Marple that matters. We've got to find her."

They'd got to find her before it was too late—but perhaps it was already too late? Those penciled words showed that she was on the track . . . But that was dangerous—horribly dangerous. And where the hell was Fletcher?

Craddock strode out of the vicarage to where he'd left his car. Search—that was all he could do—search.

A voice spoke to him out of the dripping laurels, "Sir!" said Sergeant Fletcher urgently. *"Sir . . ."*

CHAPTER 21

Three Women

Dinner was over at Little Paddocks. It had been a silent and uncomfortable meal.

Patrick, uneasily aware of having fallen from grace, only made spasmodic attempts at conversation—and such as he did make were not well received. Phillipa Haymes was sunk in abstraction. Miss Blacklock herself had abandoned the effort to behave with her normal cheerfulness. She had changed for dinner and had come down wearing her necklace of cameos but for the first time fear showed from her darkly circled eyes, and betrayed itself by her twitching hands.

Julia alone had maintained her air of cynical detachment throughout the evening.

"I'm sorry, Letty," she said, "that I can't pack my bag and go. But I presume the police wouldn't allow it. I don't suppose I'll darken your roof—or whatever the expression is—for long. I should imagine that Inspector Craddock will be round with a warrant and the handcuffs any moment. In fact, I can't imagine why something of the kind hasn't happened already."

"He's looking for the old lady—for Miss Marple," said Miss Blacklock.

"Do you think she's been murdered, too?" Patrick asked with scientific curiosity. "But why? What could she know?"

"I don't know," said Miss Blacklock dully. "Perhaps Miss Murgatroyd told her something."

"If she's been murdered, too," said Patrick, "there seems to be logically only one person who could have done it."

"Who?"

"Hinchliffe, of course," said Patrick triumphantly. "That's where she was last seen alive—at Boulders. My solution would be that she never left Boulders."

"My head aches," said Miss Blacklock in a dull voice. She pressed her fingers to her forehead. "Why should Hinch murder Miss Marple? It doesn't make sense."

"It would if Hinch had really murdered Murgatroyd," said Patrick triumphantly.

Phillipa came out of her apathy to say, "Hinch wouldn't murder Murgatroyd."

Patrick was in an argumentative mood.

"She might have if Murgatroyd had blundered on something to show that she—Hinch—was the criminal."

"Anyway, Hinch was at the station when Murgatroyd was killed."

"She could have murdered Murgatroyd before she left."

Startling them all, Letitia Blacklock suddenly screamed out, "Murder, murder, *murder*—! Can't you talk *anything* else? I'm frightened, don't you understand? I'm frightened. I wasn't before. I thought I could take care of myself . . . But what can you do against a murderer who's waiting—and watching—and biding his time! Oh, God!"

She dropped her head forward on her hands. A moment later she looked up and apologized stiffly.

"I'm sorry. I—I lost control."

"That's all right, Aunt Letty," said Patrick affectionately. "I'll look after you."

"You?" was all Letitia Blacklock said, but the disillusionment behind the word was almost an accusation.

That had been shortly before dinner, and Mitzi had then created a diversion by coming and declaring that she was not going to cook the dinner.

"I do not do anything more in this house. I go to my room. I lock myself in. I stay there until it is daylight. I am afraid—people are being killed—that Miss Murgatroyd with her stupid English face—who would want to kill her? Only a maniac! Then it is a maniac that is about! And a maniac does not care who he kills. But me, I do not want to be killed! There are shadows in that kitchen—and I hear noises—I think there is someone out in the yard, and then I think I see a shadow by the larder door and then it is footsteps I hear. So I go now to my room and I lock the door and perhaps even I put the chest of drawers against it. And in the morning I tell that cruel hard policeman that I go away from here. And if he will not let me, I say: 'I scream and I scream and I scream until you have to let me go!' "

Everybody, with a vivid recollection of what Mitzi could do in the screaming line, shuddered at the threat.

"So I go to my room," said Mitzi, repeating the statement once more to make her intention quite clear. With a symbolic action, she cast off the cretonne apron she had been wearing. "Good night, Miss Blacklock. Perhaps, in the morning, you may not be alive. So, in case that is so, I say good-by."

She departed abruptly and the door, with its usual gentle whine, closed softly after her.

Julia got up.

"I'll see to dinner," she said in a matter-of-fact way. "Rather a good arrangement—less embarrassing for you all than having me sit down at table with you. Patrick (since he's constituted himself your protector,

Aunt Letty) had better taste every dish first. I don't want to be accused of poisoning you on top of everything else."

So Julia had cooked and served a really excellent meal.

Phillipa had come out to the kitchen with an offer of assistance but Julia had said firmly that she didn't want any help.

"Julia, there's something I want to say—"

"This is no time for girlish confidences," said Julia firmly. "Go on back in the dining-room, Phillipa."

Now dinner was over and they were in the drawing-room with coffee on the small table by the fire—and nobody seemed to have anything to say. They were waiting—that was all.

At 8:30 Inspector Craddock rang up.

"I shall be with you in about a quarter of an hour's time," he announced. "I'm bringing Colonel and Mrs. Easterbrook and Mrs. Swettenham and her son with me."

"But, really, Inspector . . . I can't cope with people tonight—"

Miss Blacklock's voice sounded as though she were at the end of her tether.

"I know how you feel, Miss Blacklock. I'm sorry. But this is urgent."

"Have you—found Miss Marple?"

"No," said the Inspector and rang off.

Julia took the coffee tray out to the kichen where, to her surprise, she found Mitzi contemplating the piled-up dishes and plates by the sink.

Mitzi burst into a torrent of words:

"See what you do in my so nice kitchen! That frying pan—only, *only* for omlettes do I use it! And you, what have you used it for?"

"Frying onions."

"Ruined—*ruined!* It will have now to be *washed* and never—*never*—do I wash my omlette pan. I rub it carefully with a greasy newspaper, that is all. And this saucepan here that you have used—that one, I use him only for milk—"

"Well, I don't know what pans you use for what," said Julia crossly. "You chose to go to bed and why on earth you've chosen to get up again, I can't imagine. Go away again and leave me to wash up in peace."

"No, I will not let you use my kitchen."

"Oh, Mitzi, you *are* impossible!"

Julia stalked angrily out of the kitchen and at that moment the doorbell rang.

"I do not go to the door," Mitzi called from the kitchen. Julia muttered an impolite Continental expression under her breath and stalked to the front door.

It was Miss Hinchliffe.

"Evening," she said in her gruff voice. "Sorry to barge in. Inspector's rung up, I expect?"

"He didn't tell us you were coming," said Julia, leading the way to the drawing-room.

"He said I needn't come unless I liked," said Miss Hinchliffe. "But I do like."

Nobody offered Miss Hinchliffe sympathy or mentioned Miss Murgatroyd's death. The ravaged face of the tall vigorous woman told its own tale, and would have made any expression of sympathy an impertinence.

"Turn all the lights on," said Miss Blacklock. "And put more coal on the fire. I'm cold—horribly cold. Come and sit here by the fire, Miss Hinchliffe. The Inspector said he would be here in a quarter of an hour. It must be nearly that now."

"Mitzi's come down again," said Julia.

"Has she? Sometimes I think that girl's mad—quite mad. But then perhaps we're all mad."

"I've no patience with this saying that all people who

commit crimes are mad," barked Miss Hinchliffe. "Horribly and intelligently sane—that's what I think a criminal is!"

The sound of a car was heard outside and presently Craddock came in with Colonel and Mrs. Easterbrook and Edmund and Mrs. Swettenham.

They were all curiously subdued.

Colonel Easterbrook said in a voice that was like an echo of his usual tones. "Ha! A good fire."

Mrs. Easterbrook wouldn't take off her fur coat and sat down close to her husband. Her face, usually pretty and rather vapid, was like a little pinched weasel face. Edmund was in one of his furious moods and scowled at everybody. Mrs. Swettenham made what was evidently a great effort, and which resulted in a kind of parody of herself.

"It's awful—isn't it?" she said conversationally. "Everything, I mean. And, really, the less one says, the better. Because one doesn't know *who next*—like the plague. Dear Miss Blacklock, don't you think you ought to have a little brandy? Just half a wineglass even? I always think there's nothing like brandy—such a wonderful stimulant. I—it seems so terrible of us—forcing our way in here like this, but Inspector Craddock made us come. And it seems so terrible—she hasn't been found, you know. That poor old thing from the vicarage, I mean. Bunch Harmon is nearly frantic. Nobody knows where she went instead of going home. She didn't come to us. I've not even seen her today. And I should know if she had come to the house because I was in the drawing-room—at the back, you know, and Edmund was in his study writing—and that's at the front—so if she'd come either way we should have seen. And, oh, I do hope and pray that nothing has happened to that dear sweet old thing—all her faculties still and *everything*."

"Mother," said Edmund in a voice of acute suffering, "can't you shut up?"

"I'm sure, dear, I don't want to say a *word,*" said Mrs. Swettenham, and sat down on the sofa by Julia.

Inspector Craddock stood near the door. Facing him, almost in a row, were the three women. Julia and Mrs. Swettenham on the sofa. Mrs. Easterbrook on the arm of her husband's chair. He had not brought about this arrangement, but it suited him very well.

Miss Blacklock and Miss Hinchliffe were crouching over the fire. Edmund stood near them. Phillipa was far back in the shadows.

Craddock began without preamble.

"You all know that Miss Murgatroyd's been killed," he began. "We've reason to believe that the person who killed her was a woman. And for certain other reasons we can narrow it down still more. I'm about to ask certain ladies here to account for what they were doing between the hours of 4:00 and 4:20 this afternoon. I have already had an account of her movements from— from the young lady who has been calling herself Miss Simmons. I will ask her to repeat that statement. At the same time, Miss Simmons, I must caution you that you need not answer if you think your answers may incriminate you, and anything you say will be taken down by Constable Edwards and may be used as evidence in court."

"You have to say that, don't you?" said Julia. She was rather pale, but still composed. "I repeat that between 4:00 and 4:20 I was walking along the field leading down to the brook by Compton Farm. I came back to the road by that field with three poplars in it. I didn't meet anyone as far as I can remember. I did not go near Boulders."

"Mrs. Swettenham?"

Edmund said, "Are you cautioning all of us?"

The Inspector turned to him.

"No. At the moment only Miss Simmons. I have no reason to believe that any other statement made will be incriminating, but anyone, of course, is entitled to have a solicitor present and to refuse to answer questions unless one *is* present."

"Oh, but that would be very silly and a complete waste of time," cried Mrs. Swettenham. "I'm sure I can tell you at once exactly what I was doing. That's what you want, isn't it? Shall I begin now?"

"Yes, please, Mrs. Swettenham."

"Now let me see." Mrs. Swettenham closed her eyes, opened them again. "Of course, I had nothing *at all* to do with killing Miss Murgatroyd. I'm sure *everybody* here knows *that*. But I'm a woman of the world, I know quite well that the police have to ask all the most unnecessary questions and write the answers down very carefully, because it's all for what they call 'the record.' That's it, isn't it?" Mrs. Swettenham flashed the question at the diligent Constable Edwards and added graciously, "I'm not going too fast for you, I hope?"

Constable Edwards, a good shorthand writer, but with little social *savoir faire*, turned red to the ears and replied, "It's quite all right, madam. Well, perhaps a *little* slower would be better."

Mrs. Swettenham resumed her discourse with emphatic pauses where she considered a comma or a full stop might be appropriate.

"Well, of course, it's difficult to say—exactly—because I've not got, really, a very good sense of time. And ever since the war quite half our clocks haven't gone at all, and the ones that do go are often either fast or slow or stop because we haven't wound them up." Mrs. Swettenham paused to let this picture of confused time sink in and then went on earnestly, "What I *think* I was doing at four o'clock was turning the heel of my sock (and for some extraordinary reason I was going round the wrong way—in purl, you know, not plain), but if I *wasn't* doing that, I must have been outside, snipping off the dead chrysanthemums—no, that was earlier—before the rain."

"The rain," said the Inspector, "started at 4:10 exactly."

"Did it now? That helps a lot. Of course, I was upstairs putting a wash basin in the passage where the rain always comes through. And it was coming through so fast that I guessed at once that the gutter was stopped up again. So I came down and got my mackintosh and rubber boots. I called Edmund, but he didn't answer, so I thought perhaps he'd got to a very important place in his novel and I wouldn't disturb him, and I've done it quite often myself before. With the broom handle, you know, tied onto that long thing you push up windows with."

"You mean," said Craddock, noting bewilderment on his subordinate's face, "that you were cleaning out the gutter?"

"Yes, it was all choked up with leaves. It took a long time and I got rather wet, but I got it clear at last. And then I went in and got changed and washed—so *smelly*, dead leaves—And then I went into the kitchen and put the kettle on. It was 6:15 by the kitchen clock."

Constable Edwards blinked.

"Which means," finished Mrs. Swettenham triumphantly, "that it was exactly twenty minutes to five. Or near enough," she added.

"Did anybody see what you were doing whilst you were out cleaning the gutter?"

"No, indeed," said Mrs. Swettenham. "I'd soon have roped them in to help if they had! It's a most difficult thing to do single-handed."

"So, by your own statement, you were outside, in a

mackintosh and boots, at the time when the rain was coming down, and, according to you, you were employed during that time in cleaning out a gutter, but you have no one who can substantiate that statement?"

"You can look at the gutter," said Mrs. Swettenham. "It's beautifully clear."

"Did you hear your mother call to you, Mr. Swettenham?"

"No," said Edmund. "I was fast asleep."

"Edmund," said his mother reproachfully, "I thought you were writing."

Inspector Craddock turned to Mrs. Easterbrook.

"Now, Mrs. Easterbrook?"

"I was sitting with Archie in his study," said Mrs. Easterbrook, fixing wide innocent eyes on him. "We were listening to the radio together, weren't we, Archie?"

There was a pause. Colonel Easterbrook was very red in the face. He took his wife's hand in his.

"You don't understand these things, kitten," he said. "I—well, I must say, Inspector, you've rather sprung this business on us. My wife, you know, has been terribly upset by all this. She's nervous and highly strung and doesn't appreciate the importance of—of taking due consideration before she makes a statement."

"Archie," cried Mrs. Easterbrook reproachfully, "are you going to say you weren't with me?"

"Well, I wasn't, was I, my dear? I mean, one's got to stick to the facts. Very important in this sort of inquiry. I was talking to Lampson, the farmer at Croft End, about some chicken netting. That was about a quarter to four. I didn't get home until after the rain had stopped. Just before tea. A quarter to five. Laura was toasting the scones."

"And had *you* been out also, Mrs. Easterbrook?"

The pretty face looked more like a weasel's than ever. Her eyes had a trapped look.

"No—no, I just sat listening to the radio. I didn't go out. Not then. I'd been out earlier. About—about half past three. Just for a little walk. Not far."

She looked as though she expected more questions, but Craddock said quietly, "That's all, Mrs. Easterbrook."

He went on: "These statements will be typed out. You can read them and sign them if they are substantially correct."

Mrs. Easterbrook looked at him with sudden venom.

"Why don't you ask the others where they were? That Haymes woman? And Edmund Swettenham? How do you know he *was* asleep indoors? Nobody saw him."

Inspector Craddock said quietly, "Miss Murgatroyd, before she died, made a certain statement. On the night of the holdup here, *someone* was absent from this room. Someone who was supposed to have been in the room all the time. Miss Murgatroyd told her friend the names of the people she *did* see. By a process of elimination, she made the discovery that there was someone she did *not* see."

"Nobody could see anything," said Julia.

"Murgatroyd could," said Miss Hinchliffe, speaking suddenly in her deep voice. "She was over there behind the door, where Inspector Craddock is now. She was the only person who could see anything of what was happening."

"Aha! That is what you think, is it?" demanded Mitzi.

She had made one of her dramatic entrances, flinging open the door and almost knocking Craddock sideways. She was in a frenzy of excitement.

"Ah, you do not ask Mitzi to come in here with the others, do you, you stiff policeman? I am only Mitzi! Mitzi in the kitchen! Let her stay in the kitchen where she belongs! But I tell you that Mitzi, as well as anyone

else, perhaps better, yes, better, can see things. Yes, I
see things. I see something the night of the burglary. I
see something and I do not quite believe it, and I hold
my tongue till now. I think to myself I will not tell what
it is I have seen, not yet. I will wait."

"And when everything had calmed down, you meant
to ask for a little money from a certain person, eh?"
said Craddock.

Mitzi turned on him like an angry cat.

"And why not? Why look down your nose? Why
should I not be paid for it if I have been so generous as
to keep silence? Especially if some day there will be
money—much, *much* money. Oh! I have heard things—
I know what goes on. I know this Pippemmer—this
secret society of which *she*"—she flung a dramatic
finger towards Julia—"is an agent. Yes, I would have
waited and asked for money—but now I am afraid. I
would rather be *safe*. For soon, perhaps, someone will
kill *me*. So I will tell what I know."

"All right then," said the Inspector skeptically. "What
do you know?"

"I tell you." Mitzi spoke solemnly. "On that night
I am *not* in the pantry cleaning silver as I say—I am
already in the dining-room when I hear the gun go off.
I look through the keyhole. The hall it is black, but the
gun go off again and the flashlight it falls—and it swings
round as it falls—and I see *her*. I see *her* there close
to him, with the gun in her hand. I see Miss Blacklock."

"Me?" Miss Blacklock sat up in astonishment. "You
must be mad!"

"But that's impossible!" cried Edmund. "Mitzi
couldn't have seen Miss Blacklock—"

Craddock cut in and his voice had the corrosive quality of a deadly acid.

"Couldn't she, Mr. Swettenham? And why not? Be-

cause it *wasn't* Miss Blacklock who was standing there with the gun? It was *you,* wasn't it?"

"I? Of course not—what the *hell!*"

"*You* took Colonel Easterbrook's revolver. *You* fixed up the business with Rudi Scherz—as a good joke. You had followed Patrick Simmons into the far room and when the lights went out, you slipped out through the carefully oiled door. You shot at Miss Blacklock and then you killed Rudi Scherz. A few seconds later you were back in the drawing-room, clicking your lighter."

For a moment Edmund seemed at a loss for words, then he spluttered out, "The whole idea is *monstrous.* Why *me?* What earthly motive had I got?"

"If Miss Blacklock dies before Mrs. Goedler, two people inherit—remember? The two we know of as Pip and Emma. Julia Simmons has turned out to be Emma—"

"And you think I'm Pip?" Edmund laughed. "Fantastic—absolutely *fantastic!* I'm about the right age—nothing else. And I can prove to you, you damned fool, that I *am* Edmund Swettenham. Birth certificate, schools university—everything."

"He isn't Pip." The voice came from the shadows in the corner. Phillipa Haymes came forward, her face pale. *"I'm Pip,* Inspector."

"You, Mrs. Hamyes?"

"Yes. Everybody seems to have assumed that Pip was a boy—Julia knew, of course, that her twin was another girl—I don't know why she didn't say so this afternoon—"

"Family solidarity," said Julia. "I suddenly realized who you were. I'd had no idea till that moment."

"I'd had the same idea as Julia did," said Phillipa, her voice trembling a little. "After I—lost my husband and the war was over, I wondered what I was going to do. My mother died many years ago. I found out where Miss Blacklock lived and I—I came here. I took a job with Mrs. Lucas. I hoped that, since this Miss Blacklock was an elderly woman without relatives, she might, perhaps, be willing to help. Not me, because I could work, but help with Harry's education. After all, it *was* Goedler money and she'd no one particular of her own to spend it on.

"And then——" Phillipa spoke faster; it was as though now her long reserve had broken down, she couldn't get the words out fast enough——"that holdup happened and I began to be frightened. Because it seemed to me that the only possible person with a motive for killing Miss Blacklock was *me*. I hadn't the least idea who Julia was—we weren't identical twins and we're not much alike to look at. No, it seemed as though I was the only one bound to be suspected."

She stopped and pushed her fair hair back from her face, and Craddock suddenly realized that a faded snapshot in the box of letters must have been a photograph of Phillipa's mother. The likeness was undeniable. He knew too why that mention of closing and unclosing hands had seemed familiar—Phillipa was doing it now.

"Miss Blacklock has been good to me. Very, *very* good to me—I didn't try to kill her. I never thought of killing her. But all the same, I'm Pip." She added, "You see, you needn't suspect Edmund any more."

"Needn't I?" said Craddock. Again there was that acid biting tone in his voice. "Edmund Swettenham's a young man who's fond of money. A young man, perhaps, who would like to marry a rich wife. But she wouldn't be a rich wife *unless Miss Blacklock died before Mrs. Goedler*. And since it seemed almost certain that Mrs. Goedler would die before Miss Blacklock, well—he had to do something about it—*didn't you, Mr. Swettenham?*"

"It's a damned lie!" Edmund shouted.

And then, suddenly, a sound rose on the air. It came from the kitchen—a long unearthly shriek of terror.

"That isn't Mitzi!" cried Julia.

"No," said Inspector Craddock, "it's someone who's murdered three people . . ."

CHAPTER 22

The Truth

WHEN the Inspector turned on Edmund Swettenham, Mitzi had crept quietly out of the room and back to the kitchen. She was running water into the sink when Miss Blacklock entered.

Mitzi gave her a shame-faced sideways look.

"What a liar you are, Mitzi," said Miss Blacklock pleasantly. "Here—that isn't the way to wash up. The silver first, and fill the sink right up. You can't wash up in about two inches of water."

Mitzi turned the taps on obediently.

"You are not angry at what I say, Miss Blacklock?" she asked.

"If I were to be angry at all the lies you tell, I should never be out of a temper," said Miss Blacklock.

"I will go and say to the Inspector that I make it all up, shall I?" asked Mitzi.

"He knows that already," said Miss Blacklock pleasantly.

Mitzi turned off the taps and as she did so two hands came up behind her head and with one swift movement forced it down into the water-filled sink.

"Only *I* know that you're telling the truth for once," said Miss Blacklock viciously.

Mitzi thrashed and struggled but Miss Blacklock was

244

strong and her hands held the girl's head firmly under water.

Then, from somewhere quite close behind her, Dora Bunner's voice rose piteously on the air:

"Oh, Lotty—Lotty—don't do it . . . Lotty!"

Miss Blacklock screamed. Her hands flew up in the air, and Mitzi, released, came up choking and spluttering.

Miss Blacklock screamed again and again. For there was no one there in the kitchen with her—

"Dora, Dora, forgive me. I had to . . . I had to—"

She rushed distractedly towards the scullery door—and the bulk of Sergeant Fletcher barred her way, just as Miss Marple stepped, flushed and triumphant, out of the broom cupboard.

"I could always mimic people's voices," said Miss Marple.

"You'll have to come with me, madam," said Sergeant Fletcher. "I was a witness of your attempt to drown this girl. And there will be other charges. I must warn you, Letitia Blacklock—"

"Charlotte Blacklock," corrected Miss Marple. "That's who she is, you know. Under that choker of pearls she always wears you'll find the scar of the operation."

"Operation?"

"Operation for goiter."

Miss Blacklock, quite calm now, looked at Miss Marple.

"So you know all about it?" she said.

"Yes, I've known for some time."

Charlotte Blacklock sat down by the table and began to cry.

"You shouldn't have done that," she said. "Not made Dora's voice come. I loved Dora. I really loved Dora.

Inspector Craddock and the others had crowded in the doorway.

Constable Edwards, who added a knowledge of first aid and artificial respiration to his other accomplishments, was busy with Mitzi. As soon as Mitzi could speak she was lyrical with self-praise.

"I do that good, do I not? I am clever! And I am brave! Oh, I am brave! Very, very nearly was *I* murdered, too. But I am so brave I risk *everything.*"

With a rush Miss Hinchliffe thrust aside the others and leaped upon the weeping figure of Charlotte Blacklock by the table.

It took all Sergeant Fletcher's strength to hold her off.

"Now then—" he said. "Now then—No, no, Miss Hinchliffe—"

Between clenched teeth Miss Hinchliffe was muttering, "Let me get at her. Just let me get at her. It was she who killed Amy Murgatroyd."

Charlotte Blacklock looked up and sniffed.

"I didn't want to kill her. I didn't want to kill anybody—I had to— But it's Dora I mind about—after Dora was dead, I was all alone—ever since she died— I've been alone—oh, Dora —Dora—"

And once again she dropped her head on her hands and wept.

CHAPTER 23

Evening at the Vicarage

MISS MARPLE sat in the tall armchair. Bunch was on the floor in front of the fire with her arms round her knees.

The Reverend Julian Harmon was leaning forward and was for once looking more like a schoolboy than a man foreshadowing his own maturity. And Inspector Craddock was smoking his pipe and drinking a whisky and soda and was clearly very much off duty. An outer circle was composed of Julia, Patrick, Edmund and Phillipa.

"I think it's your story, Miss Marple," said Craddock.

"Oh, no, my dear boy. I only just helped a little, here and there. *You* were in charge of the whole thing, and conducted it all, and you know so much that I don't."

"Well, tell it together," said Bunch impatiently. "Bits each. Only let Aunt Jane start because I like the muddly way her mind works. When did you first think that the whole thing was a put-up job by the Blacklock?"

"Well, my dear Bunch, it's hard to say. Of course, right at the very beginning, it did seem as though the ideal person—or rather the *obvious* person, I should say—to have arranged the holdup *was* Miss Blacklock herself. She was the only person who was known to have been in contact with Rudi Scherz, and how much easier

247

to arrange something like that when it's your own house. The central heating for instance. No fire—because that would have meant light in the room. But the only person who could have arranged *not* to have a fire was the mistress of the house herself.

"Not that I thought of all that at the time—it just seemed to me that it was a pity it *couldn't* be as simple as that! Oh no, I was taken in like everyone else, I thought that someone really did want to kill Letitia Blacklock."

"I think I'd like to get clear first on what really happened," said Bunch. "Did this Swiss boy recognize her?"

"Yes. He'd worked in—"

She hesitated and looked at Craddock.

"In Dr. Adolf Koch's clinic in Berne," said Craddock. "Koch was a world-famous specialist on operations for goiter. Charlotte Blacklock went there to have her goiter removed and Rudi Scherz was one of the orderlies. When he came to England he recognized in the hotel a lady who had been a patient and on the spur of the moment he spoke to her. I daresay he mightn't have done that if he'd paused to think, because he left the place under a cloud, but that was sometime after Charlotte had been there, so she wouldn't know anything about it."

"So he never said anything to her about Montreux and his father being a hotel proprietor?"

"Oh, no, she made that up to account for his having spoken to her."

"It must have been a great shock to her," said Miss Marple thoughtfully. "She felt reasonably safe—and then—the almost impossible mischance of somebody turning up who had known her—not as one of the two Miss Blacklocks—she was prepared for *that*—but definitely as *Charlotte* Blacklock, a patient who'd been operated on for goiter.

"But you wanted to go through it all from the beginning. Well, the beginning, I think—if Inspector Craddock agrees with me—was when Charlotte Blacklock, a pretty, lighthearted, affectionate girl, developed that enlargement of the thyroid gland that's called a goiter. It ruined her life, because she was a very sensitive girl. A girl, too, who had always set a lot of stress on her personal appearance. And girls just at that age in their teens, are particularly sensitive about themselves. If she'd had a mother, or a reasonable father, I don't think she would have got into the morbid state she undoubtedly did get into. She had no one, you see, to take her out of herself and force her to see people and lead a normal life and not think too much about her infirmity. And, of course, in a different household, she might have been sent for an operation many years earlier.

"But Dr. Blacklock, I think, was an old-fashioned, narrow-minded, tyrannical and obstinate man. He didn't believe in these operations. Charlotte must take it from him that nothing could be done—apart from dosage with iodine and other drugs. Charlotte *did* take it from him, and I think her sister also placed more faith in Dr. Blacklock's powers as a physician than he deserved.

"Charlotte was devoted to her father in a rather weak and soppy way. She thought, definitely, that her father knew best. But she shut herself up more and more as the goiter became larger and more unsightly, and refused to see people. She was actually a kindly affectionate creature."

"That's an odd description of a murderess," said Edmund.

"I don't know that it is," said Miss Marple. "Weak and kindly people are often very treacherous. And if they've got a grudge against life it saps the little moral strength that they may possess.

"*Letitia* Blacklock, of course, had quite a different personality. Inspector Craddock told me that Belle Goedler described her as really *good*—and I think Letitia *was* good. She was a woman of great integrity who found—as she put it herself—a great difficulty in understanding how people couldn't see what was dishonest. Letitia Blacklock, however tempted, would never have contemplated any kind of fraud for a moment.

"Letitia was devoted to her sister. She wrote her long accounts of everything that happened in an effort to keep her sister in touch with life. She was worried by the morbid state Charlotte was getting into.

"Finally, Dr. Blacklock died. Letitia, without hesitation, threw up her position with Randall Goedler and devoted herself to Charlotte. She took her to Switzerland to consult authorities there on the possibility of operating. It had been left until very late—but, as we know, the operation was successful. The deformity was gone—and the scar this operation had left was easily hidden by a choker of pearls or beads.

"The war had broken out. A return to England was difficult and the two sisters stayed in Switzerland, doing various Red Cross and other work. That's right, isn't it, Inspector?"

"Yes, Miss Marple."

"They got occasional news from England—amongst other things, I expect, they heard that Belle Goedler could not live long. I'm sure it would be only human nature for them both to have planned and talked together of the days ahead when a big fortune would be theirs to spend. One has got to realize, I think, that this prospect meant much more to *Charlotte* than it did to Letitia. For the first time in her life, Charlotte could go about feeling herself a normal woman, a woman at whom no one looked with either repulsion or pity. She was free at last to enjoy life—and she had a whole lifetime, as it were, to crowd into her remaining years. To travel, to have a house and beautiful grounds—to have clothes and jewels, and go to plays and concerts, to gratify every whim—it was all a kind of fairy tale come true to Charlotte.

"And then Letitia, the strong healthy Letitia, got flu which turned to pneumonia and she died within the space of a week! Not only had Charlotte lost her sister, but the whole dream existence she had planned for herself was canceled. I think, you know, that she may have felt almost resentful towards Letitia. Why need Letitia have died, just then, when they had just had a letter saying Belle Goedler could not last long? Just one more month, perhaps, and the money would have been Letitia's—and hers when Letitia died . . .

"Now this is where I think the difference between the two came in. Charlotte didn't really feel that what she suddenly thought of doing was wrong—not really wrong. The money was meant to come to Letitia—it *would* have come to Letitia in the course of a few months—and she regarded herself and Letitia as one.

"Perhaps the idea didn't occur to her until the doctor or someone asked her sister's Christian name—and then she realized how to nearly everyone they had appeared as the two Miss Blacklocks—elderly, well-bred Englishwomen, dressed much the same, with a strong family resemblance—(and, as I pointed out to Bunch, one elderly woman is *so* like another). Why shouldn't it be *Charlotte* who had died and *Letitia* who was alive?

"It was an impulse, perhaps, more than a plan. Letitia was buried under Charlotte's name. 'Charlotte' was dead, 'Letitia' came to England. All the natural initiative and energy, dormant for so many years, were now in the ascendant. As Charlotte, she had played second fiddle. She now assumed the airs of command, the feeling of command that had been Letitia's. They were not really so unlike in mentality—though there was, I think, a big difference *morally*.

"Charlotte had, of course, to take one or two obvious precautions. She bought a house in a part of England quite unknown to her. The only people she had to avoid were a few people in her own native town in Cumberland (where, in any case, she'd lived as a recluse) and, of course, Belle Goedler, who had known Letitia so well that any impersonation would have been out of the question. Handwriting difficulties were got over by the arithritic condition of her hands. It was really very easy because so few people had ever really known Charlotte."

"But supposing she'd met people who'd known Letitia?" asked Bunch. "There must have been plenty of those."

"They wouldn't matter in the same way. Someone might say: 'I came across Letitia Blacklock the other day. She's changed so much I really wouldn't have known her.' But there still wouldn't have been any suspicion in their minds that she wasn't Letitia. People *do* change in the course of ten years. *Her* failure to recognize *them* could always be put down to her nearsightedness: and you must remember that she knew every detail of Letitia's life in London—the people she met—the places she went. She'd got Letitia's letters to refer to, and she could quickly have disarmed any suspicion by mention of some incident, or an inquiry after a mutual friend. No, it was recognition as *Charlotte* that was the only thing she had to fear.

"She settled down at Little Paddocks, got to know her neighbors and, when she got a letter asking dear Letitia to be kind, she accepted with pleasure the visit of two young cousins she had never seen. Their acceptance of her as Aunt Letty increased her security.

"The whole thing was going splendidly. And then—she made her big mistake. It was a mistake that arose solely from her kindness of heart and her naturally affectionate nature. She got a letter from an old school friend who had fallen on evil days, and she hurried to the rescue. Perhaps it may have been partly because she was, in spite of everything, lonely. Her secret kept her in a way apart from people. And she had been genuinely fond of Dora Bunner and remembered her as a symbol of her own gay carefree days at school. Anyway, on an impulse, she answered Dora's letter in person. And very surprised Dora must have been! She'd written to *Letitia* and the sister who turned up in answer to her letter was *Charlotte*. There was never any question of pretending to be Letitia to Dora. Dora was one of the few old friends who had been admitted to see Charlotte in her lonely and unhappy days.

"And because she knew that Dora would look at the matter in exactly the same way as she did herself, she told Dora what she had done. Dora approved wholeheartedly. In her confused muddle-headed mind it seemed only right that dear Lotty should not be done out of her inheritance by Letty's untimely death. Lotty *deserved* a reward for all the patient suffering she had borne so bravely. It would have been most unfair if all that money should have gone to someone nobody had ever heard of.

"She quite understood that nothing must be allowed to get out. It was like an extra pound of butter. You couldn't talk about it but there was nothing wrong about having it. So Dora came to Little Paddocks—and very soon Charlotte began to understand that she had made a terrible mistake. It was not merely the fact that Dora Bunner, with her muddles and her mistakes and her bungling, was quite maddening to live with. Charlotte could have put up with that—because she really cared for Dora, and, anyway, knew from the doctor that Dora hadn't a very long time to live. But Dora very soon became a real danger. Though Charlotte and Letitia had called each other by their full names, Dora was the kind of person who always used abbreviations. To her the sisters had always been Letty and Lotty. And though she schooled her tongue resolutely to call her friend Letty—the old name often slipped out. Memories of the past, too, were rather apt to come to her tongue—forgetful allusions. It began to get on her nerves.

"Still, nobody was likely to pay much attention to Dora's inconsistencies. The real blow to Charlotte's security came, as I say, when she was recognized and spoken to by Rudi Scherz at the Royal Spa Hotel.

"I think that the money Rudi Scherz used to replace his earlier defalcations at the hotel may have come from Charlotte Blacklock. Inspector Craddock doesn't believe—and I don't either—that Rudi Scherz applied to her for money with any idea of blackmail in his head."

"He hadn't the faintest idea he knew anything to blackmail her about," said Inspector Craddock. "He knew that he was quite a personable young man—and he was aware by experience that personable young men sometimes can get money out of elderly ladies if they tell a hard luck story convincingly enough.

"But she may have seen it differently. She may have thought that it *was* a form of insidious blackmail, that perhaps he suspected something—and that later, if there was publicity in the papers, as there might be after Belle Goedler's death, he would realize that in her he had found a gold mine.

"And she was committed to the fraud now. She'd established herself as Letitia Blacklock. With the bank. With Mrs. Goedler. The only snag was this rather dubious Swiss hotel clerk, an unreliable character and possibly a blackmailer. If only he were out of the way—she'd be safe.

"Perhaps she made it all up as a kind of fantasy first. She'd been starved of emotion and drama in her life. She pleased herself by working out the details. How would she go about getting rid of him?

"She made her plan. And at last she decided to act on it. She told her story of a sham holdup at a party to Rudi Scherz, explained that she wanted a stranger to act the part of the 'gangster,' and offered him a generous sum for his co-operation.

"And the fact that he agreed without any suspicion is what makes me quite certain that Scherz had no idea that he had any kind of hold over her. To him she was just a rather foolish old woman, very ready to part with money.

"She gave him the advertisement to insert, arranged for him to pay a visit to Little Paddocks to study the geography of the house and showed him the spot where she would meet him and let him into the house on the night in question. Dora Bunner, of course, knew nothing about all this.

"The day came—" He paused.

Miss Marple took up the tale in her gentle voice.

"She must have spent a very miserable day. You see, it still wasn't too late to draw back. . . . Dora Bunner told us that Letty was frightened that day and she must have been frightened. Frightened of what she was going to do, frightened of the plan going wrong—but not frightened enough to draw back.

"It had been fun, perhaps, getting the revolver out of Colonel Easterbrook's collar drawer. Taking along eggs, or jam—slipping upstairs in the empty house. It had been fun getting the second door in the drawing-room oiled, so that it would open and shut noiselessly. Fun suggesting the moving of the table outside the door so that Phillipa's flower arrangements would show to better advantage. It may have all seemed like a game. But what was going to happen next definitely wasn't a game any longer. Oh, yes, she was frightened . . . Dora Bunner was right about that."

"All the same, she went through with it," said Craddock. "And it all went according to plan. She went out just after six to 'shut up the ducks,' and she let Scherz in then and gave him the mask and cloak and gloves and the flashlight. Then, at 6:30, when the clock begins to strike, she's ready by that table near the archway with her hand on the cigarette box. It's all so natural. Patrick, acting as host, has gone for the drinks. She, the hostess, is fetching the cigarettes. She's judged, quite correctly, that when the clock begins to strike, everyone will look at the clock. They did. Only one person, the devoted Dora, kept her eyes fixed on her friend. And she told us, in her very first statement, exactly what Miss Blacklock did. She said that Miss Blacklock had picked up the vase of violets.

"She'd previously frayed the cord of the lamp so that the wires were nearly bare. The whole thing only took a second. The cigarette box, the vase and the little switch were all close together. She picked up the violets, spilt the water on the frayed place and switched on the lamp. Water's a good conductor of electricity. The wires burned out."

"Just like the other afternoon at the vicarage," said Bunch. "That's what startled you so, wasn't it, Aunt Jane?"

"Yes, my dear. I'd been puzzling about those lights. I'd realized that there were two lamps, a pair, and that one had been changed for the other—probably during the night."

"That's right," said Craddock. "When Fletcher examined that lamp the next morning it was, like all the others, perfectly in order, no frayed cord or burned out wires."

"I'd understood what Dora Bunner meant by saying it had been the *shepherdess* the night before," said Miss Marple, "but I fell into the error of thinking, as she thought, that *Patrick* had been responsible. The interesting thing about Dora Bunner was that she was quite unreliable in repeating things she had heard—she always used her imagination to exaggerate or distort them, and she was usually wrong in what she *thought* —but she was quite accurate about the things she *saw*. She saw Letitia pick up the violets—"

"And of course, when dear Bunch split the water from the Christmas roses onto the lamp wire—I realized at once that only Miss Blacklock herself could have put out the lights because only she was near that table."

"I could kick myself," said Craddock. "Dora Bunner even prattled about a burn on the table where someone had 'put their cigarette down'—but nobody had even lit a cigarette . . . And the violets were dead because there was no water in the vase—a slip on Letitia's part—she ought to have filled it up again. But I suppose she thought nobody would notice and, as a matter of fact, Miss Bunner was quite ready to believe that she herself had put no water in the vase to begin with."

He went on:

"She was highly suggestible, of course. And Miss Blacklock took advantage of that more than once. Bunny's suspicions of Patrick were, I think, induced by her."

"Why pick on me?" demanded Patrick in an aggrieved tone.

"It was not, I think, a serious suggestion—but it would keep Bunny distracted from any suspicion that Miss Blacklock might be stage managering the business.

Well, we know what happened next. As soon as the lights went and everyone was exclaiming, she slipped out through the previously oiled door and up behind Rudi Scherz who was turning his flashlight round the room and playing his part with gusto. I don't suppose he realized for a moment she was there behind him with her gardening gloves pulled on and the revolver in her hand. She waits till the light reaches the spot she must aim for—the wall near which she is supposed to be standing. Then she fires rapidly twice and as he swings round startled, she holds the revolver close to his body and fires again. She lets the revolver fall by his body, throws her gloves carelessly on the hall table, then back through the other door and across to where she had been standing when the light went out. She nicked her ear—I don't quite know how—"

"Nail scissors, I expect," said Miss Marple. "Just a snip on the lobe of the ear lets out a lot of blood. That was very good psychology, of course. The actual blood running down over her white blouse made it seem certain that she *had* been shot at, and that it had been a near miss."

"It ought to have gone off quite all right," said Craddock. "Dora Bunner's insistence that Scherz had definitely aimed at Miss Blacklock had it uses. Without meaning it, Dora Bunner conveyed the impression that she'd actually seen her friend wounded. It might have been brought in suicide or accidental death. And the case would have been closed. That it was kept open is due to Miss Marple here."

"Oh, no, no." Miss Marple shook her head energetically. "Any little efforts on my part were quite incidental. It was you who weren't satisfied, Mr. Craddock. It was *you* who wouldn't let the case be closed."

"I wasn't happy about it," said Craddock. "I knew it was all wrong somewhere. But I didn't see *where* it was wrong, till you showed me. And after that Miss Black-lock had a real piece of bad luck. I discovered that that second door had been tampered with. Until that moment, whatever we agreed *might* have happened—we'd nothing to go upon but a pretty theory. But that oiled door was *evidence*. And I hit upon it by pure chance—by catching hold of a handle by mistake."

"I think you were *led* to it, Inspector," said Miss Marple. "But then I'm old-fashioned."

"So the hunt was up again," said Craddock. "But this time with a difference. We were looking now for someone with a motive to kill Letitia Blacklock."

"And there *was* someone with a motive, and Miss Blacklock knew it," said Miss Marple. "I think she recognized Phillipa almost at once. Because Sonia Goedler seems to have been one of the very few people who had been admitted to Charlotte's privacy. And when one is old (you wouldn't know this yet, Mr. Craddock) one has a much better memory for a face you've seen when you were young than you have for anyone you've only met a year or two ago. Phillipa must have been just about the same age as her mother was as Charlotte remembered her, and she was very like her mother. The odd thing is that I think Charlotte was very pleased to recognize Phillipa. She became very fond of Phillipa and I think, unconsciously, it helped to stifle any qualms of conscience she may have had. She told herself that when she inherited the money, she was going to look after Phillipa. She would treat her as a daughter. Phillipa and Harry should live with her. She felt quite happy and beneficent about it. But once the Inspector began asking questions and finding out about 'Pip and Emma,' Charlotte became very uneasy. She didn't want to make a scapegoat of Phillipa. Her whole idea had been to make the business look like a holdup by a young criminal and his accidental death. But now, with the discovery of the oiled door, the whole viewpoint was changed. And, except for Phillipa, there wasn't (as far as *she* knew, for she had absolutely no idea of Julia's identity) anyone with the least possible motive for wishing to kill her. She did her best to shield Phillipa's identity. She was quick-witted enough to tell you when you asked her, that Sonia was small and dark and she took the old snapshots out of the album so that you shouldn't notice any resemblance at the same time that she removed snapshots of Letitia herself."

"And to think I suspected Mrs. Swettenham of being Sonia Goedler," said Craddock disgustedly.

"My poor mama," murmured Edmund. "A woman of blameless life—or so I have always believed."

"But, of course," Miss Marple went on, "it was Dora Bunner who was the real danger. Every day Dora got more forgetful and more talkative. I remember the way Miss Blacklock looked at her the day we went to tea there. Do you know why? Dora had just called her Lotty again. It seemed to us a mere harmless slip of the tongue. But it frightened Charlotte. And so it went on. Poor Dora could not stop herself talking. That day we had coffee together in the Bluebird, I had the oddest impression that Dora was talking about *two* people, not one—and so, of course, she was. At one moment she spoke of her friend as not pretty but having so much character—but almost at the same moment she described her as a pretty, lighthearted girl. She'd talk of Letty as so clever and so successful—and then say what a sad life she'd had, and then there was that quotation about stern affliction bravely borne—which really didn't seem to fit Letitia's life at all. Charlotte must, I think, have overheard a good deal that morning she came into the cafe. She certainly must have heard Dora mention about the lamp having been changed—about its being the shepherd and not the shepherdess. And she realized then what a very real danger to her security poor devoted Dora Bunner was.

"I'm afraid that that conversation with me in the café really sealed Dora's fate—if you'll excuse such a melodramatic expression. But I think it would have come to the same in the end . . . Because life couldn't be safe for Charlotte while Dora Bunner was alive. She loved Dora— she didn't want to kill Dora—but she couldn't see any other way. And, I expect (like Nurse Ellerton that I was telling you about, Bunch) she persuaded herself that it was really almost a *kindness*. Poor Bunny—not long to live anyway and perhaps a painful end. The queer thing is that she did her best to make Bunny's last day a happy day. The birthday party —and the special cake . . ."

"Delicious Death," said Phillipa with a shudder.

"Yes—yes, it was rather like that . . . she tried to give her friend a delicious death . . . The party, and all the things she liked to eat, and trying to stop people saying things to upset her. And then the tablets, whatever they were, in the aspirin bottle by her own bed so that Bunny, when she couldn't find the new bottle of aspirin she'd just bought, would go there to get some. And it would look, as it did look, that the tablets had been meant for *Letitia* . . .

"And so Bunny died in her sleep, quite happily, and Charlotte felt safe again. But she missed Dora Bunner —she missed her affection and her loyalty, she missed being able to talk to her about the old days . . . She cried bitterly the day I came up with that note from Julian—and her grief was quite genuine. She'd killed her own dear friend . . ."

"That's horrible," said Bunch. "Horrible."

"But it's very human," said Julian Harmon. "One forgets how human murderers are."

"I know," said Miss Marple. "Human. And often very much to be pitied. But very dangerous, too. Especially a weak, kindly murderer like Charlotte Blacklock. Because, once a weak person gets *really* frightened, they get quite savage with terror and they've no self-control at all."

"Murgatroyd?" said Julian.

"Yes, poor Miss Murgatroyd. Charlotte must have come up to the cottage and heard them rehearsing the murder. The window was open and she listened. It had never occurred to her until that moment that there was anyone else who could be a danger to her. Miss Hinchliffe was urging her friend to remember what she'd seen and until that moment Charlotte hadn't realized that anyone could have seen anything at all. She'd assumed that everybody would automatically be looking at Rudi Scherz. She must have held her breath outside the window and listened. Was it going to be all right? And then, just as Miss Hinchliffe rushed off to the station, Miss Murgatroyd got to a point which showed that she had stumbled on the truth. She called after Miss Hinchliffe: 'She wasn't *there* . . .'

"I asked Miss Hinchliffe, you know, if that was the way she said it . . . Because if she'd said '*She* wasn't there,' it wouldn't have meant the same thing."

"Now that's too subtle a point for me," said Craddock.

Miss Marple turned her eager pink and white face to him.

"Just think what's going on in Miss Murgatroyd's mind . . . One does see things, you know, and not know one sees them. In a railway accident once, I remember noticing a large blister of paint at the side of the carriage. I could have *drawn* it for you afterward. And once, when there was a fly bomb in London—splinters of glass everywhere—and the shock—but what I remember best is a woman standing in front of me who had a big hole halfway up the leg of her stocking and the stockings didn't match. So when Miss Murgatroyd stopped thinking and just tried to remember what she *saw*, she remembered a good deal.

"She started, I think, near the mantlepiece, where the torch must have hit first—then it went along the two windows and there were people in between the windows and her. Mrs. Harmon with her knuckles screwed into her eyes for instance. She went on in her mind, following the torch past Miss Bunner with her mouth open and her eyes staring—past a blank wall and a table with a lamp and a cigarette box. And then came the shots— and quite suddenly she remembered a most incredible thing. She'd seen the wall where Letitia Blacklock had been standing when she was shot, and at the moment when the revolver went off and Letty was shot, *Letty hadn't been there* . . .

"You see what I mean now? She'd been thinking of the three women Miss Hinchliffe had told her to think about. If one of them hadn't been there, it would have been the *personality* she'd have fastened upon. She'd have said—in effect—'*That's* the one! *She* wasn't there!' But it was a *place* that was in her mind—a place where someone should have been—but the place wasn't filled —there wasn't anybody there. The place was there— but the person wasn't. And she couldn't take it in all at once. 'How extraordinary, Hinch,' she said. 'She wasn't *there*' . . . So that could only mean Letitia Blacklock . . ."

"But you knew before that, didn't you?" said Bunch. "When the lamp went out. When you wrote down those things on the paper."

"Yes, my dear. It all came together then, you see— all the various isolated bits—and made a coherent pattern."

Bunch quoted softly, *"Lamp?* Yes. *Violet?* Yes. *Bottle of aspirin.* You mean that Bunny had been going to buy a new bottle that day, and so she ought not to have needed to take Letitia's?"

"Not unless her own bottle had been taken or hidden. It had to appear as though Letitia Blacklock was the one meant to be killed."

"Yes, I see. And then 'Delicious Death.' The cake—but more than the cake. The whole party setup. A happy day for Bunny before she died. Treating her rather like a dog you were going to destroy. That's what I find the most horrible thing of all—the sort of—of spurious kindness."

"She *was* quite a kindly woman. What she said at the last in the kitchen was quite true. 'I didn't want to kill anybody.' What she wanted was a great deal of money that didn't belong to her! And before that desire—(and it had become a kind of obsession—the money was to pay her back for all the suffering life had inflicted on her)—everything else went to the wall. People with a grudge against the world are always dangerous. They seem to think life owes them something. I've known many an invalid who has suffered far worse and been cut off from life much more than Charlotte Blacklock—and they've managed to lead happy contented lives. It's what's in *yourself* that makes you happy or unhappy. But, oh, dear, I'm afraid I'm straying away from what we were talking about. Where were we?"

"Going over your list," said Bunch. "What did you mean by 'Making enquiries'? Inquiries about what?"

Miss Marple shook her head playfully at Inspector Craddock.

"You ought to have seen that, Inspector Craddock. You showed me that letter from Letitia Blacklock to her sister. It had the word 'enquiries' in it twice—each time spelt with an *e*. But in the note I asked Bunch to show you, Miss Blacklock had written 'inquiries' with an *i*. People don't usually alter their spelling as they get older. It seemed to me very significant."

"Yes," Craddock agreed. "I ought to have spotted that."

Bunch was continuing: *"Severe affliction bravely borne*. That's what Bunny said to you in the café and, of course, Letitia hadn't had any affliction. *Iodine*. That put you on the track of goiter?"

"Yes, dear. Switzerland, you know, and Miss Blacklock giving the impression that her sister had died of consumption. But I remembered then that the greatest authorities on goiter and the most skillful surgeons operating on it are Swiss. And it linked up with those really rather preposterous pearls that Letitia Blacklock always wore. Not really her *style*—but just right for concealing the scar."

"I understand now her agitation the night the string broke," said Craddock. "It seemed at the time quite disproportionate."

"And after that, it was Lotty you wrote, not Letty as we thought," said Bunch.

"Yes, I remembered that the sister's name was Charlotte, and that Dora Bunner had called Miss Blacklock Lotty once or twice—and that each time she did so, she had been very upset afterwards."

"And what about Berne and Old-Age Pension?"

"Rudi Scherz had been an orderly in a hospital in Berne."

"And Old-Age Pension?"

"Oh, my dear Bunch, I mentioned that to you in the Bluebird though I didn't really see the application then. How Mrs. Wotherspoon drew Mrs. Bartlett's Old-Age Pension as well as her own—though Mrs. Bartlett had been dead for years—simply because one old woman is so like another old woman—Yes, it all made a pattern and I felt so worked up I went out to cool my head a little and think what could be done about proving all this. Then Miss Hinchliffe picked me up and we found Miss Murgatroyd . . ."

Miss Marple's voice dropped. It was no longer excited and pleased. It was quiet and remorseless.

"I knew then something had *got* to be done. Quickly! But there still wasn't any *proof*. I thought out a possible plan and I talked to Sergeant Fletcher."

"And have I had Fletcher on the carpet for it!" said Craddock. "He'd no business to go agreeing to your plans without reporting first to me."

"He didn't like it, but I talked him into it," said Miss Marple. "We went up to Little Paddocks and I got hold of Mitzi."

Julia drew a deep breath and said, "I can't imagine how you ever got her to do it."

"I worked on her, my dear," said Miss Marple. "She thinks far too much about herself anyway, and it will be good for her to have done something for others. I flattered her up, of course, and said I was sure if she'd been in her own country she'd have been in the Resistance movement, and she said, 'Yes, indeed.' And I said I could see she had got just the temperament for that sort of work. She was brave, didn't mind taking risks and could act a part. I told her stories of deeds done by girls in the Resistance movements, some of them true, and some of them, I'm afraid, invented. She got tremendously worked up!"

"Marvelous," said Patrick.

"And then I got her to agree to do her part. I rehearsed her till she was word perfect. Then I told her to go upstairs to her room and not come down until Inspector Craddock came. The worst of these excitable people is that they're apt to go off half-cocked and start the whole thing before the time."

"She did it very well," said Julia.

"I don't quite see the point," said Bunch. "Of course, I wasn't there—" she added apologetically.

"The point? It was a little complicated—and rather touch and go. The idea was that Mitzi, whilst admitting, as though casually, that blackmail *had* been in her mind, was now so worked up and terrified that she was willing to come out with the truth. She'd seen, through the keyhole of the dining-room, Miss Blacklock in the hall with a revolver behind Rudi Scherz. She'd seen, that is, *what had actually taken place*. Now the only danger was that Charlotte Blacklock might have realized that, as the key was in the keyhole, Mitzi couldn't possibly have seen anything at all. But I banked on the fact that you don't think of things like that when you've just had a bad shock. All she could take in was that Mitzi had seen her."

Craddock took over the story.

"But—and this was essential—I pretended to receive this with skepticism, and I made an immediate attack, as though unmasking my batteries at last, upon someone who had not been previously suspected. I accused Edmund—"

"And very nicely *I* played *my* part," said Edmund. "Hot denial. All according to plan. What wasn't according to plan, Phillipa, my love, was you throwing in your little chirp and coming out into the open as 'Pip.' Neither the Inspector nor I had any idea you were Pip. I was going to be Pip! It threw us off our stride for the moment, but the Inspector made a masterly comeback and made some perfectly filthy insinuations about my wanting a rich wife which will probably stick in your subconscious and make irreparable trouble between us one day."

"I don't see why that was necessary."

"Don't you? It meant that, *from Charlotte Black-lock's point of view,* the only person who suspected or knew the truth, was *Mitzi.* The suspicions of the police were elsewhere. They had treated Mitzi for the moment as a liar. But if Mitzi were to persist, they might listen to her and take her seriously. So Mitzi had got to be silenced.

"Mitzi went straight out of the room and back to the kitchen—just like I had told her," said Miss Marple. "Miss Blacklock came out after her almost immediately. Mitzi was apparently alone in the kitchen. Sergeant Fletcher was behind the scullery door. And I was in the broom cupboard in the kitchen. Luckily I'm very thin."

Bunch looked at Miss Marple.

"What did you expect to happen, Aunt Jane?"

"One of two things. Either Charlotte would offer Mitzi money to hold her tongue—and Sergeant Fletcher would be a witness to that offer, or else—or else I thought she'd try to kill Mitzi."

"But she couldn't hope to get away with *that?* She'd have been suspected at once."

"Oh, my dear, she was past reasoning. She was just a snapping, terrified, cornered rat. Think what had happened that day. The scene between Miss Hinchliffe and Miss Murgatroyd. Miss Hinchliffe driving off to the station. As soon as she comes back Miss Murgatroyd will explain that Letitia Blacklock wasn't in the room that night. That's just a few minutes in which to make sure Miss Murgatroyd can't tell anything. No time to make a plan or set a stage. Just crude murder. She greets the poor woman and strangles her. Then a quick rush home, to change, to be sitting by the fire when the others come in, as though she'd never been out.

"And then came the revelation of Julia's identity. She breaks her pearls and is terrified they may notice

her scar. Later, the Inspector telephones that he's bringing everyone there. No time to think, to rest. Up to her
neck in murder now, no mercy killing—or undesirable
young man to be put out of the way. Crude plain murder. Is she safe? Yes, so far. And then comes Mitzi—
yet *another* danger. Kill Mitzi, stop her tongue! She's
beside herself with fear. Not human any longer. Just a
dangerous animal."

"But why were you in the broom cupboard, Aunt
Jane?" asked Bunch. "Couldn't you have left it to Sergeant Fletcher?"

"It was safer with two of us, my dear. And, besides,
I knew I could mimic Dora Bunner's voice. If anything
could break Charlotte Blacklock down, that would."

"And it did . . . !"

"Yes . . . she went to pieces."

There was a long silence as memory laid hold of them
and then, speaking with determined lightness, to ease
the strain, Julia said, "It's made a wonderful difference
to Mitzi. She told me yesterday that she was taking a
post near Southampton. And she said" (Julia produced
a very good imitation of Mitzi's accent). " 'I go there
and if they say to me you have to register with the
police—you are an alien, I say to them, "Yes, I will
register! The police, they know me well. I assist the
police! Without me the police never would they have
made the arrest of a very dangerous criminal. I risked
my life because I am brave—brave like a lion—I do not
care about risks." "Mitzi," they say to me, "you are a
heroine, you are superb." "Ach! it is nothing," I say.' "

Julia stopped.

"And a great deal more," she added.

"I think," said Edmund thoughtfully, "that soon
Mitzi will have assisted the police in not one but hun-
dreds of cases!"

"She's softened toward me," said Phillipa. "She actually presented me with the recipe for Delicious Death as a kind of wedding present. She added that I was on no account to divulge the secret to Julia, because Julia had ruined her omelette pan."

"Mrs. Lucas," said Edmund, "is all over Phillipa now that since Belle Goedler's death, Phillipa and Julia have inherited the Goedler millions. She sent us some silver asparagus tongs as a wedding present. I shall have enormous pleasure in *not* asking her to the wedding!"

"And so they lived happily ever after," said Patrick. "Edmund and Phillipa—And Julia and Patrick?" he added tentatively.

"Not with me, you won't live happily ever after," said Julia. "The remarks that Inspector Craddock improvised to address to Edmund apply far more aptly to you. You *are* the sort of soft young man who would like a rich wife. Nothing doing!"

"There's gratitude for you," said Patrick. "After all I did for that girl."

"Nearly landed me in prison on a murder charge—that's what your forgetfulness nearly did for me," said Julia. "I shall never forget that evening when your sister's letter came. I really thought I was in for it. I couldn't see any way out. As it is," she added musingly, "I think I shall go on the stage."

"What? You, too?" groaned Patrick.

"Yes. I might go to Perth. See if I can get your Julia's place in the Rep there. Then, when I've learned my job, I shall go into theater management—and put on Edmund's plays, perhaps."

"I thought you wrote novels," said Julian Harmon.

"Well, so did I," said Edmund. "I began writing a novel. Rather good it was. Pages about an unshaven man getting out of bed and what he smelt like, and the gray streets, and a horrible old woman with dropsy and a vicious young tart who dribbled down her chin—and they all talked interminably about the state of the world and wondered what they were alive for. And suddenly I began to wonder, too . . . And then a rather comic idea occurred to me . . . and I jotted it down—and then I worked up rather a good little scene . . . All very obvious stuff. But, somehow, I got interested . . . and before I knew what I was doing I'd finished a roaring farce in three acts."

"What's it called?" asked Patrick. *"What the Butler Saw?"*

"Well, it easily might be . . . As a matter of fact I've called it *Elephants Do Forget*. What's more, it's been accepted and it's going to be produced!"

"Elephants Do Forget," murmured Bunch. "I thought they didn't?"

The Rev. Julian Harmon gave a guilty start.

"My goodness! I've been so interested. My *sermon . . .*"

"Detective stories again," said Bunch. "Real life ones this time."

"You might preach on *Thou Shalt Do No Murder,"* suggested Patrick.

"No," said Julian Harmon quietly, "I shan't take that as my text."

"No," said Bunch. "You're quite right, Julian. I know a much nicer text, a happy text." She quoted in her fresh voice, " 'For lo, the Spring is here and the Voice of the Turtle is heard in the Land'—I haven't got it quite right—but you know the one I mean. Though why a *turtle* I can't think. I shouldn't think turtles have got nice voices at all."

"The word turtle," explained the Rev. Julian Harmon, "is not very happily translated. It doesn't mean a reptile but the turtle dove. The Hebrew word original is—"

Bunch interrupted him by giving him a hug and saying:

"I know one thing—*You* think that the Ahasuerus of the Bible is Artaxerxes the Second, but between you and me it was Artaxerxes the Third."

As always, Julian Harmon wondered why his wife should think that story so particularly funny. . . .

"Tiglath-Pileser wants to go and help you," said Bunch. "He ought to be a very proud cat. *He* showed us how the lights went out."

Epilogue

"WE OUGHT to order some papers," said Edmund to Phillipa upon the day of their return to Chipping Cleghorn after the honeymoon. "Let's go along to Totman's."

Mr. Totman, a heavy-breathing, slow-moving man, received them with affability.

"Glad to see you back, sir. *And* madam."

"We want to order some papers."

"Certainly, sir. And your mother is keeping well, I hope? Quite settled down at Bournemouth?"

"She loves it," said Edmund who had not the faintest idea whether this was so or not, but like most sons, preferred to believe that all was well with those loved, but frequently irritating beings, parents.

"Yes, sir. Very agreeable place. Went there for my holiday last year. Mrs. Totman enjoyed it very much."

"I'm glad. About papers, we'd like—"

"And I hear you have a play on in London, sir. Very amusing so they tell me."

"Yes, it's doing very well."

"Called *Elephants Do Forget,* so I hear. You'll excuse me, sir, asking you, but I always thought that they *didn't*—forget, I mean."

"Yes—yes, exactly—I've begun to think it was a
273

mistake calling it that. So many people have said just what you say."

"A kind of natural history fact, I've always understood."

"Yes—yes. Like earwigs making good mothers."

"Do they indeed, sir? Now that's a fact I *didn't* know."

"About the papers—"

"The Times, sir, I think it was?" Mr. Totman paused with pencil uplifted.

"The Daily Worker," said Edmund firmly, "And the *Daily Telegraph,"* said Phillipa. "And the *New Statesman,"* said Edmund. "The *Radio Times,"* said Phillipa. "The *Spectator,"* said Edmund. "The *Gardener's Chronicle,"* said Phillipa.

They both paused to take breath.

"Thank you, sir," said Mr. Totman. *"And* the *Gazette,* I suppose?"

"No," said Edmund.

"No," said Phillipa.

"Excuse me, you *do* want the *Gazette?"*

"No, we don't."

"Certainly not."

"You don't want the *North Benham News and Chipping Cleghorn Gazette?"*

"No."

"You don't want me to send it along to you every week?"

"No." Edmund added: "Is that quite clear now?"

"Oh, yes, sir—yes."

Edmund and Phillipa went out, and Mr. Totman padded into his back parlor.

"Got a pencil, Mother?" he said. "My pen's run out."

"Here you are," said Mrs. Totman, seizing the order book. "I'll do it. What do they want?"

"Daily Worker, Daily Telegraph—Radio Times, New

Statesman, Spectator—let me see—*Gardener's Chronicle.*"

"*Gardener's Chronicle,*" repeated Mrs. Totman, writing busily. "And the *Gazette.*"

"They don't want the *Gazette.*"

"What?"

"They don't want the *Gazette*. They said so."

"Nonsense," said Mrs. Totman. "You don't hear properly. Of course they want the *Gazette!* Everybody has the *Gazette*. How else would they know what's going on round here?"

AGATHA CHRISTIE'S
MOST FAMOUS DETECTIVE–
HERCULE POIROT!

He is brilliant. He is dapper.
He is the star of the most fascinating –
and popular–mysteries ever written.